LIFE SHOULDN'T BE WASTED. THE EXPERIENCE of being alive is too extraordinary. To think that there was a brief moment, just ten months ago, when it had seemed that it all might end.

When I first emerged from my tunnel, I could smell the smoke from the explosion and fire, and watch the growing embers blend with the light snow. As I moved away, that faded until there was just the snow, the silence of the forest, and a single, focused thought:

Lucas Frank is a walking dead man. . . .

Books by John Philpin and Patricia Sierra

THE PRETTIEST FEATHERS
TUNNEL OF NIGHT

TUNNEL
OF NIGHT

John Philpin & Patricia Sierra

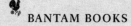

BANTAM BOOKS

New York Toronto London Sydney Auckland

Grateful acknowledgment to reprint "Phoenix," copyright © 1994 by
Steve Philpin. Reprinted by permission of the composer.

TUNNEL OF NIGHT
A Bantam Book/January 1999
All rights reserved.

ISBN 0-553-57954-1

Published simultaneously in the United States and Canada

PRINTED IN THE UNITED SATES OF AMERICA

OPM   10   9   8   7   6   5   4   3   2   1

For Katie Hall

Now is the time of the *Assassins*.

FROM *Morning of Drunkenness* BY ARTHUR RIMBAUD

TUNNEL OF NIGHT

PROLOGUE

HER HAIR WAS LIGHTER THAN I REMEMBERED, and looked as if she hadn't combed it.

I watched, absorbed every detail, as she came through the kitchen door, walked to the table, put on her glasses to read the morning paper. She was heavy, dressed in baggy black Bermuda shorts and a T-shirt. The once regal lines of her profile and her slender neck were gone, buried beneath puffy flesh.

"Hello," I said.

The coffee cup clattered to the floor as her head spun around. Her mouth opened, and she made a noise—perhaps she said my name.

She turned in her chair and stared at me as I stepped between her and the kitchen door. Then she stood, leaned against the table, and forced it backward.

"Oh, my God. Why did you come here? What do you want?"

Her body shook. Her eyes were wide, filled with terror.

"All those years," I began, thinking for a moment

that I might answer her, that I might tell her what I had become and why.

"You betrayed me," I said, slipping my hands behind my back and removing the knife from my pocket.

She gripped the shaky table. "No," she said, but it sounded more like a question.

She never had time to lift her arms. As I stepped toward her, her head snapped up and her throat accommodated my blade.

For the first time in our lives, she was totally compliant.

She never made a sound.

I OPENED THE REFRIGERATOR. THE LIGHT DIDN'T work, so I jiggled it and tightened the bulb in its socket. It went on. People don't take care of things, not even the simplest adjustments requiring the least amount of effort.

I found some lettuce, cold cuts, a jar of mustard, and a loaf of whole wheat bread. Then I opened the cupboard above the sink to get a glass and a plate. I noticed the impressionistic figurine of a bird, and remembered the beautiful young woman I had sent it to so many years ago—the woman who now rested on the kitchen floor. I placed the figurine on the table, a centerpiece.

The sunlight from the window refracted as it passed through the glass bird, cascading bands of primary color across the table. I sat with the chair facing the window so that I didn't block the light, and so that I could enjoy my own private display of all the colors of the sun.

Mine was a private celebration. I was completing

old projects, and beginning new ones. No one who had touched my life was safe.

I grabbed my knife—a heavy, folding Buck with a single four-inch blade. It was sticky with blood, so I wiped it with a paper towel. I sliced the bread, then placed the knife on the table to my right. In many ways the preparation of a meal is more important than the eating of it.

I glanced to my left. If it were not for the blood, she would have looked as if she were sleeping.

I took a bite from my sandwich, then pushed the food away and moved the short distance to her side. This complete possession, this ownership of another, carried with it certain responsibilities. With both hands, as if I were cradling something fragile, I adjusted one of her arms so that it was parallel to her side, like the other one.

Symmetry.

ONE

POP

THOMAS WOLFE WAS WRONG.

You can always find your way back home—so long as you know how much garlic to put in the marinara. That is the secret. Garlic. And, of course, the olive oil—Filippo Berio extra virgin. But even when you get the recipe right, people want to give you directions. They want to barge into your home and take over your kitchen. Miscreants. Philistines.

If Thomas Wolfe had studied marinara, if he had labored over a hot stove more than he did over a typewriter, he would have changed the title of his book—and probably his life. For one thing, he would have gotten drunk more often. Oh, yes, one cup of ale for the pot, and one for the maw. You seldom have trouble finding your way home because you hardly ever leave.

I was getting buzzed. A morning on the lake in the warm sun trying to outwit an elusive bass, followed by a stint in the kitchen starting the sauce (it has to simmer all afternoon), and I was ready for the shower. Life is grand.

I was expecting company—a rare visit from my

daughter, Lane, a detective with the New York City Police Department. She had sent a fax four days earlier. Lane was concerned that she hadn't heard from me, and sounded as if she were having a crisis of conscience. Her note said, in part:

> We wrapped up the Wolf case nearly a year ago, but I'm still not able to put it behind me. I need to talk to you about that day in Vermont. I've told the sanitized version of the story a dozen times, but you and I have never sorted out what really happened. Sometimes I think it was murder. Other times I'm sure that it was justice. I just need to know why you did what you did.

I answered the fax, assured my daughter that I was fine, and told her that I would love to see her.

Intuition had been nudging Lane with the truth—that I had murdered the killer, John Wolf. It didn't seem that long ago, but my daughter was right. It was nearly a year ago. Lane had been the lead investigator in her partner's ex-wife's murder. What began as a straightforward homicide case became a hunt for a serial killer. I had provided armchair advice to Lane and her lieutenant until it was clear that Wolf's next intended victim was my daughter. So I went after the bastard, tracked him to his lair in Vermont, and used his own bomb to blow him to pieces. Enormously rewarding justice, that.

The six-week bout with demons in the night that erupted when I returned home had nothing to do with my having dispatched a predator to the netherworld. The problem had been that even though he was dead, Wolf continued to live inside my head. In order to track him, to anticipate his moves, I had to invite him into my mind, to learn to see the world as he saw it, to think as he thought. When it was over, the task of evicting Wolf from my dreams took more time than bringing down the beast.

Killing him had caused me no confusion. I had not hesitated, and I had not lost a wink of sleep over it. But it was different for my daughter.

When she was young, Lane was always sticking bars of flowery-smelling soap in the shower. She would dump my Ivory in the wastebasket, and I would have to haul ass out of the shower, dripping wet, to retrieve it.

Soap is not the only thing that she and I see differently. I used to lure her into the kitchen when she was a child, determined to turn her into a cook. "That's men's work," she would say—and she was right, at least in our house. When it was my turn to cook, my wife, Savvy, seldom passed through the kitchen; I was not a kind cook.

As Lane grew older, she became more specific in her distaste for cooking. "Think of the time we consume driving to the grocery, picking out the food, preparing it, eating it, clearing the table, washing the dishes, drying them, putting them away. You could solve half a dozen murders in that time."

I wanted her to appreciate cooking the way I did, to appreciate cooking the way it *deserved* to be appreciated, but it was hopeless. She was too caught up in that other part of my life—my work as a practicing psychiatrist, profiling and tracking human predators. Although she always ate whatever I set before her, she remained steadfast in her indifference to the process.

"It's just food, Pop."

A heartbreaking sacrilege.

When she was transferred from her street beat to Homicide, Lane wanted to fill my head with her cases.

She expected me to offer some profound insight, some new angle on a murder that was fracturing the best minds in law enforcement. "When I quit," I always told her, "I really quit."

She insisted that she had special rights—a "biological exception" to my rule. True. I have never mastered the art of saying no to my daughter.

My daughter or my cat. I guess they are the only two creatures on earth who have me exactly where they want me.

I looked at my massive Maine coon cat and said, "Max, do you think you'll ever retire?"

I was sure that he would do a better job of it than I had.

Max flipped his tail. He was sound asleep on *his* kitchen chair, deep in a dream state—with his paws curled back and his lower jaw in a cataclysm of murder. Max is the perfect predator. The field mice, chipmunks, and squirrels that populate my ten acres have learned the hard way. When he comes inside, Max purrs, rubs against my leg, curls into my lap, sniffs my beard to determine what I have eaten in his absence. When he sleeps, he is back in the field—the cold, calculating killer that nature designed him to be.

I ran my hand down his back, from his neck to the base of his tail. "Pity your jungle friends, Max. They're capable of many things, but they can't purr. Has to do with the arrangement of cartilage in the throat. Of course, they can roar, and you can't. Maybe it all evens out."

He opened one eye, yawned, then went back to sleep.

Because I had been somewhat out of touch, Lane assumed that I had shut myself away, struggling with a bout of depression akin to what had nailed me just before I sold my practice and headed for the Michigan woods several years ago. She was just being a dear, over-protective worrywart, although I must admit to a twinge of guilt—this time I had not been struggling with anything but road maps. Janet, my friend from across the lake, and I had sneaked away to Vancouver, British Columbia, where Blues Traveler was playing in concert. Actually, I should amend that. We did not sneak, we simply did not tell anyone, including my daughter, what we were doing.

In truth, I had not lingered on the Wolf matter. After my six weeks of emotional recuperation, I pronounced myself sane, then promptly continued with the important things in life: fishing, good music, a new book by Harry Crews.

Most detectives go through an entire career without encountering a serial murderer. Lane had already dealt with one—John Wolf, who had killed dozens in a career spanning two decades—and more than a hundred had haunted me. I certainly could listen to my daughter, but I did not know how much help I could offer her.

I walked toward my bedroom at the back of the house. Lane was usually prompt, so I had perhaps an hour to get out of my fishy jeans, grab a quick shower and some clean jeans, and just generally make myself more presentable. I nipped a final time at the ale, then hit the switch on the perimeter security system. Chuck Logan was due to deliver two cords of firewood, and I didn't want him or Lane to pull up the drive and be greeted by screaming sirens.

I had installed the alarm system as soon as I moved to the lake. Back then, I was still feeling vulnerable to the outside world, surrounded by the ghosts and other incarnations of the monsters that I had wrestled over the years. I wanted, *needed*, an absolutely secure retreat.

I had also stocked the log house with a small arsenal of rifles, revolvers, and semiautomatic pistols. But security had never been a problem. I doubted that I needed any of the hardware anymore.

Everything seemed to be under control when I hit the shower. A bit blurry perhaps, but under control, with the promise of a pleasant visit ahead.

As the water splashed onto my face, my head began to clear. Muscle aches that I had been nursing since the day before responded to the warm spray. I had begun splitting my winter's firewood—a task that tests my ability to tolerate ambivalence. I always have to force myself to go out to the stump in the wood lot, but once I start wielding the twelve-pound splitting hammer, I hit a rhythm, develop a momentum, feel as if I'm thirty again. It's when I have to break out the Ben-Gay the next day that I know I am not.

I toweled off, then pulled on my jeans. I was rubbing the towel through my hair as I walked toward the sliding-glass door and stepped out onto the patio. The surface of the lake was dead calm. No boats. Not even a fish rising. Typical for an autumn day.

A sliver of light off to the right caught my eye. When I saw the source of that light, recognized it, I froze—the towel still in my hand, my arm still extended upward. I watched as a man standing a hundred yards away in my field casually lowered a rifle into firing position, then aimed in my direction.

I twisted back to my left, catching a glimpse of the muzzle flash as I threw myself to the ground. The sonofabitch was shooting at me.

A burning pain told me that the slug had slapped the right side of my head. I heard the report of the first shot as the second bullet sliced across my side.

This was no hunter mistaking me for his quarry. He was trying to kill me.

I slammed against the ground as a third shot carved a crease in the gray slate patio.

I pushed against the ground, believing that I could get up, run into the house, grab a weapon, and return fire. But I couldn't move.

My world faded rapidly. I shivered with cold. Blood pooled everywhere, but even that was fading, as if the color red were disappearing.

I could make no sense of the crazy thoughts cascading through my head.

Max came out to watch the gouge in the slate fill with blood. I remember that I wondered how long death would take.

Then everything went black.

LANE

THE TRIP FROM NEW YORK CITY TO LAKE ALBERT, Michigan, can be made in less than a day if you drive straight through. But I didn't want to pull up at Pop's place looking or feeling like a zombie, so I decided to drive only as far as Toledo on Friday. Toledo is an hour from Detroit; Lake Albert is two hours north of there. I figured that if I was behind the wheel by nine, I would be right on time for lunch. And lunch would be a piece of work, since Pop fancies himself the Galloping Gourmet.

In Toledo I stayed at the Mansion View on Collingwood Boulevard—a Victorian bed and breakfast just off the interstate, on the edge of the city's business district. It reminded me of the house in Boston where I lived when I was a little girl, back when my mom, Savvy, was still around. Lots of woodwork, sunlight filtering through antique curtains, fireplaces. Maybe a ghost or two.

I remember an autumn afternoon when someone rang the bell at that house on Beacon Hill, and Savvy went to open the door. I padded along behind her, eager to see who had come to visit. It wasn't anybody we knew—just a guy selling something. He looked at Savvy, then at me, and asked if the lady of the house was in. He had assumed that Savvy was the maid or the baby-sitter.

I didn't know then about black and white. I may have noticed that my father's skin was light, and that my mother's was more like the darkest chocolate, but I had not yet translated that information into anything racial. The first time I heard the word "biracial" applied to me, it was at school, not at home, and I wasn't sure what it meant. I did not think of myself as white or black—just closer in color to my father than to my mother. I didn't figure out until much later that apparently it mattered what color a person was.

That day when the salesman came to our door asking for the lady of the house, I didn't realize that he had insulted my mother—so it made no sense to me when she slammed the door in his face. I felt embarrassed by her behavior, and I wondered why she seemed so angry afterward. Pop never acted that way, so I decided that he must be a nicer person than Savvy was.

We were living in that house when I discovered that life with Pop was dictated by his moods, which zigzagged like the needle on a polygraph machine. I never knew from one day to the next which end of the spectrum he would be on. Most days when I came home from school, I would charge into Pop's office. He stopped whatever he was doing and wanted to hear all about my day. Usually, we drifted out to the kitchen and he fixed snacks.

Whenever Ray Bolton—a Boston homicide detective, Pop's best friend, and my godfather—was around,

the two men might be deep in conversation about a
murder, but I knew that I could walk in on them anyway. Ray and Pop would sweep away any crime-scene
photos, close their file folders, and the three of us might
talk, play Parcheesi, or, as a special treat in the summer,
head for the bleachers at Fenway Park to catch a Red
Sox game.

There were other times, though, when Pop stormed
into the house, said nothing, and locked himself in his
office. Within seconds, he had music playing loud
enough to shake the pictures on the walls, and I would
usually not see him again until dinner (which was always the same on those occasions: grilled cheese sandwiches and split pea soup—obviously a dire sign). If he
spoke at all, he might say something like, "Lanie, I really
don't care for people."

Pop never explained, but sometimes Ray did. "Your
dad was in court. Judges do moronic things sometimes.
Wearing a black robe doesn't make you God, but some
judges can't seem to keep that straight. Your dad is an
idealist. He can't tolerate stupidity in anyone ever. I
think he'd be much happier living in the woods and
talking to chipmunks."

Sounded good to me.

When I went into police work, I thought that Pop
and I would grow closer—that he would be more open,
more accessible. I assumed that the same thing driving
me was what had driven him all those years: a need to
see killers arrested and brought to trial. Get them off
the street and plug them into the system.

I quickly learned how different my father's view
of the world is. Pop does not feel bound by any rules,
and his definition of justice does not involve the criminal justice system. The brilliance that allowed him to

look into the minds of killers with such terrifying clarity also shaped the man and his view of the world. Indeed, such unprotected intimacy with the depths of violence that can lurk in men fostered an attitude free of self-quibbling. You create your own justice. Simple. But since Pop retreated into the great north woods to camp with the chipmunks and the fish and the birds and the trees, but no killers, he has mellowed out. I think.

All these things were on my mind that Saturday morning as I drove toward Lake Albert. Getting out of New York had gotten to be more than just a good idea; it was mandatory. I've never handled stress well, and I could feel it building to record levels. I had to get away, and I had to see my father. I felt that he had been avoiding me ever since Vermont, and I knew it would just get worse if we didn't talk about it.

I was about a half hour past Detroit when I saw the red strobe light in my rearview mirror. Since I wasn't speeding, I decided that they were not after me. Then the Michigan State Police vehicle pulled alongside mine and the trooper motioned for me to pull over.

I pulled off on the shoulder of the road and rolled down my window. The trooper walking toward me looked to be in his early twenties, with a face full of freckles.

"What's the problem, Officer?" I asked.

"Is your name Lane Frank?"

Something was wrong. Nobody except Pop and my boss, Captain Hanson, knew that I would be traveling that stretch of road that day. My cop-mode immediately kicked into high gear.

I flashed my shield, climbed out of my car, and stared down at the cop's sunglasses. "Trooper, I'm a homicide detective. Who notified you? What's happened?"

"We were asked to intercept you," he said, appearing unnerved by my height—a shade over six feet tall.

He pulled a paper from his pocket and read it before continuing. "Chief Semple wants you to come to City Hall, not to the house, when you arrive in Lake Albert."

Buck Semple was the chief of police in Lake Albert. He and Pop had been friends for years.

"Buck? How'd he . . ."

"There's been an accident."

Oh, no. I'd been a cop long enough to know that "accident" can mean exactly that: a collision, or maybe a pratfall on broken pavement. But it's just as likely to be a euphemism for death.

"Where's my father?"

"I'm sorry. You'll have to talk to Chief Semple about that."

Oh, my God. I slipped back into my car, hit the accelerator, and merged back onto the road. I don't know why I was in such a hurry to hear the bad news that I was sure was waiting for me, but I pushed the speedometer up to eighty-five and kept it there.

Why would Buck Semple send out an intercept order? It had to be bad. A heart attack? No. Pop's heart was fine. Besides, the cop said "accident." What could Pop do to himself splitting wood or fishing?

A drowning? No. Pop was a great swimmer, and he knew every inch of that lake.

I remembered a summer on the Cape when he taught me to swim. He was so patient—holding me in the water while I practiced the strokes he described, then letting me go, gradually, with me swallowing a little water, but exulting in the idea that I was doing it on my own.

Whatever had happened, I knew that I had to get to Lake Albert fast.

AS I PULLED INTO THE MUNICIPAL PARKING LOT in front of the converted church that served as Lake Albert's City Hall, Buck Semple stood at the curb waiting for me.

"He's gonna be okay," he said, his hands up, palms out, as if he expected me to come roaring out of the car at him.

"What happened?" I asked, surprised by how composed I sounded.

"He took a couple of superficial wounds from a hunting rifle. One creased his side, the other grazed his head. Local guy delivering cordwood found him. There was a lot of blood, but Doc Grissom says it looked worse than it was."

"A shooting? What? Who shot him?"

"We don't know that yet. That's why I didn't want you going out to the house. The shooter could still be prowling around out there."

"Where's Pop?"

"The county hospital."

"How do I get there?" I was already turning back toward my car.

"I'll drive," Buck said. "It'll probably take both of us to keep him from walking outta there. They've got him doped up, so he's been drifting in and out of consciousness. He says he wants to go home."

When Buck told me that Pop had been shot, my first thought was that an overzealous hunter had mistaken him for a deer. Then I figured that some crazy had picked him at random—that it was one of those sicko things you see reported on CNN every day. "There's no way that a lunatic with a gun hit Pop by chance," I told Buck. "Not *two* shots."

"He fired three times," Buck said. "Third shot cracked the patio. Lucas says the shooter was there to kill him. We're treating it as an attempted homicide."

He pulled the car onto the country road and drove north.

"He's helped put away a lot of killers," I said, already putting together a to-do list. "What about inmates who have escaped or been paroled?"

"That's in the works."

We drove along in silence for several minutes, the road signs, guardrails, and trees all a blur.

"After I've seen Pop, I'll want to see the house."

He turned and looked hard at me. "You can't get involved in this, Lane."

I could feel the anger rising in me. "I'm already involved. He's my father. I'm a cop."

Buck was getting heated, too. "I'll take care of the investigation, Lane. You manage your father."

I didn't say anything more. I knew better than to argue with Buck. But I did start organizing my own investigation in my mind.

POP

I WAS IN A COUNTY HOSPITAL IN UPSTATE MICHIGAN.
As contact with reality washed over me, then departed, I was also a boy again, fishing the waters off Hull, Massachusetts. I was doped-up, flirting with the edges of consciousness. My sea breeze carried the pungent odor of disinfectant.

I pushed a red pram from the sand into the shallow breakers of low tide, then climbed in, pulling the oars through the waves. A quarter mile. A half mile. The houses that lined Beach Avenue grew smaller. A mile.

I didn't bother with an anchor—just drifted—the currents and the wind pushing me first to the south, then north. I had no worries about being ripped to the east into the open sea. The currents were not that strong; the prevailing winds blew from the opposite direction.

It was all so detailed. I knew I was there, and I knew I was not.

The shallows ended, and the land was a thin stripe across the horizon. Ocean swells gently rocked the boat between two lines of lobster buoys.

Armed with an ultralight spinning rod and a Mitchell 300 reel loaded with two-pound-test line, I tried a few casts with a mackerel jig, a slender silver lure designed to move through the water like a darting bait fish. I flipped out a short cast and had a hit immediately. The fish ran hard to the left, dove once, then yielded to the slow, steady pressure I exerted. I boated a slapping one-pound mackerel.

A second and third fish followed in quick succession—all about the same size—when, without warning, the placid surface of the ocean rose to a boil. It had to be a big school. I had another one on, this time running right, when a second slam hit the line.

The rod bent in half, and the bail screamed as line tore off the pool. The slender monofilament snapped.

"What the hell was that?" I said out loud.

I looked out at the water that was in constant turbulence now. With a chill, it hit me. The hunter had become the hunted. Bluefish, maniacal killing machines with razor-sharp teeth, were chasing and devouring the mackerel, just as the smaller predator went after the shiners.

I popped off the spool of line, then snapped in one of eight-pound-test. I found a wire leader and a hook that looked about the right size. Then I took my fishing knife and cut a long, bloody slab from the side of a mackerel. I flipped the new rig and bait into the middle of the maelstrom and watched as it began a slow descent, pendulum fashion, through the clear water. This time the streak appeared from below. It looked gray, not silver, as I felt the smash on the line. I leaned back—setting the hook with several yanks on the rod and watching the blue run. Each time that I thought he was tiring, subdued, he would take off again.

By the time I had him beside the boat, my arms were weary, just about useless. I lowered a net under him as sweat ran in rivers down my neck. I had what I estimated to be about six pounds of blue, what the locals called a "chopper."

As I dragged him into the boat, the flat gray eyes of the fish seemed to look into mine. The mouth kept snapping, as if the blue were trying to wrap its teeth around my forearm. Then it did.

I watched my blood flow down my arm.

"This didn't happen," I shouted.

I heard a voice saying, "Pop, leave it alone."

My eyes opened. Lane and I were struggling over the IV in my right arm. I was trying to pull it out.

"Pop?"

"Okay."

"Leave it alone."

"His teeth," I explained.

"You must have been dreaming."

"Yeah."

"You awake now?"

"I don't know."

And I didn't. "There's fog across my bow," I said, starting to laugh, then stopping because it hurt.

"Someone shot you, Pop."

There was an edge of urgency in my daughter's voice. She was trying to tell me something that I needed to know. The fog cleared. The bow was gone. I wasn't a child anymore. I was a fifty-five-year-old man stepping outside my back door with a towel in my hand, gazing at the flat calm of Lake Albert. Then I was watching blood pool on the tiles in front of my nose.

"Someone shot me," I parroted.

"Right."

"Where am I?"

"County hospital."

"What time is it?"

"Just after midnight."

Everything faded, then snapped back into focus.

"Lane?"

"I'm here, Pop. I wish you were, too."

Then I did laugh. "I'm here. Shit. What am I on?"

"Demerol."

My head was beginning to clear. "That explains my fishing trip. What a dream. Who shot me?"

Lane shrugged and shook her head as she handed me a cup of ice chips.

"Where'd I get hit? My side?"

"Doc Grissom said it's not nearly as bad as when Hinckley shot Reagan. The shooter also grazed the side of your head. You were moving."

"Wait. I remember," I said, wishing that I had a plain old glass of water. "The sunlight reflected off the rifle scope."

I could see the flash of light, feel the damp towel in my hand, see the man casually lower his rifle into firing position. The bastard knew exactly what he was doing. "He was trying to kill me."

I also remembered the crazy thoughts that were going through my head—the words to a song that I hadn't heard in years, Chester Arthur Burnett's "Killing Floor." Weird.

"He was up in the field by the fence line. Has Buck been in?"

"He dropped me here. You must've been conscious enough to tell him I'd be staying in Toledo. He had the state highway cops stop me. Last I heard, he was still up at the house. He called once."

"Did anyone let Janet know?"

Lane and Janet Orr had met only once. The two of them seemed to get along, but I sensed an uneasiness. Savvy and I have remained married despite the years and the thousands of miles between us. I think Lane has never stopped hoping that we'll work it out—get back together—and I think she assumed that there was more to Janet's and my relationship than there was.

"I haven't seen her," Lane said. "I don't know if Buck called her. Couple of other people have been in. Chuck Logan's wife brought the flowers."

I glanced at the wildflower arrangement on the table to my right. "How long do I have to stay wired up here?"

"Pop . . ."

"With the drugs they're pumping into me, I doubt that I'll stay awake long. Let's get this worked out. Besides comparing me to a B-movie actor, what did the doctor say?"

"She says she wants you on your feet first thing in the morning. And maybe . . ."

"Provided there are no complications," I said, well aware of the drill.

"*Provided there are no complications*, you can go home in a day or two."

"Insurance company probably told her to get my ass out of here. That's fine. I don't much care for the steel and vinyl ambience. Does Buck know that this was no accident?"

"You told him that. He said he was treating it as an attempted murder."

"Sounds like you'll live," Buck Semple said as he walked through the doorway.

Semple had put in twenty-five years with the

Massachusetts State Police, retired, then took the job as Chief at the Lake Albert PD—a three-person operation (two of them part-time). Despite my tenure in the Boston area, Buck and I never crossed paths back there. He's a tall, slender man with a 1950s crew cut—one of those cops who have law enforcement in their blood. Over the years, he had been out to the house a couple of times, asking me to help unravel a series of sexual assaults and one particularly nasty homicide. On my twice-monthly trips into the village, Buck and I usually had lunch at the Lake Albert Diner.

"It wasn't a good day to die," I muttered.

I remember reading somewhere, many years ago, that a Native American tribal chief—maybe it was Crazy Horse—said that any day was a good day to die. It was a way of showing respect for life.

"Doc tells me you're gonna be sore for a while," Buck said. "You were lucky."

"Uh huh. Find anything out there?"

"I can point to the matted grass where he walked down from the fence, and the place where he stood and waited. That's about it. I tried to follow his path back toward North Road, but the guy knows the woods. He didn't leave much of a trace trail."

Lane said something, but I didn't hear it. I was drifting off—not to sleep, but to a place that my mind often visits. A compartment that is both open and confined, filled with chaos and control.

Paradox. The blood of my life.

I was groggy, and losing it, struggling to grab hold of what had happened. Why was I here? My mind slammed against a desolate reality that made no sense.

It was beginning.

That's what my dream about the bluefish had been telling me.

The hunter had become the hunted.

It was a terrible feeling.

LANE

WHEN POP AWAKENED, HE ASKED, "WHERE'D Buck go?"

"That was hours ago, Pop."

Pop looked and sounded irritated. "Usually, I don't mind not knowing what day or time it is. Right now it's pissing me off. I want to get back out to the lake. Buck's a good guy and a decent cop, but I have to get a look at this myself."

"Last thing he said was that I should stay the hell out of the investigation. That's the second time he's warned me, Pop. Anyway, how do you know the shooter won't come back and finish his business with you?"

"I don't know anything right now."

I left it at that. Pop and I were both frustrated, and nobody knew anything at the moment. It was time to start finding out a few things.

I caught a ride with a nurse who was headed into Lake Albert Village. I retrieved my car from the municipal lot, then drove along the south side of the lake, past the marina, until I found a motel—Paul's Lakeside. The place was a collection of separate cabins, each one with its own small beach, tucked into stands of pine for privacy. Mine was the last cabin at the end of a lighted walkway framed with railroad ties that had been cut into the natural slope of the land.

I brought in my suitcase and opened it. The only item I wanted was the Colt .38 I had packed. I slipped the holster clip over my belt and tucked the gun into place on my right hip, then drove back to the hospital and fell asleep in the chair beside Pop's bed. By the time the breakfast trays were being distributed the next morning, Pop was acting so cantankerous, I thought it would be safe—even pleasant—for me to escape the hospital for a few hours.

Dr. Grissom had decided to keep him another day. "The managed care outfit will probably send a hit man after her," Pop muttered. "She sure I got hit with enough bullets to rate another day? Maybe I should shoot myself a couple more times, to be sure."

"I need a decent cup of coffee," I lied, easing toward the door, "and I'm not going to find one here."

I drove out to Lake Albert. Something that Pop had said kept going through my head. He described stepping out his back door and seeing the sunlight bounce off a rifle scope. The reflection came from somewhere along the fence line, up on the hill. I wanted to go up there and take a look around.

I had no trouble finding the matted grass that Buck had described. It was midmorning when I began walking back and forth in the field, studying the ground. I walked the length of the chain-link fence, then took a half step farther away and walked the same distance again. I must have done that twenty times. Nothing.

Pop's cat, Max, sauntered up through the field and wound himself in figure eights around my legs. Finally, a little company. "Hey, big guy," I said. "I'll bet nobody thought to feed you."

I picked up the fifteen-pound cat and headed toward the house. When I used my key to open the side door, Max jumped down and led me to his dishes in the kitchen. I scooped out some dry food for him and changed his water.

It felt strange being in the house without Pop there. The place was like a slice of his life, interrupted. His keys, wallet, and pocket change were on the counter. The latest bills were thrown into a basket. There was an open box of garlic crackers, two empty ale bottles, a pot of burned pasta sauce on the stove. His leather work gloves lay crumpled on a stool.

I smiled when I saw a round, sea-polished piece of granite on top of his spice rack. Pop had accepted the baseball-sized rock from an indigent patient as payment for services. He had kept it all these years. I remembered other times that patients had paid him with baskets of tomatoes from their gardens, or jars of dilly beans from a family recipe.

I wandered to the back of the house where the control panel for the security system was. When the system was off, as it was now, a green light glowed on the panel. I hit the switch, arming the perimeter grid. The green light went out and a red light came on. Simple enough.

I disarmed the system, walked to the window, and looked down toward the driveway. I knew there was a small metal box that had something to do with the grid on a post near the entrance. And there it was, barely visible, at the southeast corner of the field—a tiny green light. It faced the house, so that it couldn't be seen by anyone coming up the drive, approaching through the woods from the east, or down low in a boat on the water. With binoculars, though, it could be easily viewed from the upper part of the field where the shooter had stood.

Whoever had come here from the north ridge had to be in good shape. It was at least a two-mile hike over ledges and through dense forest from North Lake Road to Pop's property.

"Determined sonofabitch," I muttered, letting myself out and locking the door.

POP

I COULD HEAR THE HOSPITAL'S MUTED SOUNDS as I drifted, half-conscious, in reverie.

Faces raced in front of my eyes, some colliding, some merging. I recognized one man, but could not recall his name at first. He was moving away from me when I remembered and called to him. He never turned back.

Then Lane thundered into the room.

"Wasn't Morgan Wylie the one who killed all those kids?" she asked.

"Wylie? Yeah. Why?"

"When I walked in, you were mumbling his name. Why would you be thinking about him?"

Good question. I hadn't thought about Wylie in years. I shook my head. "When I left my practice, I thought I left it all behind me. Sometimes I think we do our best jobs of deception on ourselves."

"Come on, Pop, cut the crap. I want to know about Morgan Wylie. What did you do?"

She wanted to know if I had committed yet another murder. Subtlety is a game Lane has not yet mastered.

I closed my eyes. "The killer left the kids nude, except that they always had their socks on. He didn't want their feet to be cold. Not because he was a nice guy. He was projecting. His feet were always cold because he had a circulatory problem. His father had the same problem and ended up with one foot. Morgan Wylie wore shoes a size too big so he could wear lots of socks. He was on the edge of that investigation for years. They questioned him half a dozen times. He even passed a polygraph. I spent part of a day with him. Told him that feelings of guilt worsened circulatory problems, usually ending with amputation. I said there were studies that showed that people who unburdened themselves kept their feet. Wylie didn't want to lose his feet, so he confessed."

I took a deep breath, exhaled, then opened my eyes. "It was a matter of creating a different reality for him."

My head was throbbing. I was due for another dose of Demerol, but I didn't want it. My body had to heal, and my mind had to clear. "The State of Texas executed him many years ago. I don't know why he's turning up in my head now, but I'm sure there's a reason."

Buck Semple was growling at Lane before he had walked all the way into the room. "You were seen up at the lake," he shouted. "I told you twice to stay out of this thing."

"She's a cop, Buck," I told him. "A homicide detective. Based on what I hear, she's good at what she does."

"Lane, stay the hell out of this case," he barked.

"I can't do that, Buck," she said, getting up and walking from the room.

I chuckled softly. I couldn't believe I was having to deal with these two.

Semple turned his wrath on me. "I heard a few things about what happened in that situation a year or so ago. You don't work with law enforcement, Lucas. They've gotta tag along behind while you do your thing. Lane's starting to pull the same shit, but the system doesn't work that way."

I wanted to tell Buck that the system did not work at all, but thought better of it. He was already cranked.

Police agencies, local and federal, tend to be linear. If an approach is not in the manual—if it does not pass the test of hard, unrelenting logic—it is not used. There is no role for instinct.

The courts are worse, true theaters of the absurd, with witnesses rehearsed like actors, and evidence little more than polished props. Televised trials have done better in the Nielsen ratings than the afternoon soaps.

"Lane isn't about to compromise your investigation," I told Semple. "She could be of some help to you. I'm the one who could be the pain in your ass, and I'm not doing much of anything right now."

"You switched off the security system," Buck said. "The afternoon you were hit."

"Yes, yes I did. Chuck was bringing up some wood. Lane was due to arrive. I was getting into the shower."

"How did the shooter know?"

I have no phone to tap. Never use the things. No one had been out to the house in two weeks. I use the fax sparingly.

"I don't know."

"Somebody you locked up?"

"Some of my patients weren't exactly enamored of me. So, yes. Maybe. I don't know. I've got a couple of computer disks at the house with lists of the dangerous and the delirious."

He reminded me that it was his case, told me he would be in touch, then stomped out.

Long after Buck—only somewhat mollified—had gone, I stared at the ceiling. Despite his grouchiness, the chief's arrival had interrupted a conversation that was headed in a direction I did not want to go.

My daughter needed to talk about things that two days ago were nicely straightforward in my head—and now were ominously less so.

EARLY THE NEXT AFTERNOON, LANE AND I HEADED for my place at the lake. Buck didn't want us anywhere near there, but I was not about to be evicted from my home.

"You could both end up as targets," he had said. "We don't know what we're dealing with here."

He was right, of course. I figured that I might have to break out some of my unused arsenal, but I was *not* going into Buck's version of a witness protection program over at the Lakeside Motel.

I had trouble getting into Lane's little car and was starting to hurt from bouncing around on the dirt roads in her aqua sardine can. "Why didn't you use the Jeep? Or gotten something bigger?" I complained.

"Wouldn't make any sense in the city. We'll be there soon."

"Not soon enough," I said, gripping the overhead handle as if my life depended on it. Which it did. "Buck check the house?"

"First thing this morning."

"We won't be there for long. Maybe a couple of days."

"What are you talking about?"

"My horoscope said there was a trip in my future."

"You read that stuff?"

"Religiously. That and the comics. The rest of the newspaper isn't worth a damn."

"You believe it? The horoscopes?"

"About as much as I believe the comics. They're more entertaining than reading about how Washington is finding new and creative ways to fuck over the poor, the disabled, and the elderly."

We drove in silence for several minutes, then Lane said, "Pop, we're not dealing with some asshole running around the lake taking potshots. This guy was gunning for you and we've got no idea who the hell he is. What are we gonna do?"

I looked at Lane's profile, watched as she brushed her hair back from her face. She had driven to Lake Albert expecting to relax—do some fishing, soak up some sun—and to have a serious talk with her old man about his homicidal behavior. Instead, she had found me in the hospital, the house a crime scene, and no one having any idea what murderous wretch might be wandering the woods. It was no wonder that Lane's grip on her control had slipped a notch.

"I need a little time," I said gently. "We'll get the bastard, but I have to do it my way."

She nodded and glanced over at me. "I'm just frazzled, Pop."

"Lane, the reason I said there was a trip in my future is that I'm convinced this shooter isn't a local. After my head cleared, I was able to do some thinking. In the nearly six years I've lived at the lake, I have gotten to know Buck, Janet, Chuck Logan, a few of the local merchants. That's about it. With the exception of Buck and Janet, the most anyone knows about me is that I'm a retired shrink. People here respect each other's privacy. This guy came with an agenda: kill Lucas Frank. I think that he would want to draw a minimum of attention to himself, get his job done, and get out of town. So . . ."

She snapped a quick incredulous glance at me. "So, what? You're going after him?"

"I hope it doesn't come to that," I said.

"But, it might?"

She drove into the yard, stopped the car, and switched off the ignition.

"It might," I said. "Now, would you mind opening the place? I want to go down and look at my lake."

When I had trouble getting out of the car, Lane came around and gave me a hand.

"I'll be right in," I said.

I walked down to the dock. A cold wind blew from the north end of Lake Albert. It was October, the skies wide and clear—too early for a frigid Canadian gale. Still, gusts ripped the surface of the lake into a froth of whitecaps.

I gazed across at Janet Orr's clapboard house, then north toward the ridge where my shooter had probably begun his trek to my house.

Who are you?

The wind whipped through my hair. Whoever he was, he had almost gotten me.

Death visits, but has to leave empty-handed.

"You can't have been too happy about that," I muttered.

I moved away from my windblown shore and walked

across the grass and into the house. Lane had turned down my bed. "I want to take a shower first," I said. "I feel like I've been slimed."

"Where are the computer disks Ginger sends you?" she asked.

Ginger, my former secretary in Boston, was an ardent admirer of VICAP who thought that I should have my own directory of deviants. She was still at it, sending periodic updates.

"The packages are in by the computer. I don't think I've ever opened them."

I could hear Lane fussing as I wandered into the bathroom. "Where's my Ivory?" I shouted. "I don't want stinky soap."

She couldn't hear me over the Leonard Cohen she had cranked up on the stereo. I checked the wastebasket, found my soap, then trashed the flowery stuff. I couldn't believe she had gotten to the soap so fast.

I toweled off, pulled on a pair of sweatpants, and curled onto my bed. I must have been asleep within seconds, and I doubt that I shifted position. The next thing I knew, there was a flock of chickadees doing their imitation of an orchestra of flutes and fifes in the morning sun outside my window.

LANE

I WALKED INTO POP'S ROOM DURING THE NIGHT. He was still, and peaceful, and sleeping what he had always called "the sleep of a child."

I stood in the darkness at the foot of his bed and wondered what my father's dreams were like. I decided that he was so physically exhausted that he probably was not dreaming at all.

In the morning, I got up with the birds, put the coffee on, and decided to take a crack at Pop's computer database that I had installed on my laptop. Leonard Cohen was grumbling about the Chelsea Hotel when Pop wandered into the study.

"How are you feeling?" I asked.

"Better. I didn't expect to sleep all night. Guess I just needed my own bed. Do I smell coffee?"

"I made a pot. Sit down and I'll get you some."

When I returned with the coffee, I watched as Pop prowled through his books. He yanked out a battered hardcover that looked like an antique. "What's that?"

"*The Monster of Düsseldorf*, by Margaret Seaton Wagner. It was published in 1932. I don't know what's drawing me to this particular volume, but I've learned not to second-guess my instincts. No word from Janet?"

I glanced at the empty fax machine, shook my head, and returned to my work at the computer.

"Hmphh. She didn't say anything about going out of town."

Pop curled up with his book, and I continued to bang away at the keyboard. I had installed his disks and had the software operating. Now I wanted to pump my father for characteristics related to the shooter so that I could feed them into a set of search criteria. He was more interested in Margaret Wagner's description of the exploits of Peter Kurten, a German serial killer from the 1920s and '30s.

"I'm not fond of computers anyway," he said. "I agree with the Unabomber's professed philosophy about technology. Fortunately, I have a different way of expressing it."

"It's giving me twelve spaces," I interrupted, futilely hoping to turn his attention back to the program. "What about 'crack shot'?"

"Marksman. One of the FBI's 'mind hunters' claims credit for the term 'serial killer.' Margaret Wagner came close. She called Peter Kurten a 'series killer.' In the 1980s, the feds went to categories and definitions— cooling-off periods, a minimum of three dead, that sort of nonsense. Great fun if you have the mind of an accountant, but not if you want to catch a killer. Where would we be as a civilization without labelers?"

I had a certain fondness for my father's favorite polemic but enough was enough. "You fully awake now?" I asked.

He nodded happily. "Coffee's good. Double Italian roast."

"Whatever that black stuff was in the freezer. Now, are you ready to help me with this?" I nudged, indicating the computer program.

"I'll learn more from Peter Kurten. You know, I was a labeler all those years that I went to my office. This one's schizophrenic. That one's borderline. The one who's examining the walls for thought-stealing devices is a tad paranoid. Insurance companies and health management outfits require labels so they can determine if a patient needs three sessions or five—as if anything could be cured in that time. Clerks who don't know a schizoid from a solenoid make those decisions."

"C'mon, Pop. I need some help."

"Okay," he said, sighing. "We don't know a hell of a lot. So I don't know why you're bothering me. He's bright, and he's deliberate. He had to do some homework to know that I had a security system in place. Maybe he was here before, saw the perimeter guard, and realized that it can't be disarmed outside. If you tamper with it, it goes off. So, he could have waited for me to shut down the system, or he knew that I would have it down. I don't know what that program wants, but I want to get back to my book. Peter Kurten said that the biggest disappointment in his life was that he wouldn't get to hear his own blood drip into the bucket when they decapitated him. Charming fellow."

"All right, all right, tell me about him," I said, leaning back in my chair, giving in to the inevitable. Besides, he obviously had something on his mind and it was bound to be more interesting than the database.

"Kurten fascinates me. He killed his victims in virtually every imaginable manner. He set fire to women. Stabbed them with screwdrivers. Bludgeoned children. Drowned them. He operated on the basis of what he called 'compensatory justice.' Simply stated, his sole motivation was vengeance. He believed that every slight, or perceived affront, gave him license to enter any home, to assault, maim, murder anyone he selected, so that 'society' received its payback. For years he terrorized an entire city. He said at his trial that he was sending them a message. I think I'm beginning to understand why I woke up drawn to this particular book. Vengeance is a good choice of motivation for our shooter. But for what? What did I do to him? What's *his* message?"

In his own way, Pop already was working on the case. His head never stopped working.

While he was mulling through the mind of our anonymous shooter, I pushed myself away from the desk. "I found something for you in the hospital gift shop," I said, handing him the small package.

I watched as he pulled the tissue from a stone carving of an African lowlands gorilla. He studied its hunched posture, huge hands, and black eyes, and seemed mesmerized by the precision of the artist's work.

"Why do you love them so much?" I asked.

"I've always been fascinated with the animal," he said. "When I was a kid, I identified with one particularly imposing gorilla who was locked in a stone cage at a zoo near the tenement where we lived. He was trapped, and that was how I felt then. Trapped. If he had been left alone and unprovoked in the wilds, he would have lived a relatively peaceful existence. Locked up, taunted, and tortured—as my gorilla was—he could only erupt in a destructive rage."

"The one in the zoo did?"

"Some kids threw lighted bottles of gasoline into his enclosure. He broke free. The police had to shoot him."

"God, that's horrible."

Pop looked down at the stone carving in his hand. "I imagined that my anger was like a gorilla who lived inside of me. As I grew older, I thought I could even feel him there. My sister always said that I was a fearful child—'Sad and frightened by the world,' she said. She was right. I learned fast that it was easy to transform intolerable feelings of sadness, fear, and helplessness into fury."

"Savvy told me that when you were a kid, you saw *Mighty Joe Young* about a dozen times."

"More," he said. "Do you know the story?"

I shook my head.

"Mighty Joe was a gentle, giant ape, taken from his home in the jungle by a Hollywood nightclub owner. After three drunks slipped backstage and primed Joe with whiskey, the gorilla went on a rampage—tearing the nightclub apart, terrorizing the patrons into a stampede that spilled out onto the city streets. Even his having saved children from a burning house couldn't redeem him. Joe had to die. My sister took me. I remember our trips up Dale Street to the Warren Theater in Roxbury. She didn't seem to mind."

"Is she the one who used to take you to the zoo?"

Pop looked at me with a strange intensity. "Lane, what is it that you want to know?"

"How you think. Why you think the way you do. How you came to be the person you are."

"Because I killed a man?"

"That's part of the reason," I agreed.

Pop placed the stone gorilla on the table beside him. "Well, it looks like we're finally going to have that talk. Lane, for thirty years, I immersed myself in murder and murderers. The reason I experienced the success that I did was that I never tried to deny my own violent impulses. Whenever I felt it necessary to rip into and expose a killer's secrets, to bring him to tears or rage, I did it. I had the knack of 'out-psychopathing' the psychopath. John Wolf was going to kill you. I wouldn't let that happen. Period. The criminal justice system would have diddled around with him—or he with it—for years. That was unacceptable. Does that answer your question?"

"I had more than one, Pop," I said, smiling.

"You know, it isn't a requirement of the father-daughter relationship that we agree on any of this."

"I know that."

"Good. Now, I'm going for a boat ride. I'm headed for Janet's. Want to come?"

"No, thanks," I said. "I'm gonna bang around in this database some more. You sure you should be bouncing around on the lake so soon?"

"There's just a light chop on the water this morning. I'll be fine. Back in an hour."

When he got up, Pop touched the side of my face. "I love you, Lanie," he said.

"Love you, too, Pop."

I watched him when he headed out through the sliding-glass doors. He stopped on the patio, gazed to his right, up into the field where the shooter had stood.

Only then did I notice that my father was carrying a gun.

POP

I GUIDED MY EIGHTEEN-FOOT BOSTON WHALER across Lake Albert's choppy surface. In the distance, I could see Janet's boat secured to her dock.

I remembered my first week at Lake Albert. Janet paddled across the lake in a kayak to bring me a house-warming gift. Someone had briefed her. The gift, neatly wrapped in the previous Sunday's comics section, was a book on how to make the most of an early retirement.

Janet was tall, forty-two, and wore her black hair fashionably short. She had a college student's preference for black clothes—sweaters, shirts, jeans, an occasional skirt, onyx rings, and necklaces.

"You're the prematurely tired shrink," she said, welcoming me to the lake.

"Word gets around fast."

"All the waterfronts come equipped with cans and string."

"Are you the welcome wagon?" I asked.

"Janet Orr. I've got the small clapboard place over there," she said, pointing to the northwest.

There were only four houses at our end of the lake, so I had no trouble placing it.

"Lucas Frank," I said, smiling, and we shook hands.

We talked about everything—music, the weather, cooking, her work as a potter, politics, her estranged husband in Wisconsin, my estranged wife in what was then called Zaire, and cats. I had one. She had three.

That was six years ago. We had dinner together—her place or mine—once or twice a month. Occasionally we would take off, like we had for Vancouver. We became the best of friends.

As I stepped onto the dock, I wondered again why I had not heard from Janet. News travels fast at Lake Albert, especially bad news. I walked up the steps to her deck, and when she did not respond to my knocking, I shoved at the sliding-glass door. It was locked.

I wandered around the north side of the building. She had parked her Honda in the driveway and left the garage door open, something she often did when she was working in the yard, but she wasn't in the yard.

The front door was also locked. Janet's garden gloves and a trowel rested on the brick steps. I tried the door knocker and chimes, but again there was no answer, and no sound of anyone stirring inside.

It was possible that she had locked the house and driven off with a friend, but she would not have left the garage door up.

I walked down West Shore Drive to Ann Chelsea's house. Janet's only neighbor met me on the dirt road.

"Is she back?" Ann asked. "I've been calling and getting the machine."

I shook my head. "When did you last see her?"

The gray-haired octogenarian thought for a moment. "It was right before I heard you were in the hospital. Eva Logan called me. There was a man here from a foundation, and he was looking for Janet. He showed me his business card and all. I'm worried, Lucas. I almost called Buck Semple."

For Ann Chelsea to consider calling Buck meant that she was damn near in a panic state. "Call Buck now," I told her. "Ask him to meet me at Janet's."

"Oh, God. I hope she didn't have a fall," Ann said as she turned back toward her house.

My bandaged side stinging, I jogged back up the road, went directly into Janet's garage, and tried the door to the house. Like the others, it was locked. I grabbed a screwdriver from the tool rack and pried between the doorjamb and the lock housing. On my third try, the door popped open.

The rancid stench of death knocked me back a step.

"Oh, Jesus," I muttered, grabbing the nine-millimeter semiautomatic pistol from my hip.

I stepped into the mud room and moved toward the kitchen door that I knew had no lock. The house was silent. I covered my left hand with a plastic bag from Janet's recycling bin, then grasped the knob and pulled gently. The smell came on stronger.

I saw an arm on the floor, extending out from behind the sink. The hand was palm up. The fingers were curled.

Janet's left hand. The wedding ring she still wore.

As I moved farther into the room, I could see Janet's body, facedown, her head surrounded by a pool of hardened black blood.

Janet is dead.

I didn't know what had hit me harder—the two slugs that had slammed me to the ground, or staring down at my friend's corpse.

Janet Orr was dead. I knew the words. I had the information. I saw her legs stretched out behind her in black jeans, work boots on her feet. I pulled my gaze away and scanned the kitchen. My eyes were watering, blurring my vision.

My knees threatened to buckle.

"What the hell were you doing at McDonald's?" I asked, half expecting her to answer.

I was staring at a take-out coffee cup and paper bag. Janet hated that shit.

There was blood spatter on the sink and on the few dishes stacked to the right. Janet was probably standing at the sink, with her back to her killer.

I looked again at Janet's wedding ring. After twenty years of marriage, her husband, Lou, had announced that he was gay. He had left her, and now he was dying of AIDS. Janet had been paying for his hospice care.

Who would want to kill this woman?

I reholstered my gun and dropped to one knee so that I could see the source of all the blood. Her head was turned slightly. Someone had slit her throat and she had fallen, twisting slightly on the way down.

"Why did you turn your back? Who the fuck was here?"

Had her killer toyed with her? Talked to her for a while? Lulled her into a sense of security? The cupboard door was open, revealing shelves of dishes, mugs, and tumblers. Maybe she had been reaching for a glass when he grabbed her.

I looked at Janet's hands and forearms, then glanced again around the room. There was nothing out of place, nothing that indicated struggle, no defensive wounds.

He approached her from behind and cut her throat.

The McDonald's bag stood like an ornament on her

kitchen table. In addition to the coffee cup, now I also saw a Big Mac box.

I had noticed no evidence of forced entry. She let him in, trusted him. Was it someone she knew?

She spent time with him.

"What the fuck for?"

"Lucas?" Buck called from the garage.

I ran my hand back through my hair. "In here, Buck."

He stepped through the kitchen door. "Oh, shit."

I nodded. "You'd better get whoever it is you use for crime scenes."

"You touch anything?"

"Just the doorknob," I said, holding up my left hand, still clad in its plastic bag. "Oh, and I grabbed a screwdriver off the rack out there. I had to jimmy the door."

"You okay?"

"No."

My friend was dead, and I was overwhelmed with the sense that this wasn't happening for the first time.

Buck grumbled into his handheld radio, barked commands, snapped directions.

Since I had entered the room, my eyes had focused on Janet's body, then the kitchen table, then back again—like someone watching a tennis match. I stood, walked to the table, and gazed down at what was probably a killer's residue.

Bag. Cup. Sandwich collar and wrapper. Receipt dated the day before I was shot. A single page torn from a book.

"What book?" I muttered.

"You say something?"

I waved Buck off, and he continued talking into

his radio. I leaned over the table. Page 108 from the text section of what looked like a birding field guide. Flycatchers. At the top of the page was the eastern kingbird—*Tyrannus tyrannus.* The cruel ruler. The tyrant.

"State guys are on their way," Buck said. "You been through the place?"

I shook my head.

"Lucas, if you want to go outside . . ."

"No. Let's look around."

Buck handed me a pair of latex gloves and I snapped them on. I wandered into the living room, hearing the occasional burst of noise from Buck's radio, his voice as he responded to the calls, then I wandered back to the kitchen, unable to stay away.

Janet Orr had detested the sharp edge of violence that she said she saw surrounding me. Lane often sent murder over my fax machine. It had been my work, then it was my daughter's. Janet hated it.

She had kept Max when I went to Vermont to deal with the killer John Wolf. The night I returned to the lake I stopped at her place to retrieve the cat, but he did not want any part of me. I remember how Janet stared—first at him, then at me. Standing in the dim light of a kerosene lamp, she said, "Go home, Lucas. Get human."

Now, I stood looking down at her body. Her corpse. And I, too, hated the violence. I looked up at Janet's bookcase. She had three bird books, two of them field guides—Peterson's and Audobon's. The Peterson was the right size, so I removed it from the shelf and found page 108. *Tyrannus tyrannus.* It was identical to the page on Janet's table, but not as worn.

What the hell is going on? Did this guy bring his own bird book to a murder? And why the fuck do I feel as if I should know what's going on?

"I don't think this has to do with Janet," I said.

Buck walked through the archway behind me. "So what does it have to do with?"

"Did Ann Chelsea mention some guy who was up here looking for Janet?"

"Something to do with a charitable foundation, she said. I'll get a complete statement from her later."

"I figure that was the day before my visit from our assassin."

"I'm not following."

"My perimeter security system was down. Chuck Logan was delivering wood, and Lane was arriving. Janet knew both of those things."

"Lucas, you're stressed out. We've got totally different MOs here. You were shot . . ."

"Fuck the MOs," I snapped. "You'd rather believe that somebody came here, hung out for coffee and lunch, slit Janet's throat, then went merrily on his way? And the next day, a totally different person blew me down? That gives us two assassins, unrelated, taking out two people who *do* share a relationship. Bullshit. This is Lake Albert, not the Bronx."

A call on Buck's radio pulled him away.

I remembered sitting with Janet in my den late at night a month after my return from Vermont. She said, "One day this is all going to end."

I misunderstood. "Oh, I don't know. The Berlin Wall's down, Moscow's gone democratic. Who's left to drop the bomb? North Korea, maybe, but I don't think they have a plane to fly it this far. Unless we sold it to them, of course."

Janet pushed a wisp of black hair away from her forehead. "The world is more stable, but you aren't. You're volatile. I used to wonder what you were like when you were younger. Then I saw you when you came back from New England, and I knew. There'll be another one, another killer who will twist you inside out. You say there won't, but there will."

She looked hard at me. "I don't want to be around when it happens," she said.

She was right. There was another one, and she had not been given a choice about being around when it happened.

I wandered out through the kitchen and garage, and into Janet's front yard. I could hear the trees creaking as they moved gently in the wind, and the scurrying of a small animal through the fallen leaves. I felt shock giving way to frustration and anger. I was totally bewildered, unable to make any sense out of Janet's murder or the attempt on my life, but I knew that somehow the two events were connected.

I looked back at Janet's house. Why did I feel as if I had observed this scene before?

Like someone had dropped quarters into a jukebox and played the same song over and over.

I gazed through the skeletal branches of the trees at the sky and watched as the clouds seemed to form faces.

I remembered a man in a John Deere cap, and a woman in a yellow plastic jacket with the logo of a volunteer fire department.

They were real people. Where had I seen them?

The plastic woman grasped a child with straw hair, vacant gray eyes, her thumb stuck in her candied mouth.

Buck shuffled through the leaves behind me.

Wherever I had been, I remembered loud young men at a bar. Women mud wrestled on TV. Aggression and sex were fused for humor and entertainment. And the same song played over and over on the jukebox.

"Lucas?"

Where was I?

"Yeah, Buck."

He clapped his hand on my shoulder. "State folks are on their way. I'm sorry."

I nodded, and then I remembered.

Vermont.

LANE

POP WAS DOZING IN HIS CHAIR WHEN I HEARD the knock on the door. I slipped my .38 from its hip holster and headed for the front of the house.

"It's probably Buck," Pop called after me. "Don't shoot him."

It *was* Buck.

When he had settled into the overstuffed chair opposite mine, the chief made his announcement. "The day before the shooting, Murphy's—that store up on the state road that sells everything from rubbers to Rugers—sold a Remington 30.06 to a guy named Charles S. Weathers from Nebraska. Said he was up here hunting. He had all the right papers, waited his three days, paid cash. But there's no such guy. All his IDs are genuine; they're in the computers. He left all kinds of tracks, but he isn't real."

"You can add multiple identities to your list of characteristics for the computer," Pop said. "Also, he's smooth. He was convincing in whatever role he selected for himself. Janet invited him in and spent time with him."

I hadn't seen my father look so miserable since my mother left for Africa.

"Ann Chelsea's description of the foundation guy who was looking for Janet's place sounds pretty close to what I got from Murphy's," Buck said. "White male, forties, six feet, dark hair with some gray, mustache. Lucas, you're right. He didn't bust into Janet's. It does look like they talked some. Far as we could tell, nothing was missing from the house. She was still wearing her diamond ring. The TV, VCR—everything was where it belonged. This was well organized."

"Well organized" was a quality that I had heard Pop attribute to many killers over the years. Serious killers.

"No signs of struggle," Pop said. "No defensive wounds. While he was playing his part, he knew that he was going to kill her. He chewed his hamburger, sipped his coffee. The whole fucking time he was into his own private excitement. Only he knew what he was going to do. That's an enormous amount of power—a natural for sadistic fantasies."

"We figure that when he had what he wanted, he cut her throat," Buck said. "The county doc who came to the scene said she was probably grabbed from behind. He also said the cutting was a neat job. 'Precise' was the word he used—like somebody who knew exactly what he was doing."

"I think he got his information about the security system from Janet," Pop said. "At the very least, he had to have known that it was there. How else? Nothing's making sense. My thinking is all muddy."

As Buck and I continued to examine the bits of information and the impressions that we were collecting, I noticed Pop drift away from our conversation. Finally, he left the room.

"He gonna be okay?" Buck asked.

"This has hit him hard."

"I'm beginning to think he's right about what went down over there. Janet Orr was one stop on the killer's way here."

"Pop said something about a page torn from a book."

Buck flipped through his notebook. "Peterson's *Field Guide to the Birds*. It didn't come from Janet's copy. It was on the table with the crap from McDonald's."

"Any similar crimes?" I asked.

"Nothing in-state. I haven't done the VICAP form yet. Damn thing'll take a weekend."

"So, this guy probably found out about Pop's security system—that it would be off—from Janet."

Buck thought for a moment. "At first, I didn't think so. There's no telling how he got it out of her, but I guess I have to agree."

"So he went after Janet for information. Why'd he go after Pop?"

I was thinking out loud, not necessarily asking Buck, but he answered anyway.

"Lane, I don't know why this guy has a hair across his ass about your father. But he does. He wants Lucas Frank dead. And I don't think we've heard the last of him."

POP

I WANDERED INTO THE KITCHEN, LEAVING BUCK
and Lane to compare their investigative notes. I found
a bottle of Sierra Nevada pale ale in the refrigerator,
pried off the cap, and sipped.

Messages.

The mind is always at work. We know things that
we do not realize we know, because they have not bubbled up into conscious thought. People say that something is "right on the tip of my tongue."

The more effort we exert to retrieve it, the more
elusive it seems. Later, when we're not trying to remember, that bit of information "pops" into consciousness.
My experience has been that the less effort I exert, the
less encumbered is the associative process that is always going on in one of the far corners of my mind.

I sat at my old maple table and fixed my gaze on the
stone gorilla that Lane had given me. I allowed myself
to slip into a familiar hypnotic state. Within seconds I
was drifting back to the day of the shooting.

Marinara. Pale ale for me and for the pot. Shower.
Stepping outside the back door. A flash of light. Twisting

down and away. A mental snapshot—not quite in focus—of a man dressed in black, up by the fence. And me, down on Chester Arthur Burnett's "Killing Floor"— the song that played in my head as I lost consciousness.

In 1928, as Peter Kurten terrorized Europe, Chester Arthur Burnett mounted a stage with his first band and belted out his own brand of Mississippi Delta blues. Those who heard the big man described his deep, growling voice as "lupine." It made sense that he would perform for half a century as Howlin' Wolf.

Howlin' Wolf. Charles S. Weathers from Nebraska. The inexplicable alleys of the human mind. Bruce Springsteen had written a song about a killer from Nebraska. I had stood in Janet Orr's yard staring at the clouds and seeing the face of a kid with her thumb stuck in her mouth—a kid I'd seen in Vermont.

I was beginning to have a notion of what we might be dealing with. "How could that be possible?" I muttered.

What had set everything in motion, and resulted in my trip to the northeast last year, was a crime-scene photograph—a woman lying on her living-room floor, her throat cut with surgical precision.

The wind slashed across the lake. A loose shutter on the north side of the house clattered a reminder of work I had not done. I watched as a lone, hardy sailor brought about her blue catboat and headed back down the lake toward the marina. For just a second, I was certain that I saw Janet Orr sitting in the stern, both hands gripping the tiller.

Lane had moved on to the Roger Waters CD, *Amused to Death*—a soft din in the background, receding even farther as I drifted—and thoughts, pictures cascaded through my mind as if blown by the afternoon gale that churned Lake Albert.

The thoughts and pictures slowed, in defiance of the wind, until they too floated gently through awareness.

The dream. Drifting in a small red boat.

When I was a child on a visit with my sister to my grandmother's house, I walked out alone through the woods to the brackish waters at the mouth of the Weir River. A man stood on the bridge that spanned the moving water. He gripped a fishing rod—a magic wand, I thought, because he made fish jump from the water into his hands.

Later, my sister explained what I had seen that day, but I preferred my own version of events. I wanted to be like the man on the bridge—grasping a seven-foot stick of magic, luring fish from the rivers and lakes, the bays and the seas.

A streak of gray sliced through the water, followed by a solid pull on the line. Then nothing. The predator had become the prey.

I learned about fishing the same way that I learned about everything else: on my own. From books that I withdrew from the library. From watching others. From practice.

The child that I had been remained in me now—a lover of solitude, content with a stack of books, some music, and perhaps a slant on what my next act of defiance would be. When I was in my teens, my sister's husband said that I was oppositional, a troublemaker. He was right.

I was only twelve the first time my mother grabbed the kids, left my father, and took us all to stay with my grandmother in Hull. I remember taking my first spinning rod, an outfit from Sears Roebuck mail order, and walking to a wall behind the bait house at Nantasket Pier. It was a forbidden place. Dangerous, my mother said.

"Why?" I wanted to know.

"You might fall in."

"I can swim."

"No one would be there to help you."

I resorted to my secret weapon—sarcasm. "To help me swim?"

"You are not to go near that place," she snapped in her sharp, clipped tone that signaled the end of all discussion.

My secret weapon never seemed to work with her.

Her attitude reinforced my need to claim some independence. Sure I was defiant. I was going to do it my way. Obstacles—human or otherwise—were irrelevant.

I went fishing. Alone. Grasping my good-luck charm: a large treble hook that I used for snagging shiners for bait.

The water wore a multicolored halo of oil—a virtual slick that coated my line, the bobber, eventually my hands. No fish could have survived there. But there is more to angling than the fish. Ask any twelve-year-old kid with a bamboo pole and an empty afternoon.

I sat on the pier until dusk, proving my point about fishing and not drowning.

The real danger was one that my mother knew and hadn't told me. Its name was Hector—the pedophile who ran the bait shop.

I didn't know any of the clinical words then, but I did know that there was something unmistakably threatening about Hector. The gestalt was wrong—the stale smells of beer, sweat, motor oil, and bait. The stubble on his cheeks and chin. The matted black hair protruding from his Socony cap. The dirt-encrusted hands that gripped my shoulders as I stepped off the wall at the side of the bait shop.

The hunter of fish had become a fish for the hunter.

Much later, when I asked my sister about Hector, she told me the truth.

"Why didn't Ma tell me?" I asked.

"She won't talk about bad things."

"Then how am I supposed to know?"

"She says, 'What you don't know won't hurt you.'"

"But that's what hurts the most."

When Hector's hands closed on my shoulders, he never got a chance to say a word. I turned, raked his face with the big treble hook, then ran.

"Hector's face is all bandaged," my sister told me. "They say he'll have a bad scar."

Months after my fishing expedition, I saw the scar. I was walking along the breakwater toward my cave—a shelter that I had discovered in my travels, formed by scrapped slabs of gray and black granite—when Hector drove up in his old, light green Packard.

"I'm gonna get you, kid," he said.

I shook my head.

"You're right. I can't run along them rocks after you. But later. That's when I'm gonna get you. When you don't expect it."

I shook my head again. Then Hector floored the Packard, kicking up gravel and cinders.

"He wants to give you nightmares," my sister said. "He's mean."

The bluefish closed its teeth on my arm. It was a gesture of mindless, random meanness.

Even as a twelve-year-old, when confronted with a

predatory human, I shifted into an instinctive state. Fear disappeared. Rage bubbled up in a slow simmer. Then I acted.

Late one night, when I was sure that everyone was asleep, I climbed out my bedroom window, creeping along the side of the house to the kerosene barrel. I filled a small jar, replaced the pin in the spigot, and walked down the hill to the bay.

Hector's house was in a setback near the breakwater. It was abutted on each side by a bar. The three buildings shared a backyard that was nothing more than a vacant lot of cinders and stone that the two bars used for a parking area. I knew he would be in one of the bars—either Callahan's or Surf's Up. I walked around his cottage twice, looking in the windows, seeking any sign of life. There was none, so I walked inside.

His bedroom smelled like the bait shop and resembled the town dump. Clothes strewn all over, a half-eaten cheese sandwich growing blue mold on a table beside a bed of unmade gray sheets. There was a picture of a glowing Jesus on the wall above the bed board.

I stepped into his closet and waited.

Twenty minutes later, I heard him come through the front door. Then I heard his footsteps in the hall, water running in the bathroom, the toilet flushing. When he stumbled through the bedroom door, he was naked—his limp dick wagging beneath a bulging belly full of beer.

Hector fell onto the bed and sighed. Then he did what I knew he would do: he tapped a Camel out of a pack for one last smoke before he passed out—just what my father would have done.

When Hector struck his match, I hurled my jar into

the face of Jesus. The son of God shattered, along with my jar.

And the room ignited.

What happens when the prey becomes the predator? What happens if you refuse to play the part of victim? What happens when you become more cunning and meaner than any other depravity in the world?

Later that night, my sister sat with me after the police had gone. She looked into my eyes. "He didn't die."

"I didn't want him to die. I just wanted him to know that if I'm to be afraid, and to have nightmares, then he can't sleep anymore."

Before my dream of the red boat, there was a flash of light up in the field to my right. I had stepped out the back door, a towel in my hand. A scope. A man holding a high-powered rifle. Blurred. Black pants, creased. A black shirt. Dark glasses. My height. Dark hair. So steady with his rifle, his elbow cocked out to his right. Military bearing. A sharpshooter. He shouldn't have missed.

"And maybe I, too, missed the mark," I murmured.

I was aware of Lane standing in the doorway behind me. "Buck leave?" I asked.

"He had some state people he had to talk to."

"Lane, one of the reasons you came out here was to talk about John Wolf."

"It can wait."

"No, it can't. You have questions about my actions in Vermont."

"It's like you said, Pop. We don't have to agree."

Lane, perhaps more than anyone else, knew that I worked from my own set of laws. Some were identical to those in the standard law books; the rest were more expedient or, in my opinion, more just.

Anyway, most of what was on the books represented a government's feeble attempts to regulate morality. It can't be done. People will use their drugs of
choice. They will engage in mutually consenting sexual
behavior that their neighbors consider an anatomical
atrocity. Some won't stand and salute the flag. Others
will express their discontent with government by burning the flag.

"Lanie, I *planned* to kill him. It never entered my
mind that I might not kill him, that I didn't have to kill
him. Nothing else mattered. I wanted him dead—
there's your premeditation—and he died."

She cocked her head to one side. "Afterward, when
the feds came to Michigan, what did you tell them?"

"I saw no reason to tell them the truth."

She was shaking her head, running her hands back
through her hair. "In the same situation, any other man
would have wondered if he had any reason to lie to
investigators. Your only question was, 'Do I have any
reason to tell them the truth?' You see the world so differently, Pop."

I shrugged. "Your mother used to tell me the same
thing. Lane, I want you to scribble a fax to Buck. His office is number eight on the auto-dial. He'll be getting
there soon. Ask him where in Nebraska Mr. Weathers
said he was from."

"What's this got to do with Wolf?"

It had everything to do with Wolf. I was growing increasingly convinced that my attempt to incinerate the
bastard had failed, that the most prolific killer I had
ever encountered—and the one who most needed to
die—somehow had walked away from Armageddon.

*The essential nature of the psychopath is the power
to play the shell game on a person's mind. When there*

are too many intrusions, too much abuse from too many fathers—most of them made mad from their own sense of power and mission—something snaps inside. Then, it is up to each of us to watch out for the sleight of mind game.

When I did not answer Lane, she left the room.

I walked to the kitchen counter, retrieved my copy of Peterson's *Field Guide to the Birds,* and returned to the table. I placed the book next to my stone gorilla, sat, and stared, and waited. In five minutes, Lane was back.

She looked at me and quietly asked, "What's he gonna say, Pop?"

She was playing a game that we had played since she was a child.

"Lincoln," I said. "This has everything to do with John Wolf."

I had traveled inside other people's minds. They had wandered into mine. I knew what they thought and felt and what they were going to say before they said it. When they did not want anyone to know who they were, when *they* didn't want to know who they were, I pushed their faces and their souls in front of a mirror. I exposed the fallacies in their thinking, and now, I feared, the fallacies in my own thinking were about to be put on display. I had made a monstrous mistake.

Lane stood in the doorway with a fax in her hand. "Right again, Pop," she said, according to the script for our game.

"Charles S. Weathers of *Lincoln*, Nebraska," I said, experiencing just a twinge of twisted admiration. "Charlie Starkweather? We have a killer with a sense of humor."

Starkweather, like Peter Kurten, operated according to a retribution- or vengeance-based system. With his fourteen-year-old girlfriend, Caril Fugate, in tow,

Starkweather set out from Lincoln in 1957—killing eleven times before he was finished. Every injustice that the nineteen-year-old garbage collector had experienced fueled his role as the ultimate rebel. He strode into Nebraska's death chamber, expressing only defiance right to the end. The executioner had to throw the switch on the electric chair three times—each a jolt of 2200 volts—before Starkweather agreed to die.

I flipped open my copy of Peterson and sought out the kingbird on page 108. The page was missing, excised neatly with a razor-sharp implement.

I was on my feet, grabbing my keys and moving toward the door. "You know how I feel about coincidence, Lane," I said. "There's no such thing. Like so many of Wolf's victims, Janet's throat was sliced with surgical precision. Wolf was trained as a marksman in the military. He grew up in Vermont, so he certainly knows his way around a deer rifle like a 30.06. He was consistent about signing in for his kills. Remember his fascination with birds? This time, instead of feathers, we get a page from a birding field guide—*my* fucking field guide, by the way. Who else would have the brass balls to kill Janet, shoot me, rip out a page from this book, then return to Janet's?"

"Could we have a copycat on our hands, Pop?"

"No," I said, slamming the door as I headed for my Jeep.

LANE

IT WASN'T THE FIRST TIME THAT I HAD BEEN unable to follow Pop's train of thought. He had come out of the hospital and latched on to Peter Kurten. Then it was Charles Starkweather. Now it was John Wolf.

I couldn't keep up with him.

I remember one time when I was in my teens, and I wandered into Pop's study. He was so busy poring over some photographs at his desk, he didn't notice me. His lips were moving, but I couldn't hear what he was saying. Then he got up and walked through the door that led to the garage. I followed him, passing close to his desk, glancing down at pictures of a dead young woman, her back laced with thin, bloody, parallel lines.

I kept moving, until I could see Pop on his hands and knees on the concrete garage floor. He raked his right hand across the rough surface of the cement, then stared at the bloody lines on his palm. "That's how she got those striated marks," he said. "He couldn't pick her up. He lifted her legs, dragged her across the concrete floor, then maneuvered her into the trunk."

Pop walked within feet of me, ignoring the blood

that stained his hand, and sat again at his desk. After a few minutes, he picked up the telephone receiver, and as he dialed, seemed to realize for the first time that his hand was bleeding. He balled up some tissues and gripped them, stanched the wounds, and made his call.

A few weeks later, I saw an article in the newspaper. The police had charged their prime suspect, Frank Lockerby, a mechanic, with the murder of a young woman. Pop was mentioned in the article, and so was his old police friend and my godfather, Ray Bolton.

Years later, I asked Pop about the case. "The lines on the victim's back were crucial to making the case," he explained. "We could explain every other mark on her body, but didn't know what had caused those marks, and didn't know where the crime had been committed. Once we knew how the marks were made, we had a crime scene—the gas station where Lockerby worked— and that gave Ray the additional physical evidence he needed to make the case. Lockerby was a shade over five feet tall, and had a slight build. He couldn't have lifted his victim. He had to drag her across the concrete floor."

That was only one of many times that I had learned not to question my father's erratic behavior in matters related to murder.

Now, I watched his Jeep disappear through the gate, and returned to my work at the computer.

Ginger had spent months putting together the relational database for Pop, but I wasn't having any luck making it work. I had entered all the criteria that Pop and I had been able to come up with, but every time I tried to run the program, I got the same on-screen message: GOTO:DEA.

I knew that Pop had done a lot of work for government agencies, but I had never heard him mention anything about Drug Enforcement. When I tried to call up the DEA file, the screen seemed to freeze, as if the computer were waiting for the rest of the command. After a series of tries, and just as many failures and reboots, I shut down the system and put away the disks. I was starting to agree with my father, at least as far as technology was concerned.

POP WAS GONE NEARLY TWO HOURS. I WAS READY to call Buck when I heard the Jeep pull into the yard.

"Fuckin' phones," he said as he came through the door.

"If you put one here in the house . . ."

"I'd have to talk to people."

"What about a fax with a handset? Stick an answering machine on it and turn off the ringer."

Pop ignored me as he stomped around the house. Max dove off his chair and headed for cover under the sofa.

Pop mumbled something that I couldn't hear.

"What?" I asked.

"Nothing."

"I hate it when you do that."

"I said you get more like your mother every day. She had to have a phone in every room. Even the fucking bathroom."

Pop was seething. He didn't say why he was angry, and I had long ago learned not to ask. When he's ready to talk, he talks. Not before.

"I booked a flight to Washington, D.C.," he said. "You can come if you want."

"What?"

"It's been a while since I've seen the Lincoln Memorial."

I knew that there was only one Lincoln on his mind. Lincoln, Nebraska. Charlie Starkweather—and whatever connection he had to our shooter. But the trail was here, not in Washington.

"Pop, what are you talking about? You've got a case to work. *We* do. You are somebody's target, and that somebody made Lake Albert his personal shooting gallery."

"Fine. You stay. I'll go."

He stalked into his bedroom. I could hear him yank open drawers and pull back the zippers on his duffel bag. I walked to the doorway.

"You know I'm not gonna let you go off alone," I said.

"Then go pack."

POP

THE 737 LIFTED OFF THE RUNWAY.

I looked down, watching the earth recede and race away. Lake Albert was far behind me. I was roaring toward something that I wanted nothing to do with, but I knew that I had no choice.

I was chasing a killer who consumed victims as if they were handfuls of cheese-flavored popcorn. He was a man who had operated according to his own agenda, who had lived as a god deciding who died and when, until I had tracked him down. For most of his adult life, John Wolf had sought his own justice for the physical and emotional pain inflicted on him by a sadistic stepfather. Now, a different vengeance drove him: I'd had the gall to interrupt his mayhem.

I had more questions than answers. Number one on my list was how anyone could walk away from an explosion that blew flames and debris a hundred feet into the air. I had locked him in the coal bin of his family's Vermont home and flipped a switch that triggered the load of the plastic explosives buried in the bin. Explosives *he* had planted to kill me and my daughter. Number two nudged for the top spot: Why hadn't he killed me when he had the chance?

When I first opened my practice in Boston, most of my referrals originated with the courts. Spousal homicide, familicide, patricide. I needed to know how the events of violence had evolved. The killer's dynamics could be understood only in the context of his or her relationships. Lengthy interviews with survivors—relatives, neighbors, the accused—provided a complete biography that moved inexorably toward a single convulsive moment.

Albert DeSalvo—"The Boston Strangler"—had changed everything. There were many other serial killers before him. Who knew what the werewolf legends of Europe really were? DeSalvo had brought his carnage into my neighborhood, and forced himself into my consciousness.

I was living on Beacon Hill when DeSalvo, in his cell at Bridgewater State Hospital, identified himself—first to fellow inmate George Nassar, then to the fiery young attorney, F. Lee Bailey—as Boston's most feared killer. It was close. One of the strangler's victims lived on Charles Street, within walking distance of my apartment. For me, in my practice, DeSalvo had changed the face of murder. He had known none of his thirteen homicide victims, nor had he known any of his countless "Measuring Man" or "Green Man" rape victims.

The sixties—a benchmark decade in music, political assassination, social revolution—also saw a sharp increase in the number of strangers killing strangers. How was it possible to trace the evolution of an act of violence that had no apparent context, where there was no discernible relationship? I was determined to find out, and developed my own approach to the art of identifying the characteristics of a killer from the evidence left at the crime scene, and from what I could learn about the victim's personality. It was a process of working backward.

I decided that examining the grab site and its circumstances were as important as microscopy of everything found at the kill site, the location that my colleagues in law enforcement insisted on calling the "crime scene." The crime, I decided, moved through several locations—whether within the same room, apartment, or house, or spread all over the city and throughout Suffolk County. The homicides that I studied had *scenes*, multiple locations that were equally important.

I remember one homicide detective telling me, "The perp grabbed her at a supermarket on the Cambridge side of the river, but he did her here."

"Here" was an alley in Boston's North End.

"Did he grab her inside the market, in the parking lot, what?" I asked.

"Inside. He didn't exactly *grab* her, Doc. They walked out together. What fuckin' difference does that make?"

"He established face validity," I said. "He was believable, seemed trustworthy, a nice guy."

"Nice guys don't do this shit, Doc."

The knee-jerk reaction had been to call these murders random, senseless, motiveless. They weren't. In our revulsion, our need to assign a label, and an equally strong need to distance ourselves from these killers, we hastened to dismiss them as sick, demented, insane. They weren't. Many of them were "nice guys."

What I eventually concluded offended everyone's sensibilities. It arrived one day in a blinding flash from Walt Kelly's *Pogo*: "they" were "us."

When I was young, in addition to a taste for the comics, I learned many things from my father. It is difficult to gain enlightenment from someone who is inebriated most of the time, but when he spoke in that thick brogue of his, I listened. He was uneducated, at least formally, but intelligent—a working-class drunk who imbibed philosophy when he wasn't sucking down Seagram's Seven in his tea.

He was . . . an unusual man. I wanted to know him, and I wanted him to know me. I remember wandering into his room one morning. He was reading, so I sat at the foot of his bed.

"Did you know that William Blake saw God?" he asked.

His voice had a raspy quality. It always did. Like someone shaking off the morning's alcoholic rust and trying to jump-start the day.

I shook my head.

"When he was a wee lad, about your age, he saw God looking at him. Blake wasn't crazy. He knew that the things we touch and smell and hear can matter only when they lead us back into our minds to what we can imagine. He knew that we must have evil. How else would we measure good? If we have heaven, we must have hell. He trusted his own mind, lad. He didn't wait for the priests and teachers to catch up. It's a heavy burden to bear, this trusting of your own mind."

"If I saw God," I said, "I might believe in Him."

"Aye, but ye'd probably be wrong. Maybe Blake did see the old guy. Maybe he didn't. But he definitely *felt* God inside his mind."

He coughed, lighted a Pall Mall, then added, "That never happened to me, but I remain open to the possibility."

Now, my father's words echoed in my head: *He trusted his own mind, lad.* That's what I had always tried to do, and it's what I had to do now. My mind would lead me to a killer, if I allowed it to.

After the pilot's announcement about our arrival time and the weather in D.C., Lane flipped open her laptop computer.

"You kids can't go anywhere without those things," I said, trying to focus my attention on a volume of poetry by Christina Rossetti.

"Do you think you're ever going to join the twentieth century, Pop?"

"Doubtful. I'm in the nineteenth right now."

I watched as she popped disks in and out, tapped commands, read whatever it was that the screen had to tell her.

"When did you ever work for the DEA?" she asked.

"Never did."

"When I get all of these characteristics in here and run the search, it says GOTO:DEA. But when I type DEA, nothing happens."

"Give Ginger a call when we get to D.C.," I suggested. "I don't know anything about it. We don't have those things here in the nineteenth century."

"Used properly, it saves time. Think of it as a tool."

"Technology is a drug. If we allow ourselves to become dependent on it, we're going to forget how to use our own powers of reasoning. People don't read enough anymore. They have 'multimedia experiences.' Sounds vaguely obscene, if you ask me. I'll take *Lady Chatterley's Lover* any day."

Lane laughed as she slipped the small computer back into its case.

It was time to include my daughter in my thinking,

so I started with the day of the shooting. "I saw him. He was dressed in black, dark glasses, maybe six feet tall. From his posture, I'd say that he learned to shoot in the military. He shouldn't have missed. Then he walked into the kitchen and tore the page from Peterson—an elaborate game. Put that together with all the other characteristics you were tapping into your twentieth-century toy."

I paused to allow Lane time to absorb that information, then said, "We're talking about John Wolf."

"A copycat. Like I said before. Somebody who studied Wolf, who is imitating him."

"Copycats are rare, Lanie. The concept appeals to the law enforcement community more than it equates with reality. Fear of the copycat becomes a convenient excuse to withhold more information in a case than is necessary. There have been a few. The Tylenol case comes to mind. When it does happen, it's a different pathology from what I've encountered among serial killers. Typically, it's someone at the fringes of sanity, about to tip over anyway. He hasn't had any formulated plan. There hasn't been anything to copy. The actions of the first killer serve as a catalyst, a trigger, and off he goes."

I looked at Lane and said, "We're going to see Dexter Willoughby."

Willoughby was the FBI agent who showed up at the old house in Vermont right after the explosion that I assumed had taken Wolf's life. Willoughby took over that scene, sealed it, then headed thirty-five miles north to secure Wolf's entire business operation.

"Willoughby wouldn't take my calls when I tried to reach him from Lake Albert. That's why I was . . . out of sorts when I got back from town."

"There's no way Wolf could have walked out of that inferno."

"I didn't think so, either. I'm still not convinced. Everyone, including me, assumed that Wolf was dead simply because of the force of the explosion. As far as I know, his death was never confirmed."

"How could he have survived that, Pop? No one could."

I thought about the last time that I had seen John Wolf. The killer was in the cellar of his boyhood home, sprawled on top of a bomb that was buried in the coal bin. It was the same coal bin that he had been locked in as a child—his stepfather's preferred method of discipline over the years.

"Lane, what might Wolf have done with all of those childhood hours alone in the terrifying darkness of that dungeon?"

Claw at the earth. Dig. Make your way toward freedom. Slow and steady, lad.

There was a large slab of sandstone in one corner of the coal bin. I had noticed it when I reburied Wolf's own explosives and changed his timing device. What would I have found if I had lifted it?

Wolf was fascinated with birds. The killdeer is a bird that builds its nest in a depression in the earth. If someone comes too near the nest, the bird emerges, feigns injury, hobbles with bent wing. I could see Wolf collapsing to the ground, wounded, like the killdeer only pretends to be. I could see him tunneling free from the cellar, dragging himself far away from the house.

Alive. Healed now. Taking flight. Seeking vengeance.

"If Willoughby wouldn't take your calls, he's not gonna let us through the front door."

"I'm confident that he already regrets not talking with me."

"Huh? Pop, he shut me out of the Wolf case totally. He didn't let the Vermont authorities in on any of it, either. After the first couple of days, he even began keeping his partner, Susan Walker, out of it. I hear he got all the credit for a major case cleared. He probably landed in a corner office, and sits behind a mahogany desk."

"I called a friend," I said. "Agent Willoughby will see us. If Wolf did get out of there alive, Willoughby is the one person who would know."

SHE WAS RIGHT ABOUT THE CORNER OFFICE. Willoughby's secretary ushered us in. But the desk that the FBI special agent was sitting behind was walnut, not mahogany. I nodded at the desk.

"Win some, lose some," I mumbled to Lane.

The small, slender man had been with the FBI for twenty years. He had worked with John Douglas, the legendary profiler who later retired and went to work trying to catch up with Robert Ressler in the book and sound-bite business. Both men regurgitated the same cases over and over—the famous felons they had visited and felt threatened by—without contributing anything new to understanding why any of them had done what they had done.

Willoughby had the requisite credentials, and because he was in the right places when the pictures were snapped, he was thought to be heir-apparent to those Quantico gurus. Willoughby was a political animal. He didn't want any part of the Behavioral Science Unit's windowless offices sixty feet beneath the earth at the

FBI Academy in Virginia. Slithering around Washington was more his style.

He had the requisite flag, the photograph of the president, the customary "praise" and "thank you" plaques, what I assumed was a photo of his family—posed like a Rockwell painting around a fireplace that could exist only on the cover of *The Saturday Evening Post*—and a framed snapshot of himself as a child, shaking hands with J. Edgar Hoover.

Willoughby was a linear thinker—A leads to B leads to C. It's the curse of the Western intellectual tradition, but our public schools keep shoving it down our throats anyway. I had told Lane that I imagined Dexter Willoughby doing the *New York Times* crossword in precise numerical order, never leaping ahead to the word at the heart of the puzzle—the one item that led to its solution. I also doubted that he had ever finished any of the puzzles.

"The senator called," Willoughby said.

"Ah . . . yes. A friend of mine from college," I told him.

The agent's face was the color of sourdough. "He threatened me with Boise if I didn't cooperate."

For a fed, that's worse than Havana. "They even take shots at the forest service people out there," I said.

I wanted this bastard to squirm, and he was well on the way.

"What is it you want?"

"Wolf."

The room was silent.

"Snows a lot in Boise," I reminded him gently. I am perfectly capable of being diplomatic.

"We found five discrete sets of partial remains buried in the cellar. We were able to identify four. We still don't know who the fifth victim was. They were all female, of course."

"What else did you find?"

"The place was incinerated. Completely demolished."

Silence again. So I cracked my knuckles. One at a time. Diplomacy.

Finally Willoughby spoke. "There was a tunnel."

I flashed on the slab of sandstone in the right rear corner of the coal bin.

"It ran parallel to the foundation for about twenty feet, then cut away," Willoughby went on. "The first ten feet collapsed in the explosion. The rest was intact."

Toward the crawl space beneath your parents' bedroom. If you couldn't get through the bolted door, you'd come up through the floor. Once you had tunneled that far, you didn't stop. You kept digging, excavating an escape route that led far from the house.

"We figure that he worked on it over a number of years. He probably used a knife and a spoon. We found a spoon down there. We do not, however, consider the tunnel a means of egress for a six-foot adult of medium build."

The determination, the absolute will, the consideration of every contingency. Kill them all, lad, then crawl away to a world you created.

"What else did you find?"

"Nothing," he said, looking directly into my eyes.

"Did it occur to you that Wolf might not be dead?"

Willoughby cleared his throat, but continued to look at me. "I never saw any basis for that assumption. Our official position is that he is dead. No one could have survived the devastation caused by that bomb."

"What's your unofficial position?"

"I wanted proof," he said. "I didn't get it. I had to be content with the circumstantial evidence which, as I've indicated, was quite compelling."

"Another woman has been murdered," Lane said.

Willoughby nodded. "Yes. I was sorry to hear about that."

"She was a friend of Pop's. He tried to kill Pop, and nearly succeeded."

Willoughby's eyes widened. He looked confused. "A month ago, Wolf's sister, Sarah Humphrey, was killed in her home near Orlando. That's who I thought you meant."

I stared into the agent's muddy brown eyes. "Let me guess. The local cops worked it as an isolated case. As what? Home intrusion? Sexual assault?"

"There was extensive postmortem cutting, and evidence of rape."

Sarah Humphrey. Once a young, slender, attractive object of her brother's fantasies, but approaching middle age now. Remember when you lusted for a taste of her, lad?

"We never found anything that suggested that Wolf sexually assaulted any of his victims," Lane said. "Why would he rape her, Pop?"

You have gone beyond power, control, humiliation— even beyond destruction. "Extensive postmortem cutting," Willoughby said. *You hacked her to pieces.*

"He was consummating a relationship that had existed only in his mind," I told her.

"Wolf couldn't be alive," the agent was saying.

"Willoughby, you're a sonofabitch," Lane snapped. "You suspected that Wolf might not have died in the explosion. When you couldn't match up any of the remains in that cellar with Wolf, why the hell didn't you tell someone? Why didn't you warn Pop? And why didn't you tell anyone when Sarah Humphrey turned up dead?"

Willoughby was shaking his head. "Wolf is dead," he said.

You have always re-created yourself, lad. What are you now? And where?

LANE AND I STOOD IN THE ELEVATOR. "LET'S get a couple of rooms at the Willard," I said. "I'd like a comfortable bed and some sleep."

"You hurting?"

"No. I'm just tired."

"Do you really think that Wolf is alive?"

"I'm never certain of anything, Lane. I don't think anyone could do a perfect impression of a Paul Sierra painting, or one of Clapton's riffs. As you know, I also don't believe in coincidence. Sarah Humphrey? Why would Willoughby even have been informed about that case? It's a local matter. Somebody must have thought he should know."

I was already hating every minute of what I was doing. I wanted it over.

"Can't you get Willoughby to help us?" Lane asked.

"I don't want him to. I don't want to muck around in some federal bureaucracy. I want to resolve this and get back to the lake."

Janet Orr had been reduced to a case number, unsolved. A killer who wouldn't stop killing until he was dead was free to methodically slake himself like a shark at a shipwreck.

"If Wolf survived," Lane said, "you've got no business going after him. He'd be at the top of his form. You're hurting. You need rest."

Autumn bass fishing on Lake Albert is about as good as it gets, at least until winter crashes into the back end of October. I wanted to reclaim my home, build a fire in the woodstove, curl up with a good book and a cold bottle of ale. But there was a killer in my way.

"Whoever it is could still be at the lake," Lane went on.

You're here, aren't you, lad? And you want me here.

I had been played like a fine-tuned piano, manipulated, misled.

"No," I told Lane. "I don't think so."

WHEN POP SAID WE WERE GOING TO STAY AT the Willard, my heart did a little dance in my chest. For years, I had been wanting to stay there—ever since I learned who Emily Dickinson was. The Willard is where she slept when she visited Washington a century and a half ago. I just wished that the circumstances of our stay were different.

"Can we get a couple of the expensive rooms?" I asked.

"At the Willard, there isn't any other kind. Let's not go crazy. We don't need any presidential suites. Just beds and indoor plumbing."

Pop was in a foul mood. But it didn't faze me at all—it's actually rather endearing when he stomps around and acts all sullen. I suspected that he was wondering how to convince a bureaucracy that someone it has listed as dead, is not dead. Or, more likely, how to avoid dealing with that bureaucracy at all.

"If this is official business, is there anybody we can pass the bill along to?" I asked.

I was about two paychecks away from going on public assistance.

"This is *my* business. Nobody else's. I'll take care of the tab."

It's a little unsettling when Pop gets that tone in his voice. He seems to turn into one of those military tanks, the kind that can roll right over anything in its path. It isn't that he's necessarily loud or crashing around, although I've seen his mad elephant impression many times in my life.

This particular tone is almost too calm, too void of emotion.

A PROMENADE CALLED PEACOCK ALLEY. THE Round Robin Bar. The Nest Lounge. Surrounded by so many feather connotations, it was hard to keep my mind off murder and John Wolf. Leaving a feather at the scene of a homicide had been one of Wolf's favorite signatures. I was determined not to let him ruin my stay at the Willard—the home of the promenade, the bar, and the lounge.

When I first read about Emily Dickinson staying there, I pictured the Willard as a dowdy hotel, a dusty, dirty hole in the wall where legislators parked themselves while in D.C. on government business. Emily's father was in politics. She accompanied him to Washington one spring, which is how she happened to stay at the Willard.

Because of my preconceptions, I was unprepared for the grandeur of the place. Mosaic tile floors, giant chandeliers, velvet-covered chairs, marble columns supporting the massive ornate ceiling of the lobby, potted

palms that were even taller than I am—it was like stepping onto a lavish movie set.

Pop and I had side-by-side rooms. He made immediate use of the bed, deciding to take a nap as soon as
we got our luggage upstairs. "Wake me for dinner," he
said, pushing me out the door.

I went into my own room then, for the first time.
Once again I was struck by what a class act the Willard
was. My own private minibar, a bed big enough for an
orgy, and a telephone in the bathroom. Savvy would
have liked that.

WHILE POP NAPPED, I CALLED GINGER AND EX-
plained that I needed her help with the relational database. The message "GOTO:DEA" meant that I should pull
up the dead file, she said.

"What's that?" I asked her.

"The file where I put all the cases that are in God's
hands. The perp's dead. The program's just directing
you to someone with characteristics similar to what
you're looking for."

She explained how to open the file, I thanked her
and hung up the phone. I located the disk that I had
been working on when we were still at the lake, and
popped it into my laptop. I went through all the steps
that led to the GOTO:DEA message, then I typed DEAD.DOC,
according to Ginger's instructions.

John Wolf's dossier appeared on my screen.

I kept rerunning the database—using different
combinations of the characteristics that Pop and I had
discussed—and each time it came out the same. John
Wolf. Maybe this would boost Pop's faith in technology.

I called Pop's room.

He picked up the phone and said, "You know I hate these things."

"Time for dinner," I said. "I'll be over in a minute."

POP OPENED THE DOOR AND ASKED, "DID YOU bring a weapon?"

"My thirty-eight."

"Good. I have a nine-millimeter. I'll call my friend the senator and arrange to have a D.C. detective work with us. When I talked with him yesterday, he told me about a cop named Williams."

"What about somebody else from the Bureau?"

"Their official position is that Wolf is dead. I told you that I don't want to waste a lot of time getting shunted from one paper-pusher to another. I'm going to take care of this. Now."

"Pop, I came out to the lake because—"

"This time it will be different," he interrupted.

"Very different."

HOURS LATER, ALONE IN MY ROOM, I TRIED TO fall asleep. I don't know what bothered me more—the bulge of the .38 under my pillow, or the hotel's ambient creakings that I attributed either to the ghost of Emily Dickinson or to death unkindly stopping for me in the guise of John Wolf.

I also realized that I didn't know what Pop had meant by "different." Would his method of dealing with Wolf be more legal?

Or would it be more final?

POP

I HAD NOT NAPPED.

I had no intention of wasting time sleeping, coddling myself over a couple of superficial wounds.

When Lane went to her room, I made arrangements for a car and drove to Vienna, Virginia. There, I sat on the curb of a tree-lined street, watching a green Volvo station wagon approach.

It was time to deal with asshole number one.

Dexter Willoughby pulled his car to the curb, then stood behind the open door. "What the hell are you doing here?"

He glanced at his house.

"I didn't ring the bell," I said. "Why don't you go inside, check your messages, then rejoin me here at curbside."

"Listen," he began.

"I suggest you check your messages," I said again.

The little federal cop grabbed his briefcase, slammed the car door, and did his best impression of an indignant, angry man striding up his driveway toward the rear of his house.

I was in no mood to play games with Willoughby. I was convinced that John Wolf was busy stalking his next victim. Despite his killing Janet Orr, and his shots at me, I didn't think I was next on his immediate list, but neither did I know who that next victim would be.

Willoughby came down the walk, having shed his briefcase and suit jacket. His vest and school tie were still immaculately in place as he stood behind my left shoulder.

"Be a shame to have to sell a place like this," I said. "Nice neighborhood."

"Senator Storrs said that I was to cooperate fully," he said, dropping two files on the sidewalk next to me.

One was labeled Humphrey, the second, Chadwick. I looked up at Willoughby. "Alan Chadwick?"

"Two months ago, Dr. Chadwick died in a fall from the roof of Boston City Hospital."

Shit. Chadwick was the pathologist whose identity John Wolf had stolen and used for years in Hasty Hills, Connecticut. Without opening the file, I was already convinced that Wolf had killed Chadwick in the same way that he had killed Chadwick's girlfriend years earlier—when all three of them were students in Cambridge. Wolf had hurled her from the roof of her dorm.

"What else do you want?" Willoughby asked.

I had to exert every ounce of my energy to refrain from throttling the little prick. I patted the curb. "Pull up a slab."

"I'll stand."

"The superiority that affords is an illusion, Willoughby."

"There wasn't any trace of Wolf. He's dead. Totally incinerated."

I stood up, staring down into the agent's eyes—the eyes that had betrayed him.

When Lane and I were in his office earlier in the day, I had watched his eyes, determined the pattern of his eye movements as they related to what he was saying. At some time in his career, Willoughby had taken a course in Neuro-Linguistic Programming, and knew about the involuntary movements of eye muscles. He had countered his own orientation, switching left with right, and had embellished that with a technique I had seen only once or twice before. When they lie, most people avoid eye contact. When Willoughby lied, it was the only time that he made eye contact.

"What else did you find in Vermont?"

He stared into my eyes and said nothing.

"Good luck out west," I said, turning to leave.

"There was a sheet of paper in the loft that he used for an office. Is that what you want? It was stuck in a book. It was dated, and he wrote down the time. It was just before you got there."

"You found it in *The Collector*. The John Fowles book."

A year ago, expecting Wolf to have a copy of the same book that cross-country killer Christopher Wilder considered a bible was pure hunch on my part. It had been one of those intuitive grabs based only on my feeling for Wolf's mind before I had ever laid eyes on him. I had been right.

Willoughby went pale. "You're a fucking nightmare. Yes. He said he was reaching the end. It was crazy. It didn't make any sense."

"What were the words?"

Willoughby sighed. "He had reached the end of the road, and he had to die. There was something about entering the long tunnel of night, then killing everyone who had destroyed him. You can't kill anybody after you die. He's dead. How can it mean anything?"

You anticipated my every move, didn't you, lad?

Wolf had drawn me to Vermont, just as he had drawn me to Washington. *He* had set the elaborate scene, not me. I even had to wonder whether he gave a shit about the Fowles book, or if that had been for my benefit, too.

Shaken, I backed away from Willoughby.

"I told you it was crazy," he said.

Death, after all, had been on Wolf's terms, not mine.

He had planned "to die." The bastard knew I would shove him into the coal bin, just as his stepfather had done countless times. He knew that he would have to use his tunnel.

There was no point in trying to educate Willoughby. What he was, he would always be. He would never understand the absolute, maniacal brilliance of a man like John Wolf. Willoughby was just plain, fucking dumb when it came to a killer who had the perfect combination of intelligence, determination, and belief in his own justification.

"Crazy? I don't think so." I said, hearing the tremor in my voice.

I turned and walked away down the suburban street.

YEARS AGO, WHEN I TALKED WITH MORGAN WYLIE, he was a man who needed an audience. He sat in a dank jail cell, three pairs of socks covering his forever frigid feet. He was doing three months for retail theft, but the cops wanted him for a lot more than that.

He knew how to manipulate his interviewers. Others had talked with him, so he had honed his skills. He expected me to ask him about the murders, to try to wheedle a confession out of him. Instead, I encouraged him to tell me about his life, about the police harassing him, about how hard it was to make a living. I urged him to tell me his complaints about the jail—lousy food, no medical or dental care—the usual laments of the jailhouse lost.

The approach is elementary. Create a positive response set. Get the guy talking about anything. Keep him talking. The more he determines his agenda, the better. Do not try to direct him.

My training and experience had also taught me that when a man uses the same number in situations where any random number will do, the repeated number holds some significance for him—a date, an age, an accumulation of something that he has been counting. Wylie's number was ten—maybe ten times a month they had a decent meal; there was often a ten-day wait to see the doctor; he had about ten of his own teeth left in his head.

Having listened to him ramble for over two hours, it was time to take a chance.

"Morgan, what I'm really interested in hearing is what happened to you when you were ten years old."

He didn't hesitate. "I found a five-dollar bill in the road. Ma said I stole it from her jar. I didn't, though. She got Jake, her boyfriend, to beat me so I wouldn't steal no more."

There was more emotion in Wylie's voice than anyone had previously reported about any of the elaborate stories he told. "I came in the door with the fuckin' thing in my hand. If I was gonna hide it or spend it, would I do that? I wanted to give it to her to help with the bills. She didn't believe me. I was so happy that day. She was always tellin' me I weren't no good, that I was a drain because I ate too much. I was gonna give her this to make some of it right. She turned Jake on me. He hammered me real bad. Then he made me suck him off."

There was a glaze over Wylie's eyes. His acne-scarred face contorted in rage. "After that, he did it whenever he felt like it. I ran away some—made it all the way to El Paso once, but they brought me back."

"You made a decision then," I said.

He was nodding. Wylie believed that no one had ever cared enough about him to listen to him—certainly not the local cops who wanted him dead, or his federal visitors with their checklists. Now, here was a stranger who was willing to listen. A stranger who even seemed to understand. "Weren't no way anyone ever again was gonna put me one down. *I* was gonna be the one who said, 'Down on your knees, boy.' 'Assume the position, boy.' "

It was pure vengeance thinking. His treatment at Jake's hands was his worst secret, the one event in his sordid life that he would not want anyone to know. Despite the fact that he was in a positive response set, I knew that he was not going to write his own death warrant. I asked him when he had developed his circulatory problem. That question would seem to him as if he were moving away from a topic that was painful for him, toward something like our original agenda—his health and welfare. Then I redefined his reality, equating unburdening himself with saving his feet from amputation. Lethal injection was a remote thought for Morgan at that moment, but his feet were cold.

Seventeen times across Louisiana and East Texas, Morgan Wylie played "Jake" to a boy between eight and eleven years old. He gave each victim a five-dollar bill, then killed him.

While awaiting execution, Morgan had woven lengths of bedsheet together and tried to hang himself. He nearly succeeded. Emergency medical personnel resuscitated him—brought him back to life so that the state could kill him.

I was convinced that someone had brought Wolf back to life. He had made it clear that he would never be caged. So someone had to kill him—again.

Wolf was not only the perfect psychopath. He was also a narcissist—a not uncommon combination of pathologies. Wolf would never accept the ego bruises that he had sustained in Vermont. He expected all people on their knees in worshipful pose before him. When they were not, he was enraged. It festered as a "kiss-my-feet-or-I'll-slit-your-throat" situation.

I had failed to kiss his feet.

BEFORE I LEFT LAKE ALBERT, WHEN I WAS STUCK with having to use a telephone anyway, I had placed a call to the Vermont State Police. The dispatcher put me through to a captain named Braxton. I explained who I was and why I was calling. The captain hesitated, then said he didn't see any harm in telling me that a car had been stolen in Saxtons River about three hours after Wolf's house exploded. "We get a few kids joyriding down that way occasionally, but this car never turned up."

It made sense to me that it would have taken Wolf a couple of hours to get to the village. He was wounded; I had shot him. He had to stumble his way through the woods. If he did take the car, where did he go?

Two of his bullet wounds had been superficial. He could treat those himself. I did not know exactly where I had hit him the third time, but it was somewhere in the abdomen. He would have needed help with that one.

Alan Chadwick had landed on the pavement twenty feet away from Boston City Hospital. He had not fallen or jumped, nor had Wolf simply pushed him off the roof. He had thrown Chadwick like a rag doll.

Sarah Humphrey had sustained thirty-one wounds. All but three—two in the chest, and one in the throat— were postmortem.

Wolf was close to tipping over. There seemed to be little of his former finesse. In the past, he had been meticulous in his planning, meticulous in his execution, and consistent about signing his work—a feather, a piece of music, a volume of poetry. In one young woman's apartment he had arranged a Scrabble board to appear as if a game were in progress. There were two interlocking words: *danse macabre*.

You've gone beyond the dance, haven't you? You are no longer interested in the flowing choreography, the beauty of murder. You're driven by rage. Get the players where you want them, and think only of their destruction.

On our way to the hotel after seeing Willoughby, I had warned Lane about the psychological condition I expected Wolf to be in. "He'll be as far out there as any of these killers has ever been. Lucid and organized for a period time, then he crumbles. He feels it happening, like he's coming apart. It's a repeating cycle, generally with increasing extremes in the swings, and longer periods of disintegration. A similar thing happened with Wylie, Bundy, Ramirez."

I told her a little-known story about Danny Rolling, the killer of five students in Gainesville, Florida. After his seventy-two-hour killing spree, he fled the city in a stolen car, only to see that shot to pieces during a holdup in Tampa. He was coming apart, close to the end, when he met a woman in a park. She sensed something about him. She didn't know who he was. Nobody did at that point. To her, he was just another lost soul who, for whatever reason, was brittle, ready to crack.

"She took him home," I told Lane. "Fed him. Fixed a place on her couch for him. He spent the night there, thanked her in the morning, and left. She was still alive, but not because he had discovered God, or a new sense of morality. What had always been a comfortable identity for him—the outlaw—was disintegrating. He had to heal, to repair that persona. All of us were fortunate that the Ocala police caught him when they did."

I SAT IN THE DARK, LISTENING TO THE SOUNDS of the Willard and the muted noise of the city from beyond the hotel's walls. Lane had wanted to know why I did what I did that day in Vermont. Had I murdered John Wolf? My intent is what mattered. By any definition, my actions had been premeditated.

For my entire life, I had wandered close to the edge—of the law, and of madness—occasionally drifting across the line on both counts. No one had taken me to the extremes that John Wolf had. Now he was going to do it again.

Lane had asked me to promise that it would be different this time. It already was different. I was not hunting him. He was hunting me. And he was here.

The sonofabitch had written his own script, and we

were dutifully moving onstage on cue, preparing to read our lines. That was my fault. If I had taken care of him when I had the chance, none of this would be happening.

As I sat in the darkness of my room in Washington, part of me was ready to jump up, pack, and go home. The rest of me was inert. No matter where I went, Wolf would eventually follow—unless I crawled inside my mind, to that familiar place with its own darkness, its own eyes looking back at me. I had to confront the beast who lives there. Whenever fear has shaken my soul into pieces, he has made me whole.

"So, come on then, lad," I muttered. "Let's have a go at it."

TWO

WOLF

WHEN I WAS A CHILD, MY MOTHER OFTEN TOLD me, "You don't wait well."

It was true. I did not wait well at all, but only when someone told me that I had to wait.

Like you, I had saxophone in the sixth grade. I was coerced, so it was a waste of time and money. To me, what the grown-ups called "patience" always meant enduring something distasteful.

My mother asked, "Why don't you stick with any one thing?"

"I don't wait well," I reminded her.

The truth was that if I *chose* to wait, if *I* elected to be patient, I was eminently capable of allowing years to pass between thought and deed.

Time became irrelevant.

Whether moments stretch out behind in an amorphous mass called the past, or extend ahead in an even more vague and formless future, time has meaning only when I shape its passage. My mark is frequently bloody, always indelible.

Consider this. What if there was a Web site on the

Internet where all you had to do was enter your name
and date of birth, or just your social security number.
Then, in confidence and complete detail—a narrated
documentary pouring from the speakers fixed to the
sides of your monitor—you could discover the particu-
lars of your ending.

Date of death; cause of death; manner of death.

Will you travel through cyberspace to that location? Or will you tease yourself with the knowledge that
it is there, somewhere in the ether?

Perhaps there are other names with your same date
of death—clusters of names suggesting an airline di-
saster, a small war, or an act of genocide.

Or maybe you are alone on your particular journey,
in your particular war. Perhaps you are driving north-
bound on a snow-covered Interstate 91 when you leave
the highway, go airborne, and collide with your granite wall.

Death is entertainment. That's all it has ever been.

Other drivers inch by, craning their necks to peer in
at you—a pudding of blood, cartilage, brain.

Life and death.

Maybe you slip on a wet floor and die in your
kitchen. So many of us greet the tunnel of night in our
own homes, struggling up out of the tub only to splash
backward in a concussive blast against the porcelain.

What if a killer chooses your back door? You become an episode of *Unsolved Mysteries*, a segment on
Inside Edition. From your box beneath the earth, you
claim your fifteen minutes of fame.

Planes fall out of the sky; rivers roar over their
banks; the earth's tectonic plates slip a bit to one side
and the world cracks open; and don't forget the men

who carry knives in the night—all receive their media forums because you are so fascinated by violence, fear, and death.

You choose not to contemplate your own ending. You don't rush to that Web site on the Internet. You tune your TV to someone else's tragic demise because you are frightened, and can tolerate only a vicarious brush with death.

I am no voyeur.

If I had the power to break the earth, crack the skies, bring the tides of a different moon crashing onto your streets—I would not hesitate. I would kill you all.

Unfortunately, I must make do with the limited power I have—the guns, the knives, and the mettle to approach your back door.

IN LAKE ALBERT, MICHIGAN, I CARRIED MY BRIEF-case and my McDonald's bag to Janet Orr's house. She was working in her yard, fussing with some flower beds.

"Bark mulch works wonders," I said.

She looked up, tucking some fallen hair under a black headband. "I've always preferred hay. Bark makes the beds look like every other yard near any body of water."

"True. Maybe that's why I thought of it."

"Are you walking?"

"I parked at a pull-out. I wasn't sure which of the two houses was yours, Mrs. Orr."

"Who are you?"

"My name is Charles Weathers," I said, handing her a business card. "I'm a field interviewer for the Kurmont Foundation. Perhaps you've heard of us."

"Of course. Kurmont awards grants. To individuals, right? People who are making some sort of social contribution with their work."

I nodded. "A neighbor of yours, Dr. Lucas Frank, has been nominated for an award."

"He's retired."

I laughed. "I've been up here for two days, and that's the first thing that people tell me. Dr. Frank has continued to write since his retirement, and . . ."

"Lucas? He chases fish."

"I have copies of two of his papers in my briefcase."

"I'm sorry. It's not that I don't believe you. He's never said anything about writing. I've always been under the impression that when he left his practice, he just quit. Well, why don't you bring your fast-food sack and come in, Mr. Weathers. I don't know how much help I'll be, though."

We deferred the formal interview while I ate my lunch. I chatted about my problems finding a dependable security system for my suburban home. She recommended the company that Dr. Frank had used for his perimeter system.

Janet Orr was most helpful.

Then I killed her.

I HAVE BEEN IN WASHINGTON FOR TWO DAYS, waiting for my players, collecting my props. There is a drama to unfold here, one that will eliminate superfluous actors and bring the most powerful law enforcement agency in the world to its knees.

Four days, a mere ninety-six hours, remain.

I was eager for those hours to pass, but I was not

pissing away time when I entered Yazgur Park in north-west D.C. Fall Fest, the neighborhood's celebration of music, food, and crafts, surrounded me. The fair and its sponsors were listed in a newsletter that I found on the sidewalk. Serendipity always provides.

Cops on horseback confiscated beer from under-age drinkers. When the cops had gone, other kids sup-plied their bereft friends. It worked better than the welfare system, and no one was obliged to chase after nonexistent jobs.

I stopped at a Volkswagen bus, its back and side doors open. A crude, Day-Glo sign on the vehicle's roof proclaimed, "Oliver's Brass Works: Beads, Earrings, and Comestibles." The owner was a large, bearded man with greasy red hair to his shoulders. He was selling teriyaki beef on a stick, assorted strands of colored beads, wood carvings, and brass figures. His woman stood a short distance away, swaying to music, tapping out a crude approximation of rhythm with finger cymbals.

I watched the woman—her eyes closed, her silver hair spilling over her black dress to her waist, her face turned up to the darkening skies—wondering if it was possible to kill someone in front of two thousand po-tential witnesses, and have no one notice.

But I rejected the notion. The bead-seller's woman was spinning in the space of a music only she could hear. I doubted that she was grounded enough to ap-preciate that death might be happening to her, and I in-sist on that much from all my victims. I wanted a victim, but not a middle-aged woman still tripping on a sixties high.

I made my purchase, a nondescript shore bird carved from driftwood, and moved slowly away. I still heard the chimes, still saw the woman in my mind as she swung her hips from side to side. And I still wanted some amusement.

The crowd surged toward a narrow gateway, and an even narrower foot bridge leading to a small amphitheater. I was forced through a funnel of obstreperous humanity, shoved from one side of the bridge to the other, and always forward. I felt trapped.

I remembered reading about the young man in Texas who climbed to the top of a tall building on a college campus and began shooting. He had the same name as the poet, Whitman. Walt embraced mainstream America. Charles Whitman mowed them down. Which is precisely what I felt like doing at that moment. But I restrained myself. The satisfaction would have been short-lived, and my plans would have been disrupted.

I decided then that I did not want Oliver's softwood sanderling. I wanted something else, something perfect, and I was certain that I would find it here.

I stood to one side and watched the mob spill into an amphitheater where a popular, local rock band stood on a makeshift stage and created deafening noise. The audience cheered. I avoided the music venue, turned, and stepped back onto the bridge.

Suddenly I was disoriented, adrift in time, as I watched a young woman leaning against the bridge's concrete parapet. I stopped and stared at her profile. For only seconds—although it seemed like much longer—the years dropped away, a dead woman returned to life, and I stared at my past. This girl was a youthful version of a woman I had met at a fire in Cambridge when we were both students there. I smiled, walked onto the bridge, and almost called her "Annie" before I snapped away from the hypnotic beckoning of a false reality.

"I will give you a wooden figure," I said. "I want something back."

She shook her head and turned away.

I felt a sharp pain behind my eyes, a familiar stab of rage. This woman had disoriented me, then turned her back. I grabbed her by her black hair, swung her around, and placed a knife against her throat. "I want an object," I said.

"What?" she gasped as she struggled ineffectively.

"I want to make a trade. Give me something of yours, and I, in return, will give something to you."

"The bird."

"What bird?"

"In my pocket. Please don't hurt me."

I searched through her pockets and found a brass bird—one that married past with present, and foretold the future. It was the phoenix, rising from its flames—its wings partially unfurled, its eyes filled with fire glaring at an open sky.

"Where did you get this?"

"In the parking lot. I got it from Oliver at the red VW bus. His wife was making music with her fingers."

I flipped her over the wall into the brook below. By the time she found a way up, I would be long gone.

I could have killed her—slit her throat and then dumped her over the wall. Stoned hordes would have stumbled across the bridge after the concert and never looked down. But it didn't seem . . . *just*. She and I had made a fair trade. I had committed an act of *justice*— she was alive, after all. It was my gift to her.

I laughed to myself as I strode into the parking lot.

The cops on horses had gone, although there were cruisers parked in the distance near the exit. The VW was there, its canopy still up. Oliver sat on a blanket next to his van, smoking a bong. I didn't want his woman. I wanted him.

I sat cross-legged, opposite the burly man.

"What do you want?" Oliver asked.

"Balance. Order. A kind of justice, perhaps."

"You a cop?"

I shook my head. "I guess you could say that I'm the opposite of a doctor."

Oliver's face clouded with confusion. He stopped sucking on his pipe, placed his hands flat on the blanket, and leaned toward me. "Get the fuck out of here."

I liked his attitude. That was exactly what I required.

"When you aren't feeling well," I said as I gripped the bone handle of my knife, "you go to see the doctor and he makes you feel better. I look for people who are feeling good, even ethereal, and I bring them down."

I plunged the knife through the back of Oliver's right hand, through the blanket and down into the dirt. His hand was pinned to the earth. I was sure that his roar of pain could be heard by the cops out near the road, and equally certain that they would pay no attention. Tears creased the big man's twisted face as he leaned agonizingly to one side. His howl faded to a whimper.

"Balance," I repeated, breathing against his tear-stained face. "Order. A kind of justice. I've just given you a gift, Oliver. Your life. This is my final charitable act. Make sure you tell the police that. Tell them that Wolf said there will be no more kindness."

I grabbed a handful of his trinkets, pushed myself up, and walked away.

I stroked the brass bird, knowing that the piece of metal was why I had been drawn to the Fall Fest, and aware of the place that it would have in my future.

I had a gift for Lucas Frank, but I would not be as generous with him as I had been with Oliver.

I WATCHED THE DOCTOR AND HIS DAUGHTER enter and leave the J. Edgar Hoover Building, the theoretical repository of justice and the home of the FBI. Then I followed them to the Willard. Both of them entered; a short time later, he left. I suspected that he was not satisfied with whatever scraps Dexter Willoughby had thrown to him.

I did not follow the retired psychiatrist. When I wanted to find him, I knew where to look.

If I had wanted Dr. Frank dead in Michigan, he would be dead. I control his world. He continues to exist only because my design dictates that he stumble around the capital for a few days.

I have an absolute wealth of patience. My mother would be proud.

I wonder if the Franks have made my hypothetical cybertrip—if they know the precise moments that they will die.

I do.

POP

JUST AFTER DAWN, I SIPPED COFFEE AND SCANNED the two files that Willoughby had dropped beside me on the sidewalk the previous afternoon. Lane tapped on my door carrying her own coffee.

"You're up early," I said.

She nodded. "What's that?"

"Copies of the case files on Sarah Humphrey and Alan Chadwick."

"Chadwick?"

"He's dead. Two months ago. Willoughby said it was a fall from a roof."

Lane sat across from me on the sofa and made room for her cup on the table where I had the reports spread out. "Where did you get that stuff?"

"I was out for a while yesterday afternoon."

"You didn't take a nap."

"I visited Willoughby at his home."

Lane's eyes widened. "Let me get this straight. Wolf killed Chadwick *and* his sister."

Three dead and one almost dead in two months, and all connected because of a single man who had been presumed dead. For me, that was coincidence overload.

"I think he killed both of them," I said. "I think Willoughby is still holding back. I have no idea what he isn't telling me, but I don't think we're through counting the dead."

"Do the files tell you anything?"

For all the years that I had made a living developing personality profiles, tracking killers, interviewing them, each new case had brought a rush. This one gave me a headache.

"Alan Chadwick was in his office doing what we're doing now," I said. "Drinking coffee. He fell, jumped, or was thrown from the roof of the hospital. When the police got there, the coffee cup was still warm. I figure that if you enjoy strolling the roof among piles of pigeon shit, you take your coffee with you. If you're planning a swan dive, you're too distracted to care about coffee in the first place. The autopsy report indicates some bruising on Chadwick's body that wasn't consistent with the fall. The way I see it, Wolf struggled briefly with him and threw him off."

As I recited the details to Lane, a feeling of helplessness washed over me. Sweat beaded on the back of my neck. It was just as I had felt in Janet Orr's kitchen when I looked down at her corpse.

"Chadwick helped us track Wolf a year ago," Lane said.

"They had their past history, too. Wolf killed Chadwick's girlfriend in Cambridge when they were all students there. Threw her off the roof of her dorm. Since Vermont, Wolf has had plenty of time to brood. I think that while he was on the mend, he developed his current script. These files are incomplete. Pages are missing.

Willoughby probably pulled them out. I can't make much sense of it."

Incomplete? Shit. Trying to make sense of the files was like working on an unnumbered acrostic.

"What about the material on Sarah Humphrey?" Lane asked.

"That file isn't quite as fragmented. Wolf drove a rental car into her trailer park in the middle of the day. He went in, raped her, killed her, then kept cutting. He also helped himself to a postmortem sandwich; there was blood on the crusts of bread. He took a shower and walked out to his car in front of a half-dozen witnesses. Their description is close enough. He even stopped and chatted with one woman about what a pleasant day it was."

"Jesus Christ."

"Sarah had just filled a prescription for diet pills. The medication was gone. Is Wolf concerned about his weight? That's laughable. Is he physiologically priming himself? That's a good bet. Swallowing uppers reinforces his belief that he is invincible."

Lane finished the last of her coffee and shook her head. "I thought that control was critical to him, Pop."

When Wolf killed his sister, he was closing the book on something that had been rattling around in his head since they were kids. All the power that he had attributed to her, he took away. He strode out her door, waved to his audience, and drove off.

"I'm not sure that Wolf has ever been able to distinguish between control and the illusion of control," I said.

When I worked the Wolf case a year earlier, I suspected that Wolf's emotional development had taken a sharp turn with Sarah's birth. She effectively displaced him in the family. Sarah became the focus of her parents' attention. All she had to do was exist. Then she grew into an attractive teenager. Young men paid attention to her, falling all over themselves.

Her brother was bright, but socially awkward, a loner. No one had any interest in him. While she was out playing around with the boys in their cars, Wolf was cooling his heels in the coal bin. He got repeated lessons about just how powerless he was. So he dug his tunnel.

"Wolf couldn't tolerate his own helplessness," I told Lane. "As he grew older, he wouldn't even entertain the notion that he was not the center of the universe. He had a sexual interest in Sarah, and a resentment that smoldered into a hatred. He loved and loathed his sister, and detested himself for feeling dependent on her. He didn't want to feel the way he did, but there was nothing he could do about it—except in his mind."

"I remember when I went to Florida and interviewed Sarah Humphrey last year," Lane said. "It was strange. She had loved her brother. She also hated him. Mostly, I think she pitied him because of the way her father treated him."

"Feeling sorry for him was probably her biggest mistake. Wolf can ignore or dismiss adoration and loathing. Pity suggests condescension, that she was above him. In his mind, no one holds that position."

"So," Lane said, "when the time came to act on what had been festering in his mind, killing her wasn't enough."

I shook my head. "He cut her up the same way he did animals when he was a boy. Committing murder at midafternoon in the close quarters of a trailer park hardly seems like the mark of a meticulous predator. When he's up, he acts on his fantasies, the rehearsals that he plays over and over in his head. I think that Florida brought him down. The satisfaction he anticipated never happened. He required the illusion of mastery offered by the amphetamines."

I stood and began pacing the room.

"What is it, Pop?"

Yeah. What was it? Wolf had collected his justification to do whatever he pleased a long time ago. He had been cashing in on it for years. Then we had humiliated him in Vermont. That degradation would be far worse than any physical pain he had ever suffered. Now, anything was enough reason for a killing season.

Shit. Wolf didn't need a reason.

"He won't stop," I said. "He can't. Killing is how he has defined his life. I think that for him to move on to whatever life he has in mind for himself, he has to first eliminate everyone who had anything to do with Vermont."

But there's more to it, isn't there, lad? It wouldn't be enough for you to simply wipe us out. You need a grand finale, a great explosion of fireworks in the sky, color and thunder that shake the earth.

"You, me, Willoughby," Lane began.

"What was his partner's name?"

"Susan Walker. Did you warn Willoughby?"

"How do I warn a man who insists that Wolf is dead, that the dead man might be coming after him?"

Now Lane was on her feet and wandering around the room. Pretty soon we would need someone to direct traffic.

"Pop, why didn't Wolf just take you out at the lake?"

It was a damn good question. He had me in his

sights, and knocked me down—even stepped over me to get the page from my Peterson. He had demonstrated that he *could* kill me. Anyplace. Anytime.

"I think there's some fucking twisted game that he's playing," I said. "We have to play. We don't get a choice in that, nor do we get to know the rules. We don't even know who all the players are. Wolf knew that as soon as I made the connection to him, I would head for Willoughby, for D.C. He would also assume that I'd find out about his sister and Chadwick."

"How do we stop him?"

There had to be a million ways that Wolf could get us, and we didn't even know where to find him. "He's somewhere in the city. He'll make an effort at anonymity, but he can't be anywhere without leaving some sort of trail. We have to lock on to that trail."

It was also possible that I was talking through my hat—trying to impose reason on an unreasonable situation. I dropped onto the sofa and planted my legs across the coffee table, scattering papers onto the floor.

"I'd like you to make contact with the local police," I said. "Start with that detective I mentioned."

"Williams?"

"Right. Give him everything we've got, including Willoughby's connection to the case. Call your Lieutenant Swartz and ask him to send copies of the composites of Wolf that he did for us last year. Do we have a list of Wolf's aliases?"

"It's in the computer."

Lane flipped open a small notebook and jotted down items.

"Add Charles S. Weathers, and share the list with the D.C. police."

She looked up from her writing. "You think he'd use a name he's used before?"

I shrugged. "I don't know. We have to start with a shotgun approach—make use of what we've got. I'd also like a hard copy of your NYPD file on Wolf, and that computer journal he kept in his office in Vermont. I have to go back to the beginning with this bastard."

"That's all in the same file. No problem. I'll get started right away."

"The dialogue that any killer has with his world can be understood," I said, as if I were trying to convince myself.

John Wolf was not "any killer." While I was thinking about him, he was thinking about me. Wolf wanted me here. I was convinced that he had planned some performance, and that I was his audience. After the show, he could move to his endgame: killing Lucas Frank.

"He will want us to hear," I muttered, "but not understand. We have to be ready to hear, to see, to comprehend."

I stared up at the ceiling.

Long ago, I had learned to trust all the dimensions of the mind, to accept that I might not know where my thoughts were leading me, but to believe that they were offering something that I needed to experience. As the textured ceiling in my room began to resemble a pale version of the surface of the moon, I was only vaguely aware of Lane closing the door on her way out.

Willoughby was the key to this case. I still felt that there was more he could tell me, but would not. When he retrieved the Humphrey and Chadwick files, he had walked up his driveway, around the house to the back. I watched as he disappeared through the trees. The guy obviously had an outbuilding that served him as an office.

I glanced at the clock and decided that it was time for a return to Vienna. This time, I didn't want to talk to anyone. I wanted only to prowl.

WOLF

I HAVE KILLED MANY TIMES, BUT I HAVE DIED only once. It happened in Vermont, just a few days less than a year ago. Soon, I will celebrate the anniversary of my death.

On that day last fall, there was dirt in my mouth, in my eyes, my nose. All that was left of my world was a moist, loamy blackness. The earth shook, and more soil broke loose. A rush of shock waves and fiery air rolled over me from behind. The tunnel that I had dug as a child—the long, narrow hollow that I had scraped out of the muck with a spoon, a knife, and my fingernails—remained intact.

All of it was real. It happened.

Now, as I traveled the streets of Washington, that experience came back to me like an anecdote—a story that I had merely overheard, not one that I had lived.

When Lucas Frank threw me into the coal bin, and when I heard the hasp click shut on the door, I experienced only a moment's panic. I took a deep breath, thinking that the good doctor had found the bomb that I had buried in the cellar. It was to have been the vehicle of his death, but then he had discovered it, and I was certain that he had dismantled it.

He must be calling the police, I thought.

I even imagined heavily armed, uniformed, intensely dedicated, muscular young men with short hair and fierce eyes whipping open the coal-bin door to find that I had dematerialized.

I had underestimated Lucas Frank. The man had murder in him. He had not notified the police. He had not disconnected my device. He had moved it and changed the timer, intending to kill me. We were more alike than I had imagined.

I lifted the slab of sandstone, unsure if I would fit into the tunnel that I had dug so many years before. It was tight and my progress was slow, but I did manage to scrape my way down. When the earth moved, and my path to freedom survived the tremors, I remember smiling, continuing to inch my way toward safety.

I shoved through the thick cover of leaves and branches that concealed the tunnel's exit. When I was free from the waist up, I slipped onto my back, turned my face toward the blowing snow, and inhaled the first clean air of a new life.

Pain ripped at my gut. There seemed to be as much blood as dirt crusted on my body.

When confronted by an experience that is accompanied by any strong feeling—pleasant or unpleasant—I leave the confines of my body and soar, like a soul, looking down and watching myself.

That's what I did then, in that moment, in that pain.

When I crawled out into the light, I knew that my injuries were serious. I had no time to examine them. I began to walk, then lope, across the side of the hill and into the woods. If my strength held, I knew that I could reach the village of Saxtons River in an hour, maybe two. And I did.

I crouched in a stand of snow-covered quince and lilac, watching the post office and general store. I had no sense of time. I guessed it to be midafternoon.

The bleeding had slowed, almost stopped. I don't know how long I waited—minutes, a half hour—until an old man parked his Subaru in front of the store, leaving the engine running as he ambled inside.

This, like so much else, was meant to be.

The car was warm, stocked with five cans of Budweiser and a bag of corn chips. The radio spewed a bilge of country music and a local DJ's musings on the state of the world. The verbose president said this. The pig-faced Speaker of the House said that. Then they shook hands. All was well.

There was no mention of any explosion. The world moves fast, but the local media move slow. My death would not be announced for hours—maybe not until the TV news at six P.M.

I remember picking up Route 11 at North Windham, and heading west. I drank a couple of the tasteless beers, ate some chips, and found a different radio station, a familiar piece of music.

> *"Like a phoenix,*
> *rising from the flame,*
> *I will return . . .*
> *I will not burn."*

I was alive, and the first order of business was to stay alive. That meant making it to Swanton.

My biological father was Gary Pease, an Abenaki Indian. He died in a logging accident the year I was born, but his brother lived in Bellows Falls when I was growing up. "If you ever need help," he had told me many times, "our people will take you in."

He knew about Corrigan, my stepfather. "The guy's a shit," he said.

As I turned north on Route 7 near Manchester, headlights shot at me through the snow. I had rolled down the window so the cold air would keep me awake.

I sensed a leering presence beside me in the Subaru. Lucas Frank. I hammered my fist into the space the phantom occupied, sending my shoulder into spasms of searing pain.

It was a little after two in the morning when I reached Swanton, the largest Abenaki settlement remaining in Vermont. The loose association of native people who lived there was still not recognized by the state or federal governments. They, in turn, recognized no government but their own.

My people.

I turned right onto Linda Street, then drove until I came to an isolated trailer.

That was all I remembered, until I was lying on an overstuffed sofa that reeked of baby shit and sweat. I thought I was falling off—on my way to the floor. Each time I faded out, I was driving on Vermont 7 again.

A woman hovered above me—a blur of blue skirt, red jacket, long black hair. She didn't say much, but she seemed to know what she was doing—as if she had treated gunshot wounds many times before. There were moments of clarity. I told her that my father was Abenaki, and I mentioned that the Subaru was stolen.

"My brother will know what to do with it," she said.

I drifted off. When I opened my eyes again, a light flickered somewhere in the room. I was shivering.

I thought I saw Lucas Frank standing beside the gun cabinet.

I growled.

"Hey," she said. "You're burning up."

"Are you real?"

"It's the fever."

She wiped my face with a cloth. I thought she said she was an echo—a sound coming back to me, a sound that I had sent into the wild. Then I understood that Echo was her name.

Sometime later, I looked up into the black eyes of Echo's fifteen-year-old daughter. She stared back at me, not flinching.

The kid gestured with her hands.

"She doesn't speak," Echo explained. "Her name is Terry. She wants to know what animal you are."

The Abenakis are the people of the wolf, so I said, "Like you."

The girl read my lips and backed away. She sensed the danger that had entered their trailer. Her hands fluttered, then she walked off. She paused in the doorway, looked back, then disappeared.

I glanced around at what I could see from the sofa. There was an old TV, but they couldn't use it because the electricity had been disconnected. There were kerosene lamps for light, but nothing to read by that light. It was unlikely that these people would know of, or care about, the drama that had begun to unfold 150 miles away.

Echo saw me staring at the cheap walnut-colored paneling. It was riddled with holes. "My husband was a drunk," she said, standing beside me, her hands on her hips.

"Was?"

She shrugged. "He's dead."

"There was a man here earlier."

"That's Herb, my brother. He took care of the car. It's at the bottom of Maquam Lake. Those are his clothes you're wearing."

I looked down at the plaid flannel shirt and jeans.

The trailer was clean, but in the disrepair and decay that accompany poverty. I asked about an odd collection of twigs and string that hung above the sofa.

"A dream catcher," Echo said. "It holds the bad dreams, and lets only the good ones pass through."

"Are those feathers?" I asked, trying to focus my eyes.

She nodded. "One is from the neck of a golden eagle. There's a native legend that says if you find such a feather, you'll always have good luck, never lose your way in the world. Terry put it there after you came. The power of the eagle cleanses your soul. She thinks you're evil."

"What about you?"

"I don't know. I only know that it's the way of my people to help our own. If my husband were alive, I would still take him in—despite the beatings. It's what I was taught. I don't know who shot you, or why. It doesn't matter."

I looked at her expressionless face. Echo was telling the truth.

I watched through the window as the snow continued to drift down. I knew that my body would heal, but my thoughts were in disarray. Disorganized. I didn't know how long I had been in the trailer, or where it was that I thought I should be—but I felt as if time were slipping away, and I was late for an appointment. I felt a need to hurry—but hurry to where?

One morning while I was recuperating in Swanton,

Echo's brother sat at the kitchen counter, cleaning his deer rifle. I still moved with difficulty, but gained strength each day.

"Where are you from?" Herb asked.

He was a tall, slender man with a weathered face, dressed in clothes similar to what his sister had given me.

"Bellows Falls," I told him.

"Any work down that way?"

"Just over at the ski areas."

"Shit work. Flatlanders in their pink and purple snow suits."

He got up and walked to the door. "Goin' huntin'," he said. "I'll be back by dark. Echo said she's comin' home right after the noon rush at the diner."

"That's where she works?"

"Waitress. Pushes plates of food in front of the down-country assholes on their way to Jay Peak. Dime tips. Quarters. That's why she ain't got no lights."

I watched through the door as Herb climbed into an old Chevy pickup. The germ of an idea flashed through my mind, the first organized thought that I'd had since the explosion. It was the beginning of a plan, something to fit into a design.

I sat at the counter sipping tea and thinking back on better days. I'd had to re-create myself often over the years. Each time, I felt as if I had lost a piece of myself. The closest I ever came to losing myself entirely was at the hands of Lucas Frank in the cellar of the old house.

There would be another encounter. I knew that even then. This time, I would choose the time and place, and I would shake the earth. There were people who had betrayed me, placed me in a position where I was forced to crawl through dirt and muck. They had disrupted the order of my life, the symmetry that I had labored to achieve. Each had provided Frank with a piece of his puzzle. When I gave them the opportunity to relive a small slice of their past, they would provide me with pieces of my own design.

MY DAYS IN THE TRAILER TURNED INTO WEEKS, then months. On a Saturday near the end of March, I borrowed Herb's truck and drove to a logging road, west of the town of Highgate. I parked, walked through snow to the crest of a small hill, then stepped through a line of maples and went to the stone wall that I knew was there.

I counted the trees and walked beside the rock barrier until I found the spot that I was looking for. I brushed away the snow, pulled out some stones at the base of the wall, and reached into the hole I had scooped out of softer earth months earlier.

I removed a box wrapped in plastic. I stuffed twenty-five thousand dollars cash into one coat pocket, and the loaded .44 Magnum with extra shells into the other, along with two complete sets of identification—one for Charles S. Weathers of Lincoln, Nebraska, and the other for Dr. John Krogh, anthropology department, Harvard.

When I returned to the trailer, Herb was sitting at the kitchen counter with his rifle. He was not cleaning it. The weapon simply rested there.

Something was wrong.

"Echo at the diner?" I asked.

"She called. Said she might be late."

"Where's Terry?"

"Don't know," Herb said, standing and cradling the .30-.30 in his arms. "You know, Terry can't talk, but she senses things in other ways. She says you're a killer. You ever kill anyone?"

"Plenty I wanted to kill," I said. "Guess I just never got around to it."

While Herb nodded, pondering that, I removed the .44 from my pocket. I watched as his expression changed from thoughtful to quizzical to alarmed. It was strange. He seemed to have forgotten that he was holding a weapon.

I squeezed off a single round. Herb fell backward, then down.

It had been a long time since I had killed.

I sat at the counter until night came. Echo appeared in the open doorway, a silhouette against the moonlit sky.

"Where's Herb?" she asked, a tremor in her voice.

"Who did you talk to?"

"I wanted to know. I went to the library, looked at old newspapers. Your name is John Wolf. Terry said . . ."

"You made a mistake."

I fired Herb's rifle twice, two slugs dead center into Echo's chest. She fell back through the open door, out onto the snow, where her blood leached designs down along the walk.

I grabbed what I needed, stepped over Echo's body, climbed into Herb's truck, and drove south.

NOW, WITH LUCAS FRANK ENSCONSED IN THE Willard and my plan falling into place, I drove into Virginia, waiting until I had found the perfect location for what I had in mind. Then I placed my call.

"Special Agent Dexter Willoughby," I said into the cellular phone.

"May I tell him who's calling?"

"No."

There was a pause. "I doubt that he'll take the call, sir."

"I have some information for him. If he wants to know why the Bureau took the heat for an ATF screwup, he'll take the call. If not, I'll sell what I have to the media."

"Hold for one moment, please."

Within seconds the thin-voiced man said, "Special Agent Willoughby. How can I help you?"

"You and I both know that the Baker matter was the ATF's problem. Your agency got slammed because there was no proof. ATF covered it up. Ten grand in cash buys you audio and videotapes that document the entire episode, and the only copy of the Baker file that never got shredded."

"Who is this?"

I ignored his question, gave him directions to a car lot where we were to meet, told him he had a half hour to get there, then clicked off. He would have no time to think it over, no time to arrange backup. If the little dick's ambition was the driving force I believed it to be, he would show up with ten thousand dollars in cash, salivating at the prospect of dumping all over a competing agency.

Willoughby had used my presumed death to advance his career. He was hardly someone to work up a sweat about, but I resented his bureaucratic ascent at my expense. He offended me. His agency offended me, especially its elite spawn in Quantico. They weren't "mind hunters." In alleys and closets and other dark places, they engaged in games of mutual masturbation. They were fucking each other's hands and getting paid to do it.

The name of the auto dealer—Featherstone Ford— was serendipitous, but couldn't have been more fitting. Clearly, it was one of those things meant to be. I knew that it would not be wasted on Lucas Frank.

At the appointed time, Special Agent Dexter Willoughby stepped out of his car and walked toward me, unbuttoning his suit jacket. When he put his arms down to his sides again, I moved forward.

"We've never been formally introduced," I said, extending my hand, smiling.

Willoughby kept his hands at his side. His expression was pained, as if he were straining to remember how and why we should know one another.

"Wouldn't you agree, Mr. Willoughby, that a life requires a certain order, a dependable if not predictable balance?"

"Who are you?"

"When the flow of a life being lived is disrupted, torn apart, and crumbles into dust, reparations are necessary, don't you think? It's only just. That's your business, isn't it? Justice."

"I don't know you."

"My name is Wolf," I said. "John Wolf."

Willoughby's right hand snapped up toward his shoulder holster. I grabbed his hand before he could draw his weapon, and spun him around. I grasped him under the chin and twisted until I heard a familiar crack. Then I propelled his limp body into the backseat of my car. I had a few more details to attend to—a final touch that I knew would give me pleasure.

The commuter traffic was heavy. I don't enjoy driving on crowded highways.

It is annoying.

Vexing.

POP

AFTER LANE HAD GONE, I MANAGED TO OVER-
come my aversion to the phone and call Dexter Willoughby's office.

His secretary remembered me. "He's in the field,
Dr. Frank," she said. "He left shortly after you did yesterday. I'm not sure when he'll be back."

When I tried the agent's home phone, I reached his
voice mail. So far, so good.

I drove to Vienna, and parked in a branch library lot
that abutted the rear of Willoughby's property. I could
barely make out the brick ranch house through the
trees and dense undergrowth. I waited in my car until
library traffic was nonexistent, then slipped over a low,
split-rail fence and disappeared into the brush, where it
was impossible to be quiet. I was sure I must sound like
Virginia's own "Bigfoot" tromping through the suburb's
fallen leaves.

Twenty-five yards in, I arrived at the side of a small,
cedar-shingled building. As I approached the door, I
was prepared to find some creative way of opening it,

and considered some of the more imaginative forced entries I've performed over the years. Most of them were legal—in my capacity as a consultant to various law enforcement agencies. A few of them—like this one—could have bought me five to ten years in a steel and stone hotel.

This time, I had no need to be concerned. The door was open. If I got nailed as a trespasser, I could talk my way out of it.

I stepped into a small, neat room. Three tan filing cabinets, neatly and clearly labeled, lined the back wall. Stacking trays on top of the cabinets also wore block-lettered tags. A large window at the front of the building offered a view of the trees. Willoughby's desk was there.

So was the agent.

He sat motionless, his semiclenched hands on his desk, his head tilted awkwardly to one side. He looked like he was staring thoughtfully into his stand of pines. I nearly said his name before I realized that he would never answer anyone again.

The agent's head sat at too odd an angle to his body to allow for life. Someone had broken his neck, then propped him in place like a gray-suited doll. His legs had been taped to the desk. A thin wire wrapped around his chest and the chair held his upper body in place.

"Jesus Christ," I muttered, staring at the man who had so infuriated me the previous day.

I looked away from the dead agent and surveyed the desktop in front of him. His hands had been placed on either side of a large notebook, as if he were about to open it. I lifted it and glanced quickly at police reports, plastic sleeves of computer disks, hand-drawn diagrams of what looked like a bomb, audiotape transcripts. It was Willoughby's case file on John Wolf.

As I closed the notebook, I noticed the printed message on the agent's Windows Marquee screen saver: "Now is the time of the *assassins*."

I could give the dead man no credit for having been that literate. The words that scrolled by were from a work by Arthur Rimbaud, one of John Wolf's favorite poets.

I grabbed some paper towels and wiped down the few areas where I might have left fingerprints. Then, carrying the notebook that I was sure Wolf had left for me, I headed back through the woods to my car.

I drove to a convenience store and used an outside phone to call 911. I knew that the call would be taped, so I held the phone away from my mouth, spoke with as much of an accent as I could muster, and gave the dispatcher all the information he would need.

Then I retraced my path to the Willard, wondering who would visit me first: Willoughby's colleagues, or his assassin.

LANE HAD DROPPED OFF A PRINT COPY OF THE NYPD file on Wolf. It was similar to Willoughby's notebook, but not nearly so complete. Lane had sent disk copies of her Wolf files to me at the lake last year, but I hadn't bothered with the stuff. I knew that the feds had edited it for our consumption.

Besides, Wolf was dead and I was going fishing.

Now, I skimmed through the early pages of both logs—names, dates, police reports, interview summaries.

Lane's partner at the NYPD, Robert Sinclair, had confirmed forty-two of Wolf's victims. Willoughby had confirmed fifty-one.

I scanned Willoughby's list, and one name immediately grabbed my attention: Cora Riordan.

"I don't believe this," I muttered, reaching for a nonexistent pack of cigarettes.

Even after six years of nonsmoking, the habit was there. People who smoke know their cues. Mine was anger.

Cora Riordan was a Boston case from the seventies. Christmas Eve. A brutal homicide that I knew well.

My wife, Savvy, and I were stringing the last of the popcorn for the tree, cutting shapes from cardboard, and coating them with glue and glittery sprinkles, or painting them with green and red acrylics. Lane was asleep. We were laughing and loving what we had made of our scrawny balsam and its single set of lights that I had bought at Woolworth's. At eleven P.M., the phone rang.

"I have to go out," I told Savvy.

"The hospital?"

I shook my head.

"What is it?" she asked.

"That was Ray Bolton," I said. "They have an unusual homicide. They don't know what to make of it."

"If killers aren't going to take the holidays, the least they can do is commit the usual murders," Savvy said, her voice sharp with sarcasm and disapproval.

I saw the squad cars and the small crowd that had gathered along Huntington Avenue. A light snow was falling—a Christmas card for the city, but filled with splashing lights and large men bulked out in blue wool suits, wearing guns. One of the uniformed officers checked my ID and directed me to the second floor. I found Ray Bolton in the kitchen area of the small apartment.

"Sorry to drag you out," Ray said. "You always say it's better if you can see it."

I nodded.

Ray pointed toward the living room, and I followed him. "Cora Riordan," he said.

Now I skimmed the original report that Ray Bolton, one of my oldest friends, had filed. Cora was thirty, divorced, and had lived in her apartment for ten months. She worked in a coffee shop near Brigham Circle.

The woman lay on her back on the floor between her sofa and coffee table, her throat cut in three places, her chest and abdomen pierced a dozen times.

"The rear windows are secure," Bolton told me. "Snow on the fire escape hasn't been disturbed. No forced entry at the front door."

"What else?"

"On the counter," he went on. "One cup, one container of cocoa. Pan of warm milk on the stove."

We walked back into the kitchen. Cora's white work shoes were placed neatly on a mat to one side of the door. "So she walked in," I said, "slipped out of her shoes, poured milk, switched on the stove."

I scanned the apartment. It was clean. Neat. Things were put away. The sink was spotless, but there was a smear of blood on the stove switch for the right front burner.

"He switched off the stove," I said as I wandered again toward the living room.

There was blood spatter on the sofa and coffee table. Blood had pooled on the carpet around Cora. I looked up and saw spatter on the ceiling. He had flailed away at the woman's body, but the killing cuts to the throat were surgically precise.

"What were you saying about the stove?" Bolton asked.

"Just wondering why he'd bother switching it off. He left the door open. Any similar cases?"

"None."

"What about prowlers in the neighborhood? Peeping Toms?"

"We haven't had any complaints like that. This isn't a neighborhood, Lucas. There are four buildings like this one. Everything else is commercial or hospital."

I looked in at Cora Riordan. She had planned a quiet Christmas Eve at home.

I remembered that Ray had an immediate suspect, Jeremy Stoneham, a young man who lived in the apartment below Cora's. Stoneham worked as an orderly at one of the hospitals in the area.

Another tenant, Lucy Wilder, reported that she had seen Stoneham walking the stairs, muttering incoherently to himself—"crazy talk," she called it. A week before the murder, Stoneham was standing inside the door when Wilder walked into the building. He had looked straight into her eyes and said, "The wolfman came. He spoke to me."

Later that night, the young man said the same thing to Ray Bolton. Bolton tapped on the door to apartment one. No one answered. He reached for the knob, and it turned. The door glided open, revealing an apartment with a floor plan identical to Cora's.

"May I come in?" Ray asked.

A slender, young, sandy-haired Jeremy Stoneham

sat on the floor rocking back and forth. He looked up from his study of a bloody kitchen knife. His clothes and face were also blood-smeared.

"The wolfman came. He spoke to me."

Stoneham had been shipped to the infamous Bridgewater State Hospital for psychiatric evaluation. He never stood trial for Cora's murder. Stoneham was deemed mentally incompetent, incapable of assisting with his own defense. Instead, he bounced around inside the mental health system for years until he finally took his own life.

Ray Bolton had done what he had to do in that case. The lab determined that the knife Stoneham cradled was the murder weapon. Blood on the knife was the same type as Cora Riordan's. Stoneham never denied the homicide.

Many psychotics experience auditory hallucinations. These voices—Jesus, Satan, or, in this case, "the wolfman"—direct the action. Stoneham's evaluators believed that the confused young man had responded to "command hallucinations" to kill Cora Riordan.

I remember telling Ray that something was very wrong about the case. I could not reconstruct her death with that young man as the killer.

Whoever had killed Cora Riordan talked his way in. She unlocked the door for him.

Albert DeSalvo could talk his way in anywhere. He also staged set pieces for the police to find. He took his time. He was methodical.

So was this killer.

The scene in Cora Riordan's apartment had been arranged by someone in total control, someone who wanted to appear totally out of control. He had killed before. Cora's murder was savagery by design. It was efficient.

As he left, the milk warming on the stove caught his attention. He couldn't leave it like that. His rigidity required that he correct the situation.

Had Stoneham's auditory command included murder and switching off the stove, but leaving the apartment door open? Absurd.

Dexter Willoughby had made the connection. He had tracked Wolf's movements, his various identities, the jobs he had held. As if he were connecting numbered dots, Willoughby patiently linked one homicide to another.

Willoughby's notes indicated that when Cora Riordan was murdered, Wolf, as "Warren Rayle," was working at a small, private hospital in the Jamaica Plain section of Boston. His job was to scrub and sterilize surgical instruments. Wolf had an apartment on Fenwood Road, two blocks from Riordan's place on Huntington Avenue.

Willoughby also discovered a Wolf kill in Harrisburg, Pennsylvania—a woman who had worked with Cora Riordan's sister.

He had not been able to link Wolf to Stoneham, but I could imagine the relationship between these distant psychological cousins. The psychopathic "wolfman" had manipulated the psychotic Stoneham, further distorted the flimsy reality on which the young man had held such a tentative grasp.

The federal agent's final paragraph was jarring:

Computer enhancement of crime-scene photograph #11 revealed one feather in victim's hair. Lab analysis (contact Harold Raiche) identified feather as originating from "common rock dove" (pigeon).

Neither Ray nor I had noticed the feather, and even if we had, it would have meant nothing.

LATE THAT AFTERNOON, AS I STUDIED WILLOUGH-by's history of Wolf, Lane arrived at my door with two FBI agents. They were faster that I had anticipated.

"We met in the hall," Lane explained.

Hiram Jackson had been around the Bureau for a while. I had never met him, but I had heard of him. He was one of the first African Americans to be absorbed into the agency in an effort to make it look like an equal opportunity employer. He was tall, my height, with as much gray in his hair as I had in mine, although he sported a Bureau-prescribed cut and my locks draped over my collar.

I had never heard of his partner, Rexford Landry, a younger, surly, acne-scarred agent. His large class ring told me that he, like many of his peers, had been sucked out of the University of Virginia, then crafted into the champion of justice that he considered himself to be.

Landry got right to the point. "Special Agent Dexter Willoughby is dead."

Cops watch for reactions when they make announcements like that, so I did my best to drop my jaw. Lane's shock was genuine.

"God. We just talked to him," she said, sitting down. "This is hard to believe."

She looked up at Jackson. "What happened to him?"

"Someone broke his neck," Jackson said.

They had found Willoughby's car parked in Falls Church, Virginia. Vienna police had notified the Bureau after they responded to an anonymous 911 tip called in by "an Eastern European," and determined that the victim was an FBI agent.

Lane shuddered, covering her mouth with her hand.

"You went to see him about John Wolf," Landry was saying. "Whatever it is you're working, you didn't want him in. The Bureau *is* in."

"What about Wolf?" I asked.

"Willoughby shut everybody out of the case up north," Jackson said, cutting off Landry. "That was his way of playing the political game. I was coordinating support for him down here while that investigation was going on. My impression has always been that no one could have walked away from the explosion."

"That's not the impression that Willoughby left me with."

"Huh?" Landry asked, his eyes shifting, gliding over Lane, no doubt mentally stripping her of jeans and sweater.

With Rexford Landry around, no one had to make the trip to the Smithsonian to find out what Neanderthal meant.

I looked at Jackson. "It was more convenient for Willoughby to believe in Wolf's death," I said. "He never found the piece of bone or flesh that would have given him that certainty. He was, however, abiding by the Bureau's official line, which makes me wonder why he had been informed of the deaths of Sarah Humphrey and Alan Chadwick."

The two agents exchanged looks. Feds never give information. They especially don't let on when they don't know something. This pair had not known about the two murders.

This was not the first time that I had been on the wrong side of an argument with law enforcement officials. Usually I did my best to cooperate, to jump through whatever hoops they held out, until everyone got comfortable with the idea that, civilian or not, I had something to contribute and was seeking the same end that they were. Now, there was no time to screw around with federal etiquette.

When neither man spoke, I continued. "Despite Willoughby's intransigence, I think he was distressed by the events in Boston and Orlando."

"What exactly did he say?" Landry asked.

"I didn't memorize the conversation."

Landry clenched and unclenched his fists in an apparent effort to fight off his own anger. "None of us see any reason to think that we're dealing with John Wolf," he said. "The Bureau's position is that he died in Vermont last year. You're chasing ghosts, Doc."

"Then why are you here?"

"We are willing to look at any possible connection to that investigation," Jackson said, skillfully avoiding my question. "If there is any connection to the Wolf case, of course, you could be someone's target. The same is true of Detective Frank. I hope we can work together on that one aspect of our investigation into Agent Willoughby's murder."

"I've already been a target," I told Jackson. "I don't usually part my hair just above my ear. A friend of mine is dead. Someone saw to it that Willoughby received files on two other murders that connect to John Wolf. It's obvious to me that neither of you were aware of that. What about Willoughby's former partner, Susan Walker? Has she been informed?"

Neither man said a word.

"I would prefer to not see her become one of Wolf's victims," I said.

Unlike the subtle connections shared by Wolf's earlier victims, this group shared an obvious link. All of us had attempted to stop Wolf. I didn't know why he had chosen the victim order he had, but I believed that he had a script, and Walker seemed an appropriate next choice.

"Wolf is dead," Landry snapped.

"If you persist in that belief, Susan Walker will be dead. Think about it. But don't think too long. The Bureau can't operate under the weight of its own paperwork. By the time you get clearance to take what you folks like to call a 'proactive' step, we could all be dead."

"This isn't getting us anywhere," Landry said. "Technically, you're a suspect, Doc. You had no use for Willoughby. You were one of the last people to see him alive. Killing a federal agent is a capital offense. Withholding information in a case like this is a felony. So is obstruction. If I decide that you're getting in my way, I will personally jump in your shit and snap the cuffs on you. I don't give much of a fuck who you think you are."

Landry was one of the agency's mistakes. Some federal hiring process had ingested raw human matter, spit out this unpleasant operative, then stuffed him into an ill-fitting suit. He never should have been hired, and probably should have been fired a long time ago.

I looked at Jackson. "Where is Agent Walker?"

"She's part of the team working this case."

I nodded. "I'd like to talk with her."

"I can tell her that. It's up to her."

"Thank you," I said. "Now, if you would, take your snapping dog down to a hydrant. Tell him he has to piss somewhere else."

Landry was slow to get it, but when he did, he started moving in my direction. Jackson grabbed him. Good man.

Jackson had just saved all of us a hell of a lot more unpleasantness that what had already gone down.

I CONSIDERED TELLING LANE ABOUT FINDING Willoughby's body, but decided that would place her in a compromising position. What I had done in Vienna was interpretable as a criminal act. If I had not eliminated all traces of myself from the agent's home office, Lane could be considered an accessory.

"This is fucking crazy," Lane said as she sat on the sofa, running her hands back through her long hair. "First Willoughby, now you think he'll go after Walker?"

She was distressed over Willoughby and frightened by Wolf, but I couldn't help her. The killer had to be stopped. That task was mine, since the rest of the world seemed content to believe that Wolf had been vaporized. I needed Lane's help. "It makes sense that Walker will be next," I said. "So, who's going to bring him down?"

After a moment, Lane looked up at me. "Okay, Pop," she said with a deep sigh, staring at me with a quizzical and appraising expression.

I had seen the look many times before. It conveyed more than a hint of disapproval.

"Human predators seldom take time off to mourn," I said.

"We're alone in this, Pop."

"Then I guess we have to work overtime."

She continued to study my eyes, then nodded slowly. "I wasn't impressed with the D.C. detective, Williams."

"The District isn't known for investigative brilliance, but according to my friend the senator, Williams would be a star in any department. I understand that he's a bit unorthodox. Sometimes that's an indication of creative thinking."

"He looks to me like a candidate for the cover of *Sports Illustrated*. Another African American with a shaved head trying to look like Michael Jordan. He's almost as tall as Jordan, in fact."

I shook my head. "Should I know who Michael Jordan is?"

Lane laughed. "Sure. He starred in a movie with Bugs Bunny."

"I know you're 'frazzled,' as your generation likes to call it, but I think you're departing from reality. Please get 'unfrazzled.' What were you able to accomplish?"

"Everything you asked me to. Williams is skeptical. We can't blame him for that. He's also an undercover drug cop. They don't believe anybody about anything."

"Lane, the first hints about Wolf's possible movements around this city are going to come from street cops or informants. That makes Williams a good contact. Getting the word onto the street is tedious and time-consuming, but it's more likely to produce results than anything else we could do right now."

Lane grabbed her notebook from her purse. "I gave him what we have. I also called Swartz. The composites of Wolf that Swartz did last year will be here in the morning. Williams has the list of Wolf's aliases. He wanted to know what to do with 'all this shit,' as he put it. I figured car rental agencies, the airports, neighborhood hangouts, hotels, that sort of thing. At least for a start."

"Good. Be sure to inform Williams that Willoughby is dead."

"What about the feds, Pop? They're investigating the murder of one of their own. We haven't heard the last of them."

Jackson impressed me as reasonable. Rexford Landry was another matter. I felt certain that the volatile agent was going to be a problem.

"They'll be around again," I said.

I also had a sneaking feeling that John Wolf was going to be of assistance in convincing the Bureau that he had not died in Vermont. He had signed in at his murders; for years, he left messages behind. The signatures were often subtle; his messages varied. He had many names, and all the necessary numbers and IDs to go with those names. The law enforcement computers never detected his work.

Linkage blindness. That pissed you off, didn't it, lad? You had your freedom, but nobody knew your name.

Now, he had returned from the dead. He had to sign in, had to leave his mark in some unmistakable manner. He would want the computers to light up, short out, and crash.

He needed one cop—preferably a fed—to look at another and say, "He is here."

Just like the Second Coming.

"You and Susan Walker were friends, weren't you?" I asked.

"I can try to reach her. We never got to be friends, exactly, but I'm sure she'd be willing to talk to me."

"Please see her before you do anything else. She is in danger. Jackson will deliver my message to Agent Walker, but neither one of them believes in the reality of that danger. Be certain that she understands."

WOLF

VENGEANCE IS AN ART.

There is a stimulus. Someone offends you, causes you inconvenience, or harms you. What follows is what the shrinks like to call "brooding."

I prefer to describe it as preparation.

When I was in my teens, the state put me in a place they referred to as a "therapeutic educational environment." I was a model student—or inmate—and I had a mental list of the people I intended to kill.

I spent the first month in that institution mastering the game, learning what the teachers and counselors wanted to hear. Then, as I said all the correct phrases, and performed for them, I perfected my ability to slip in an out of the place as I pleased. I also mastered the art of car theft. Away from the campus, I could be in any one of five different states in three hours.

I killed in all of them.

They suspected me in one murder—questioned me, accused me, almost arrested me. It was a joke.

As a juvenile in the custody of the state, the laws

were on my side. Confidentiality protected me. All legal proceedings were held behind closed doors, and court records referred to me only by first name and the initial of my last name. The records of all proceedings were sealed. The social service agencies were my partners in crime.

One of my forays into the night was even more of a close call than my near arrest, although I was the only one who knew it. One night after bed check at eleven P.M., I slipped out of the dorm, jogged into the village, hot-wired an old Chevy, and drove to Sanford, Maine. My quarry was the former receptionist at the mental health clinic that I had been forced to attend.

Anita Baines would check my name on a list when I entered the waiting room, then stare at me until it was my time to go in with the social worker. "I ain't gonna rip off the *Newsweek*," I told her.

"You think you got everybody fooled," she said. "You're nothing but a fuckin' killer."

Anita was perceptive but dumb, and had sealed her own fate. I smiled at her. "You might be next," I said.

"You don't scare me, punk."

Anita married, left the clinic, and moved to Maine. I waited what I considered an appropriate time, then followed her. It wouldn't have mattered where she went. Only the timing of her death might have changed. Had she moved to Denver or Dallas, Anita might have bought herself a couple of years. But she was going to die.

It was two A.M. when I drove into a quiet Sanford. I had no trouble finding her apartment building, then slipping the lock on the front door. They lived on the second floor, without a dead bolt. I slipped the lock and stepped inside, closing the door behind me. Then I waited in the darkness until I heard the sound of breathing—two distinct sets of muscles drawing air in, pushing it out—then walked to the open bedroom door.

He was the bulk on the right side of the bed. I remember wondering why so many men insist on sleeping on the right side. Even in the movies.

When I was sure of the position of his head, I brought my recently sharpened ax down hard. There was a spasm of movement on his side of the bed; nothing on hers.

I went to Anita, slipped the wire loop around her neck, yanked on the two wooden handles, and waited for her to open her eyes. When she did—her arms struggling to come out of the blankets—I smiled and said, "Read about it in *Newsweek*."

Then I pulled tighter and waited for her to die.

I knew that I didn't have much time, but I lingered in the apartment long enough to take a brief inventory of the things these two people had acquired—the objects that were somehow necessary to their identity or their existence. A TV set. A stereo. Two matching, molded plastic candy dishes. A clock in the shape of a fish. A framed photograph of the pope.

I could only shake my head. None of it made any sense to me.

I left the place with some reluctance. I wanted to explore, to learn more about my victims. Who had they been, and why? There wasn't time. I slipped out of the apartment, and started the long drive back to Vermont.

On Route 4, just before Concord, New Hampshire, an officer from the Epsom police department pulled me over.

"Oh, shit," I said to the cop, "my aunt is gonna kill

me. I'm supposed to get this back before my uncle has to go to work. I swear I haven't been drinking. I'll take the breath test. Anything."

He glanced at my fraudulent license, then studied the registration. "Where you been?" he asked.

"My girl," I said. "She just moved over here."

"Real lady killer, huh?"

I gave him my best goofy smile. "She's okay with my aunt, but my uncle . . ."

"Slow it down," he said, handing the papers back to me. "Gettin' laid ain't worth gettin' killed over, or killin' somebody else."

"Yes, sir."

It wasn't an Academy Award performance, but it got me back on the road, and it was my first lesson in how crudely law enforcement agencies operate. Had he opened the trunk, the officer would have found a bloody ax, a wire strangulation loop, and Anita's head.

It's never enough to commit murder. The artistic touch is a necessity. I buried her head at the edge of the mental health clinic's parking lot, beneath a forsythia bush. I assume it's still there.

I WATCHED THE FEDERAL AGENTS LEAVE THE Willard. Judging from the white cop's expression, he had not enjoyed his meeting with Dr. Frank. He stood on the sidewalk, hands on his hips, glancing up and down Pennsylvania Avenue. The black man stood behind him, writing in a narrow notebook.

All cops are assholes.

Feds are worse than most local police departments, but they are all incompetent. Wife kills husband, or husband kills wife, the locals can handle that reasonably well—provided that the assailant is sitting there, covered with blood, with the weapon in his or her hand, confessing.

But don't count on it.

And don't count on federal agents investigating anything. That's a bad joke. The only technological claptrap they don't have are cruise missiles, but they never caught the "Green River Killer."

Despite a profile by John Douglas, and extensive interviews with that master sleuth and law enforcement consultant Theodore Robert Bundy—a Vermont native more famous than Calvin Coolidge—the feds have no idea who patrolled the Seattle-Tacoma strip wiping out its female population. They don't know who killed the prostitutes in New Bedford, Massachusetts, or the ones in San Diego.

Of course, whores don't matter. They're typically of some hue, ethnicity, and religion other than WASP, and they carry disease. Clearly, they are part of what Charles Dickens called "the surplus population," and in need of elimination. A predominantly white, Christian government agency really can't be expected to give a shit.

The white fed—I heard his partner call him Landry—lit a cigarette. The other one pocketed his notebook and started walking toward the car.

"Hey," Landry called. "That broad's tough. She's bi-racial, huh? What is she? You figure maybe a quadroon?"

"There's something very black about her, Landry," his partner said. "It's the belt that I understand she has in karate. You want to be sucking on your own testicles, you go ahead and mess with her."

Landry flicked his cigarette into the gutter, and walked to the Ford.

· · ·

WHEN THE TWO FEDS HAD DRIVEN OFF, I WALKED
back into the Willard and strode directly to the elevator. There, I joined a mother and daughter going up.
The woman gripped her child's hand and stared rigidly
at the elevator door. The little girl looked up at me.
"What's your name, mister?" she asked.

The mother yanked at her daughter's arm and hissed,
"Missy."

I smiled. "John," I said. "I guess you're Missy."

"Don't bother the man," Missy's mother said.

A drama wrote itself in my mind. I would kill the
mother. Missy might experience a moment or two of
distress, but then she would be relieved. Then, thera-
pists would fuck everything up. They would arrive by
the busload to convince Missy that she had been traumatized, and had repressed her memories of horror.
She would oblige these manipulative hordes and ex-
hibit symptoms, attend groups, and live her life out as a
victim, a survivor of Elevator Mother Murder. The
truth of it all—that the kid had wished the old bitch
dead a thousand times—would be lost.

I have standards.

When the elevator door opened at my floor, I said
good-bye to Missy, then left the two of them to their
parent-child wars.

I stepped into the carpeted hall and walked toward
Lucas Frank's room. I entertained myself with the
thought that I was in the Coen brothers' film, *Barton
Fink,* and that I was about to ignite the world, beginning
there in that long, silent corridor.

I slipped my hand around my .44 Magnum, not because I was concerned with Lucas Frank's door spring-
ing open. I was considering a substantial variation in
my script.

POP

THERE WAS A KNOCK ON THE DOOR AND THE phone rang.

"Everyone wants us at once," I said to Lane, pointing at the phone and walking to the door.

I could hear Lane talking as a member of the hotel staff entered with a tray of coffee that I had ordered. He placed the tray on a table and handed me a small package. "This was on the floor, Dr. Frank, right outside your door."

I thanked him, and closed the door.

"Who's it from, Pop?" Lane asked as she replaced the receiver.

"Doesn't say. Who was on the phone?"

"Not good. A reporter at the Washington *Blade*. Her name is Darla Michaels. She wants to talk to you about Willoughby's death. I remember her name. She covered the Wolf case last year."

"Did you tell her to call the feds?" I asked as I opened the box and unwrapped a small sheet of stiff paper—mockingbirds and thrashers, page 124 of Peterson's *Field Guide*.

I froze.

"Yeah, but how does she even know you're here?" Lane asked. "Pop? What is it?"

I held up a small brass figure, about the size of the stone gorilla that Lane had found for me in Lake Albert. A sticker on the base of the figure said only "Oliver."

"It's the phoenix," I said. "Know your mythology?"

"The phoenix rises out of the ashes of its own funeral pyre, doesn't it?"

"Yes. Death and resurrection."

Lane shot up out of her chair. "The sonofabitch *is* here. He knows where we're staying."

I rubbed my fingers across the rough surface of the mythical bird's partially unfurled wings, then placed the brass figure on the coffee table, sat, and stared at it.

You watch from a silent distance as you pull the strings on your marionettes, don't you, lad? You are a patient assassin.

"He's close," I said, feeling suddenly weak, as if I couldn't get enough air. "We have our personal notice of his ascension. If I had any question about what was motivating him, it's gone now. I 'killed' him in Vermont. Now it's my turn to die."

"He was outside that fucking door, Pop," Lane said, crossing the room and examining the page from Peterson. "What the hell does *this* mean?"

I shrugged. "Janet got kingbirds. We get mockingbirds."

Law enforcement is not equipped to deal with the wolves of the world. Traditional investigation misses them more often than not. They're invisible. Most are caught by accident—usually because of something minor like the traffic violations of a Bundy, Joel Rifkin, or David Berkowitz.

Wolf was a cut above the pack. Back at the lake, I knew that I would be the one to bring him down. He would not allow himself to be taken alive, and ultimately there was only one confrontation that he wanted.

I could feel myself pulling away from Lane. It was a familiar sensation, one that I had experienced many times over the years, whenever a killer summoned me.

I walked to the window and pushed aside the curtain. "It's raining," I said, looking down at the street. "Did you notice how wet that cellar was in the old house in Vermont? Smelled like grave dirt. Sometimes I think about what it must have been like for Wolf as a kid, when his stepfather locked him in the coal bin down there. I've tried to imagine, to put myself there, to feel what he must have felt. I can't."

I glanced back at Lane. "I can't because he didn't feel anything. He thought a lot, reasoned, planned, but he didn't feel a damn thing."

Childhood trauma is only one possible ingredient in the recipe that produces a serial killer. Most children who survive abusive home lives do not go on to careers in homicide. How they perceive their experiences, and how they reason their world, have as much or more to do with shaping them as the experiences themselves. For years, our microscopes had been trained on the family, and we had ignored the subject of our study.

Lane walked up behind me. "So, Wolf makes his announcement," she said. "He's back from the dead. What do the bird book pages mean?"

"Janet's kingbird, *Tyrannus tyrannus*, the tyrant—is Wolf saying that he's the tyrant, the evil lord of all?"

"And what? 'Mocking' you?"

"I don't know what else it could mean."

I continued to gaze out at the city, at the crazy collections of lights blurred by the rain. As frightening and ominous as Wolf's gift was, it had also triggered a strange sense of resolve.

I moved closer to the window, touched the pane of glass with my fingertips, and tried to feel the drops of rain.

LATER, AFTER SAYING GOOD NIGHT TO MY DAUGHTER, I slipped out for the evening.

I was restless, and I had some business to attend to. I also wanted to explore the city, to visit those parts of D.C. that would be most hospitable to someone who needs to preserve his anonymity. I knew that Wolf would not hang out in any part of the capital where the paparazzi did, and that eliminated a good portion of the city. He was on a mission; he couldn't afford to be caught in a casual photo that turned up on the front page of the *Blade*.

A gray sedan—my federal escort, I surmised—was parked on the opposite side of Pennsylvania Avenue, thirty yards north of the Willard's entrance. I walked over and tapped on the window. It slid down, revealing two thirty-something white men in matching tan suits. The one on the passenger side was Special Agent Rexford Landry.

"If John Wolf is dead," I said, "why are you following me?"

The driver stared at me, then hit a button and the tinted window closed. I felt like putting my fist through it.

My first chore, then, would be to dump the feds, and for that I needed a well-situated, but seedy public bathroom with a window on an alley. I'd had twenty years to master my defenestration techniques, and they had never failed me. My favorite "emergency exit"—in Neil's Beer Garden—had been demolished when Boston built its government center. Poor trade, if you ask me.

A half hour later, I sipped a beer at Jewell Howard's, a bar that my nephew, Lymann Murr, had recommended if I was ever in D.C. The bouncer, Oscar Bell, a tall, muscular black man, had played drums in one of Lymann's short-lived reggae bands. We had met only once, when I was in New York visiting Lane, but Oscar remembered me.

When I walked in, he nodded, cracked what passed for a smile, and said, "Lymann's uncle."

"You have a good memory."

"After we met, Lymann told me all about you." He grinned. "I don't like bad guys either."

Oscar got paid to make sure that violence didn't happen, or if it did, that it didn't erupt in Jewell's. Because of his massive size, he was well qualified for the job.

With the advent of Uzi-toting gangs in the city, Oscar's job had gotten complicated. If he had red headbands in the bar, no blues got in. When the blues caught an early table, the reds had to walk down the block to another bar.

It was Nina Simone night in Jewell's—nothing but Nina on the cranked-up jukebox, and drafts at half price.

"I have a couple of feds following me," I said, handing him a twenty and explaining what I had in mind.

"The feds will pay the cover," Oscar said. "They never drink. They don't even loosen their neckties. They come in here and they fuck up the mood."

I sat at the bar, sipped my beer, and watched as Oscar collected a five from each of the agents. Landry remained near the front door. His partner stood at the side exit.

I tapped my fingers to Nina doing "Black Swan."

Each time that Landry glanced in my direction, he found me staring at him. It was a conditioned response for him to look my way less often. I wasn't supposed to see him. People do have a bit of the ostrich in them. When he was taking as long as thirty seconds between glances, I slipped off the stool and headed for the bathroom.

I opened the window in the small, dingy room, climbed through, and moved into the darkness next to Jewell's Dumpster. I heard noise in the bathroom behind me, pulled my nine-millimeter, and stepped back to the window.

Landry was sprawled on the pissy linoleum floor. Oscar stood over him.

"Man slipped," Oscar said, smiling his cracked smile. "Hit his head on the sink, I guess."

So much for losing the feds, I chuckled.

I nodded, then walked back through the alley's darkness.

AS I WANDERED THE CITY STREETS THROUGH A steady, light rain, I struggled with the uncompromising feeling that I was lost in an urban wasteland. I passed housing projects, liquor stores, burned-out wrecks of cars, buildings that housed whores, Tarot readers, and the Church of the Laughing God. This dismal land came with its own soundtrack—the soprano wail of sirens, the thrumming bass of a police helicopter, the staccato burst of an automatic weapon somewhere in the city's maze of dark corridors.

This was a territory where Wolf could disappear. I teased myself with the notion that I was bait, that Wolf was following me, that I was accomplishing something. I pictured him stepping out of the shadows, saw myself raise my weapon and drop him with a single shot.

It was delusion.

All I was doing was traveling through a long, dark tunnel, its walls decorated with snapshots of the scarred remains of a land more destroyed than Dresden after the bombing. But I was certain my travels were preordained.

This city was the center of power for the entire world. The perfect place to bring to its knees. But how?

At an intersection, I saw a pile of burning debris in the middle of the road. There were mattresses, a broken banister, pieces of furniture—all smoldering. Sparks shot up, but the light rain muted the prospect of any conflagration. Instead, blinding smoke billowed out from the makeshift inferno.

Two uniformed officers and five civilians stood there. I joined the group, my eyes watering, nearly blinded.

A third cop arrived. "Tactical's on their way," she said. "Who's out there?"

"Neighborhood guy. He's wasted. Killed his girlfriend, and now he's got her three-year-old daughter with him. We've got to move these people back."

Rain matted my hair, running in rivers beneath my shirt collar.

"Tactical wants to know what he's got for weapons," the officer said.

There was no response. I felt a slight breeze begin to move the late summer air as I strained to see beyond the group of cops. A small, barefoot child in pink pants and a white shirt stepped out of the smoke. She had her thumb stuck in her mouth, and grasped a rag doll shaped like an owl. The female officer rushed over, knelt, and said, "You okay, honey?"

The little girl yanked out her thumb. "Billy in the smoke," she said.

At that instant, I heard a savage roar—like a wounded animal—as a small, slender black man wielding a kitchen knife ran from the smoke directly at the cop kneeling with the child. Reflexively, my hand went to my gun.

A woman threw herself over the front end of a parked car. Two men dropped to the wet pavement.

One of the cops had much faster reflexes than I. His nine-millimeter exploded, and the running man smashed to the asphalt, his blood—briefly red in the firelight, then blue, and finally black—flowed into the pools of water.

If there had been any hesitation, the outcome would have been different.

The little girl had her fingers plugged in her ears.

"C'mon," the officer said, picking up the girl and her doll.

"Billy didn't make chicken noodle," she said. "Mama said what Billy made had okra in it. Mama's 'lergic to okra, so she went to heaven."

Each member of the small crowd had an opinion on why Billy "snapped."

"He was dead in his head from that crack," one said.

"He couldn't find no work," another contributed.

"That woman didn't want Billy 'round there."

"Why he damn near kill the baby?"

"What was his last name? Billy what?"

The last speaker's question was the answer. Billy had no recognition. These were neighborhood people, and they didn't know who he was. He lived among them, but he was a nobody. The man had been powerless. Just another crackhead.

In the end, Billy had settled for "suicide by cop."

I turned away from the D.C. smoke and the slowly growing crowd, and watched as a black Lincoln pulled to the curb.

WHEN WE WERE COLLEGE ROOMMATES, HARRY Storrs had no intention of entering politics. He had majored in comparative literature, toyed with joining SDS, and, along with hundreds of others, hurled unflattering epithets at then Secretary of Defense Robert McNamara, until the Cambridge cops turned their dogs loose on the demonstrators. The Dobermans and shepherds had sent us scurrying up the trees along the Charles River. We chanted, "Dogs need trees."

Now, in the rear seat of his Lincoln, Senator Harry Storrs handed me a bottle of microbrewed ale from his home state. He popped the cap off another for himself.

"What was the commotion back there?" he asked.

"Neighborhood guy killed his girlfriend and was going to kill her daughter. The cops got him first."

Harry lowered his bottle and stared at me. "You saw that?"

"I saw a skilled police officer kill a 'Billy' with no last name before Billy had a chance to hurt a child or another cop who was crouched next to the child."

"Jesus Christ."

I had seen the expression on Billy's face as he emerged from the smoke. Rage. "Every person he could reach was going to die. No work, a crack habit, domestic problems. He had to dig himself out. This was his chance to taste power, to tell the world to go fuck itself. I think he believed that if he created an intolerable horror, people would stop dead in their tracks and notice him. It was his justice, his way of bringing down the shithouse."

Harry shook his head. "Neighborhoods like these are bad for your health," he said, raising his bottle and drinking.

"Do something about it."

"That's up to Marion Barry. My constituents are concerned about farm subsidies. They don't give a shit whether there's any toilet paper in the District Building. How's Savvy?"

"She's fine, as far as I know. I had a card about six months ago. Vera?"

He laughed. "I think I see her about as often as you see Savvy. Ever think we might've planned it that way? You're the shrink, Lucas."

"What's going on with the Willoughby investigation?"

He shook his head. "You never did play enough. The FBI will be back on your doorstep. The Bureau's had a rough couple of years. The Olympics thing didn't help. The problems with the lab. Now this. Publicity goes down the tubes. Morale suffers. Then, of course, funding becomes a problem. They don't have anything in this Wolf matter. Is that his name?"

I nodded.

"Nothing. They're running a routine investigation on the agent's death. Intensive, but routine, and no wolves. You think he'd be in a neighborhood like this?"

"I do. He'd blend in here."

Storrs drank again from his ale, and I watched as his head went back—the mane of white hair, the familiar profile.

"What do you think of this ale?" he asked.

"It's almost an India pale," I said.

"Not bad, though, huh?"

I smiled at my old college friend. "For something they ship to the legions in a foreign land, it's excellent."

He laughed, then looked at his bottle. "You prick. You're right."

"Too bitter," I said. "What else do they make?"

"I don't know. I'd rather drink bourbon anyway. I read about that business last year, Lucas. I thought you were finished with this crime stuff."

"Wolf killed a friend of mine. He almost got me. But that isn't all of it."

"You can't leave it alone, can you?"

"Could you walk away from politics?"

He laughed. "They'll carry me away."

I sighed. "I'm starting to feel the same way. Maybe I can't quit."

THE SENATOR'S DRIVER DROPPED ME AT THE Willard.

I sat in my darkened room, smoking a cigarette, running my fingers over the brass phoenix. I had picked up the cigarettes at Jewell's. I was pissed off. It was that simple. Even after six years, smoking was an easy habit to fall back into, and it was comforting.

I tossed the brass figure of the phoenix onto the foot of the bed. Wolf was inside my head. We were going to play mind games.

As I watched the smoke circle toward the ceiling, I drifted back to that Christmas Day in the seventies, when Ray Bolton arrested Jeremy Stoneham for the murder of Cora Riordan. Late that night I sat in my study and scribbled a note to Ray.

This killer is pure predator, a brilliant one, unlike anyone we have encountered. He is Stoneham's "wolfman." He spoke to Jeremy, whispered in his ear. The voice that young man heard is real.

I grabbed the brass phoenix from the bed.

When you want to deliver a message, nobody can stop you, lad, can they? You don't guess at anything. You reason everything through, then skate around the edges, soften us up, and have one hell of a good time for yourself.

I stubbed out my cigarette, walked to the window, and gazed into the distance.

"Whisper in my ears, lad," I muttered. "Talk to me. Tell me how you got Dexter Willoughby, an FBI agent, to walk into your arms."

WOLF

AFTER LEAVING MY GIFT FOR DR. FRANK, I WENT prowling. I had work to do.

I found a gray van with white magnetic signs stuck to both doors: Valley Carpet. It was parked at the end of an alley off lower Pennsylvania Avenue.

I walked down a short flight of concrete steps illuminated by a blue, overhead light and pulled open a heavy metal door. The interior held its own shades of gray and blue—cigarette smoke, and the unmistakable aroma of marijuana.

A black man my size, perhaps a bit heavier, sat in his coveralls at the bar sipping watered whiskey and chain-smoking Camels. The Valley Carpet emblem decorated his left pocket. A patch on his right pocket advertised that he was Nick.

I slipped onto the stool next to Nick's, ordered a draft, then turned to watch the black drinkers and smokers watch me.

"You a cop?" the bartender asked.

She was a slender, young woman in a hot pink halter top, sitting in a wheelchair. There was a wooden platform built behind the bar to raise her up, and the shelves of glasses and bottles had been lowered so that she could reach them.

"Nick here can vouch for me," I said.

"What?" he asked, twisting around to look at me. "I don't know you."

"You installed my carpet about six months ago. I guess I shouldn't expect you to remember that. You lay carpet every day."

From somewhere inside his alcohol-fogged brain, he studied my face. The desire to agree with what has been presented as friendly and familiar is great. "You look like somebody I seen before. Northwest somewhere?"

"Georgetown."

He avoided calling me by a name that he thought would be wrong. He had no way to know that I would have responded to any name.

"What are you doing down here?" he asked.

"The music," I said. "I've got the 'Blues Velvet' CD. Only heard them live a couple of times."

"You got good taste, my man," Nick said, nodding toward the trio on the small stage, then turning to the bartender. "I'll vouch for this guy, Wheels. He ain't gonna be no trouble."

"Thanks, Nick," I said.

He waved me off. "No big deal. Wheels sees a white guy walk in, she figures it's the law or some other kind of trouble. Can't blame her."

I nodded, sipped my beer, listened to the music.

"What kind of carpet did I put down?"

"Pardon?"

"The rug I laid."

"The wife picked it out," I said. "It's beige. That's all I know. I hate beige."

Nick laughed. "I laid some shit today, I swear it was the color of pea soup. The lady loved that stuff. Guy looked like he was gonna puke."

We both laughed.

I left the bar seconds after Nick did. I walked up the three concrete steps outside the door and watched as the big man staggered down the alley to the parking area. As I considered the most efficient way to obtain Nick's van, I could feel a smile curl up at the corner of my mouth. I didn't have to kill him. I wanted to.

I walked quickly down the slight incline, then started to run, and caught up with him beside the door of his van. He was talking to himself, fumbling with his keys, as I jumped and landed on his back. He grunted, emptied his lungs of air.

I reached from behind and found his throat with a razor-sharp, six-inch Schrade knife that I keep for taking down larger members of the species.

Nick went down.

His blood was purple, almost black, in the soft glow of blue light. I watched the blood spread across Nick's throat like a Rorschach ink blot, changing shape as it moved.

It altered the color of his brown skin.

Purple, almost black in blue light.

Symmetry.

I stripped Nick of his coveralls, left him in the alley, and climbed into the van. As I drove slowly away, a fat black woman stepped outside the bar. Her screams shattered the silence in that dismal asphalt corridor.

It's strange how people react to events like this. They seem driven to emit noise, to touch, to move in a rapid, frantic manner. What animates them tends to calm me.

Scenes like this are what make my work worthwhile, and I wanted to savor it. I wanted to replay the memory over a glass of wine. I drove north on Pennsylvania because I could think of no better place to do this than in the Willard's bar, the one called The Nest.

THE SUBJECT OF ONE OF MY FORAYS INTO THE night, so long ago, was Cora Riordan. She raised a feeble hand as I approached her, wanting to scream, but not seeming to know how.

Jeremy Stoneham sat mute with his feckless mind and multiple realities as I caressed him with my whispers.

Lucas Frank sniveled to his favorite reporter from one of the Boston newspapers that the findings of the court in the Stoneham case were wrong. Dr. Frank was ahead of his time back then. He used a language that no one understood, a language that became common parlance in the crime-solving business twenty years later.

I'd already had several homicidal experiences when I first read about Lucas Frank. It was at a time when the best that cops or politicians could do was condemn all wet art as heinous, senseless, vicious, evil. Then, along came Dr. Frank to say that there was a logic, a system of thought at work in any apparently random homicide.

"We have to suspend our own biases about what constitutes rational behavior," Frank told reporter Anthony Michaels, "and seek to understand the killer's reasoning. His crime meant something to him. What?"

In the Michaels interview, Frank's example was a case in western Massachusetts. The killer of five young women had injected himself into the investigation with offers of assistance. Police and a university-connected shrink stated flatly that the killer had wanted to be caught, that he had a subconscious need or desire to be apprehended.

Lucas Frank disagreed. "This man seized the opportunity to be at center stage," he said. "The sense of power afforded him by the murders was enhanced by being among those who sought him."

He was right, of course. But it was years before that particular insight was routinely applied—first in arson cases, then in child abductions.

In a strange way, it was a comfort for me, a killer, to know there was someone who did not practice the art, but was on intimate terms with it. It was also unbelievable and, after some thought, threatening.

If such a man could think like I did, what was to prevent him from tracking me down? It was then that I decided to learn everything I could about this man. I have always been a believer in the preemptive strike.

The professional community demanded that Dr. Frank's notion of power as the prime mover of retributive justice be validated. Research psychologists who had never dealt with humans slapped studies together. Rats and rhesus monkeys. Mazes. Pellets of food. Electric shocks.

They had not completed their work when the genius giant, Edmund Kemper, blabbed to his buddies, the cops, listened to their frustrations as they investigated Kemper's homicides, then entertained the troops from Quantico.

The light began to dawn.

Those of us in the field love to play cops and robbers almost as much as we enjoy the stalking, the anticipation of murder, and the killing. We dismissed the notion of "studies" by textbook experts a long time ago.

There is law, and there is justice. The former is codified and fills large, dusty books. The latter is entirely subjective. I have my justice; Lucas Frank has his.

He never solved the Cora Riordan case. He never knew what he was dealing with.

How could he? She was mine.

The circle remains unbroken.

Symmetry.

I CLIMBED THE SPIRAL STAIRCASE IN THE NEST and found a table by the window, overlooking Fourteenth Street.

They had changed the decor a bit since my last visit. The trees that they bring in are changed every few weeks, and there were other small shifts in the room's appearance. The carved woodwork, the mirrored walls, and the fine wine are constant.

I prefer consistency. A sense of order. Balance.

A woman with upswept hair and pale skin sat at the piano playing "Blue Moon." A man at a nearby table sang softly to his companion.

In my mind, I could still hear the commotion in the alley as the blues club emptied and a crowd gathered, waiting for the police and paramedics.

I didn't look back. I seldom look back. Vermont was one of the exceptions.

I was thinking of that day almost a year ago, of the pain and the exhaustion and the adrenaline, when the waiter came to take my order. "A glass of the house red, please," I told him.

It is important, even necessary, to have a design in mind, preferably one composed of smaller designs. It has to do with symmetry, but it is more than that. It is the consonance of multiple forms—each within the other, cascading toward infinity. The Mandelbrot set. Fractal curves. Designs that replicate themselves repeatedly, yet are merely hinted at when given too casual a glance.

The perfect design is one that fractures time, that allows free movement between past and present. It is like the screenwriter's creation, a vision that is complete before the first word is typed.

I sipped my wine, enjoyed the ambience, and absorbed all the dimensions of my perfect design.

Two young women approached my table.

"We always sit here," the first one said, "because of the window."

"Do you mind if we join you?" the second one asked.

I expected better of the Willard—a more restrained clientele—but I smiled and nodded. They sat down, plunging instantly into the mindless gabble that characterizes their gender and age. I leaned back, not listening, allowing their chatter to become part of the background din.

Like them, I appreciated the window. I glanced outside just as Dr. Frank was making his way into the hotel. He looked disheveled—his ragged mane and beard synchronous with his faded jeans, and his gait that of a weary man.

One of my self-invited companions tapped my wrist. I looked at her with gentle eyes.

"Do you teach at George Washington?" she asked. "Philosophy, maybe?"

"No, I'm at Harvard," I said. "Anthropology."

"Bones."

"Not all of our remaining frontiers are in the heavens," I told her.

She shrugged. "You go to digs and stuff?"

"Perhaps you're thinking of archaeology."

"Oh. Maybe that. You do bones, though, right?"

"Yes," I agreed. "I do bones."

"Like that Russian czar they dug up."

"Nicholas," I said.

"Yeah."

"I didn't *do* his bones, but that *is* my work. Forensic anthropology."

"Oh, yuck. *Crime* victims?"

She turned to her friend before I could respond. Young women seem to swirl their way through life—moving along on the tips of their toes, almost dancing, never glancing to one side or another.

Someone was paying these two vacuous specimens enough money so that they could afford to sit at the Willard and drink frothy, blended concoctions, *sine* umbrellas. Who paid their salaries? For what? And where, in all the national debris, had they originated? Arkansas? Ohio? Kansas? Vermont?

"What do you do?" I asked Bones.

"What?"

"Your work."

"Oh," she said, "I'm an editorial assistant at the Washington *Blade*. She—Jeannie—is a senatorial aide. I'm Courtney."

"John," I said, wondering if Courtney knew the *Blade*'s investigative reporter, Darla Michaels, another member of my cast. "What does an editorial assistant do?"

"Oh, like, it's really complicated. I mean, there are

all these *different* things you have to do. And they don't tell you everything when they hire you. It's like, *hello*, this isn't what you *described*. Filing and stuff. I was an *English* major. I thought I'd be checking punctuation, spelling, grammar—you know?"

I heard a siren in the distance. Could be that they were wasting their time rushing to Nick, or maybe Washington was devouring more of itself.

"What does a senatorial aide do?" I asked Jeannie.

"I'd rather not say," she said.

I knew that was her canned response, a way of sounding self-important. She probably practiced it in front of a mirror, like DeNiro in *Taxi Driver*. Her clipped answer was more than just a pose.

Although it didn't happen often, I had seen this phenomenon before. I meet a woman, and she picks up on something, feels the danger from the outset. I see it in her eyes, hear it in her voice. It had been like that with Terry, Echo's daughter, in Swanton, Vermont.

I knew that Jeannie would be bounding out of there at any moment.

She looked at my sleeve. "Is that blood?" she asked.

"Did you hear the siren?"

"Yes."

"There was an automobile accident. It was a few blocks from here. I helped extract the survivors from the wreck—led them away and sat with them. One was just a child. I held her. But she died."

"Oh, *God*," Courtney said.

"I wanted to have a glass of wine, try to settle my nerves. I didn't pay any attention to my appearance. Could I be in shock and not know it?"

Jeannie said, "I want to *go*."

The two of them got up.

"Let me take care of the tab," I said. "It's the least I can do. I've ruined your evening."

"No," Jeannie said, pushing past her friend and heading for the door.

Courtney looked at me with moist, sad eyes. "I don't know what to say. We'll just go, I guess. Will you be all right?"

"Without a doubt."

I watched her sway her way on the tips of her toes toward the door, where Jeannie was waiting—looking as if she didn't feel safe at the Willard.

Abraham Lincoln had chosen the hotel as his haven when the assassination threats were mounting. He was smuggled in by the famous detective, Pinkerton, to await his inauguration. He lived through that, only to be undone by his faulty decision to attend a performance at Ford's Theater.

Then and now.

Symmetry.

I left the Willard, and stepped back into the night on Pennsylvania Avenue—watching, listening.

No sirens. The two women were gone, but the sense of the country having been culturally razed lingered on.

Life should not be wasted on such ciphers. The experience of being alive is too extraordinary for them. Life is an education, a "trip" without chemical assistance.

In a few days, it will be exactly a year since that brief moment when it seemed that my life might end. When I first emerged from my tunnel, I could smell the smoke from the explosion and fire. I watched the glowing embers blend with the light snow. As I moved away, that faded until there was just snow and the silence of the forest.

On the anniversary of my rebirth, it will not snow in Washington. But there will be a blast from beneath the earth—an explosion and fire—and then there will be the silence of the thousands numbed by my audacity.

"Perfection," I said into the cool night air.

POP

SUSAN WALKER HAD NOT RETURNED LANE'S CALLS.

"I'm not even sure she's getting the messages," Lane said. "They keep transferring my calls to that prick, Landry."

Early that morning, she had gone to find Walker. After that, she planned to do some follow-up work with the D.C. police. I intended to attack more of Willoughby's files and Wolf's journal, but Special Agent Hiram Jackson showed up at my door.

"I have to drive down to Quantico," he said. "I thought if you weren't busy, you might want to join me."

I had no interest in a tour of their underground quarters, but I did want to continue my conversation with Jackson.

As we drove south on I-95, he said, "I want to apologize for Agent Landry's behavior yesterday."

"Accepted."

"I also feel like I have to defend him. He's a South Florida veteran. I wonder sometimes if he has one of those post-traumatic stress problems. He spent five years in Miami, most of the time never knowing who was a

cop and who wasn't. He cornered one guy in an alley—
both of them had their weapons drawn—and the man
turns out to be DEA. That kind of stuff can get to you.
We all want the dope off the street, but the agencies
don't always work real well together."

My own feeling was that the war on drugs was long
lost. Tons of cocaine were removed from the trade. Millions of dollars never made their way back to Colombia.
But there were always more than enough kilos to go
around, and more than enough money to build palaces
and establish personal armies in Cali or Medellín. If
Miami got too hot, there was Galveston or L.A., and
new shipping techniques to foil customs. I was familiar
with the pressures that Landry must have experienced
working in a situation like that, but the entire enter-
prise struck me as a waste of time and money.

"He's even less happy with you now than he was before, however," Jackson said.

"Oh?"

"You picked him out last night. You knew we had a
tail on you."

"Yes. I did."

"He doesn't believe he slipped on the bathroom
floor in Jewell Howard's."

"I wouldn't know. The floor was soaked when I
went through. Looked like somebody missed the bowl."

"He says the bouncer whacked him."

"Oscar? Landry missing any money? His identification? His weapon?"

Jackson shook his head and sighed. "Let's just say
he slipped."

"Agent Jackson, I don't give a shit what happened
to your protégé while he was in the pisser. I also have
nothing but antipathy for his abuses of my tax dollars in

Florida. He told me I was chasing a ghost. If he thought he was going to put a cork in the cocaine trade in Miami, *he* was delusional. If you alphabet agencies can't work together, and really want to shoot one another, please have at it. Just try to be more efficient about it. Now, I'll ask you the same question I asked Landry. If Wolf is dead, why follow me?"

Jackson was silent.

"Did you talk with Susan Walker?"

Jackson sighed. "Before Willoughby shut her out, she got a good look at what was left of that old house. She also saw some of the preliminary reports. She's not concerned about John Wolf."

"She's comfortable with coincidence?"

"Apparently so."

"Is that why she hasn't returned Lane's calls?"

Jackson looked at me. "She didn't say anything about Lane calling."

Another reason for me to stick pins in my Rexford Landry doll.

We drove along in silence for several minutes.

"You are not comfortable with coincidence," I said. "Otherwise, you wouldn't tap on my door and invite me out."

He nodded. "I reviewed the material on Sarah Humphrey and Alan Chadwick. I remembered Wolf's fascination with birds and feathers. His sister's killer ate a meal in the trailer after cutting her. He placed an odd glass bird on the table, like it was supposed to be a centerpiece. None of her neighbors remember seeing the thing before. Her husband said he vaguely remembered it. Hadn't seen it in years. Said he thought it was a gift from her brother. I also called Boston. Spoke to a guy who said he's an old friend of yours. Ray Bolton."

"Ray brought me my first case," I said. "We go back a lot of years."

"He was kind enough to do some checking on Chadwick's death, which was ruled a suicide, by the way. There was a compact disk on a chair in the pathologist's office. Stravinsky's *Firebird*. Chadwick preferred classical music, but according to his colleagues, he purchased only vinyl recordings."

I shook my head and silently saluted my opponent. Stravinsky's ballet is the story of the phoenix. I slipped the brass figure from my pocket. "This was delivered to me at the hotel. It's the phoenix, rising out of the ashes, returning to life. It was wrapped in a page from Peterson's *Field Guide to the Birds*—mockingbirds. Janet Orr, my friend at the lake, received kingbirds. The page was torn from my copy of the book while I was unconscious on the patio."

Jackson glanced at the brass rendition of the mythical bird, then at me. "I told you that I was willing to consider any overlap in our investigations. Chadwick also received a page from Peterson—coots, page sixty-one. Humphrey's was page thirty-four, old squaws."

I knew that Wolf's signature in Willoughby's office had not been a page from Peterson. The line from the poet Rimbaud scrolling across the agent's computer screen had marked the murder as Wolf's. I also knew that my not asking about that crime scene would appear strange.

"What about Willoughby?"

"Nothing from the bird books," Jackson said, shaking his head, "but someone is involved in an elaborate charade. Maybe an ardent admirer, a fan of Wolf's. We've seen a couple of cases like that before."

That had been Lane's initial reaction—that we were

dealing with a copycat. I respected Jackson's intelligence enough to believe he knew that Willoughby's body had been propped in place for a reason. Something should have been resting between the agent's two cupped hands. I also believed that he was aware of the Rimbaud reference. He had to know.

"I don't buy it," I said. "The pathologist was connected to Wolf's late teens and early twenties. The sister connects to his childhood. Both of them played significant roles in our ability to understand Wolf, and to find him. Neither was ever identified in the media. Willoughby became one of your investigative superstars at Wolf's expense. John Wolf is motivated by vengeance."

"Why didn't Wolf kill you in Michigan?"

"I think because he wanted me here for the rest of his show."

"Willoughby."

"And Susan Walker, Lane—whatever else he has planned."

"What else *does* he have in mind?" Jackson asked. "And when?"

I gazed out the window. Something was nudging at the back of my mind, but I couldn't get a grasp on it. "I don't know," I said.

Jackson slid a photograph out of an envelope and handed it to me. I stared at the picture. An auto dealership. Willoughby's Volvo with the driver's door open. A group of cops standing around. Lab techs going through the agent's car. High on a pole, at the end of the lot, was the owner's sign: FEATHERSTONE FORD.

"I don't think that's a stretch," Jackson said.

"Neither do I."

"Officially, I can't look for John Wolf. I don't think

that matters. If it isn't someone doing a damn decent imitation of Wolf, that leaves the original article, right?"

What Jackson was offering was much better than nothing. "Right," I agreed.

THE BSU, IN ITS UNDERGROUND QUARTERS AT THE FBI Academy in Quantico, was even more institutional and depressing than I had imagined. The place was sixty feet down, ill-lighted, tomblike.

Special Agent Landry sat in one of the cramped cubicles. As we passed, he looked up, displaying a bandage on his forehead, a blackened eye, and a vicious scowl.

"Landry's reviewing all of Willoughby's files," Jackson said.

"So, I'll have a different tail tonight?"

"Depends on where you go. Why not just file an itinerary with me? Be easier on all of us."

"My sister once told me that life wasn't fair. Think she was right?"

We both smiled, and walked in silence through the hall.

"This is Herb Cooper's office," Jackson said, pointing at one of the small rooms. "He's working a case in Oklahoma, homicide victims buried in a Native American burial grounds. We have to identify the victims, two entire families, without disturbing the site."

"Is this a recent case?"

"It's from the sixties," Jackson said. "The Winklers and the Parmenters. Both families had sixteen-year-old daughters. We think the kids were the targets, and we figure the same perps did both. It's a little like the

Clutters in Kansas, the Truman Capote book, but money wasn't an issue here. Also, whoever killed them didn't leave the bodies to be found. We were lucky to stumble onto this thing—local guy found a jawbone and a femur—but it's a tough one to work. We can't disturb the burial grounds, and there could be all kinds of evidence in there."

I met so many agents on my tour that the names flew by. Lawrence, Draper, Bowers, Gannet, Means. Always, I was the intruder, the outsider. The women and men that I met were polite, but distant. I wasn't a visiting official who needed to be impressed. I was a civilian critic and competitor.

When Jackson and I sat over sandwiches and beers in the cafeteria called the Boardroom, he said, "I thought you were retired."

"I was. I liked it that way. I'm slowly realizing that I can't stay retired."

"We're not doing the job?" Jackson asked, with a twinkle in his eye.

I laughed. "You're asking me? Jesus. Of course you're not. Your press releases and your movies and the way you treat the local PDs—all of that says you know something nobody else does. You don't. None of us can do the job alone, Jackson. I think you know that."

He nodded. "The Bureau is changing," he said. "For the better, I mean. It's a slow process."

"I have no patience with any bureaucracy," I told him. "I'm not saying that I don't have my own quirks and limitations. Wolf is certainly teaching me a lesson. When you turn your back on the predators, they snap at your heels. Given a choice like that, I'd much rather be the aggressor, and I don't have time to wait for a committee decision to turn me loose."

Jackson grinned. "Everybody said you were a pissant."

"Damn right," I said, taking a bite from my sandwich. "Lane says I should be in the *Guinness Book* under 'strangest humanoid creatures.' "

"What about the pages from Peterson?"

"Good question. We could say that Alan Chadwick was a coot, Sarah Humphrey was an old squaw, and so forth. Those were just the first entries on the pages, though, right?"

Jackson nodded.

"That would be cute, but it wouldn't be Wolf."

"Or a fan," the agent added.

"Or a fan," I echoed, "since that's your price of admission. The references are inconsistent. The kingbird and mockingbird would be references to him, not his victims, like the other two. He's too rigid for that. They'd all have to be the same."

"So?"

"You gonna make me do all the work?"

Jackson laughed. "Two of the pages have text carried over from previous pages," he said. "There are other birds mentioned on all the pages. How can we be sure about what he wants us to see?"

I didn't know the answer, but I liked the idea that I was not the only one thinking about the question.

JACKSON DROPPED ME AT THE WILLARD. LANE still wasn't back from the District PD.

I began reading selections from the journal that Wolf had kept on his office computer. Several times there was an entire page that contained only the words: "I speak to you."

The audacious prick.

There were accounts of numerous murders, a long section about his sister, brief entries dealing with his mother and stepfather. One of the computer files was a lengthy, anecdotal report written by Dr. Elbert Bernard, a psychiatrist at the private school where Wolf had been confined in his late teens, just before he departed for Harvard. Authorities even then suspected him of terrible things.

Bernard was a nondirective therapist who allowed the relationships with his patients to evolve naturally. His taped sessions with the young Wolf began as a chess tutorial, with the teenager advising the older man on how to improve his game.

Wolf had rebuked his student: "Don't think one or two moves ahead. Six, eight, ten—there is no limit to how far you can anticipate. The game is finite, after all. The moves must conform to certain rules. The area of the board is quite small. You tend to view it as a series of narrow corridors. These passages intersect, Dr. Bernard. Each one opens into others, creating new and different possibilities. Corridors confine. We must break out, then consider the whole. It's a Zen sort of thing. I nurture my capacity to see not merely to the end, but beyond. Those who lecture us that perfection is not possible are wrong, of course. Perfection can be achieved, but to stay with any one thing that long would be rather boring."

Dr. Bernard asked Wolf to illustrate his point. The young man scribbled on a sheet of paper, then turned the paper facedown and slid it across to the psychiatrist.

"My move has created a number of possible moves for you," Wolf said. "If I entertain, say, the two or three most likely moves, then I can anticipate their impact, my subsequent move, your options, mine, and so forth. Try it."

"Amazing," Bernard said. "You're very clever."

"And you, unless you change your self-limiting style of thinking, are six moves from check, seven from checkmate."

"Are you willing to entertain a hypothetical?"

"Of course."

"If you had done what others have alleged—if you were killing people—would you approach such acts in the same manner that you approach this game?"

"Generally speaking. But chess is a game for simpletons, Dr. Bernard. So is life. They are most comfortable in their sameness, somewhat challenging because of what passes for complexity. I could be as adept at taking chess pieces, or lives, as I am alleged to be, only if I were to play these games according to the prevailing customs. Does that address your hypothetical?"

"It does."

Wolf cleared his throat. "The two officers who were here came equipped with their own biases of thought and behavior. One operated by the basic rules of interrogation. He asked questions, waited for answers, took notes. The other was something of a Neanderthal. Very physical. Crowding my personal space, even bumping against me. As if he could force responses. It's amusing and disconcerting at the same time. These are the people to whom we have delegated the task of protecting us. I don't feel terribly well protected. Do you recall the Heirens case from the 1940s?"

"I do."

"The authorities assumed that Heirens's writing on the mirror—some business about 'catch me before I kill more'—was a plea from a sick man. Now, if he's sick, Dr. Bernard, well, that's an aberration from the mean. The thin end of the bell curve. That explains everything. He's not like the rest of us. He's mentally ill. Interesting. I read Heirens's message as a challenge. There's another aspect of his case that intrigues me. He was caught for a number of burglaries and placed in a strict Catholic boarding school with lots of nasty nuns. Did they turn a burglar into a killer? I assaulted my parents, Dr. Bernard. What will I become here? Do you suppose that the state might have made a terrible mistake with me?"

It was a rhetorical and argumentative question. Bernard knew enough to not answer.

After a long pause, Wolf said, "Make your move."

WOLF

I WOKE UP SOMETIME IN THE AFTERNOON.

The sun pissed its way in through the only window in the apartment. I was drained, running on empty.

I didn't move, just stared at the ceiling. A lightbulb hung from a single strand of wire that disappeared through a crack in the plaster. The crack, shaped like the contour of a woman's breast, was filled with cobwebs. Stains from the last century's rains formed other patterns on the ceiling and walls.

The ratcheting of rodent teeth emanated from somewhere behind the lath.

Shit.

I swung my legs over the side of the bed and lurched to a sitting position. I swallowed the last of the pills I had taken from my sister.

Last night I drank wine at the Willard. A cheap taxi ride transported me here, light-years away from the splendor of the hotel and into a zone of marginal people. Sometimes it's necessary to live like this, beyond the edge of what passes for civilized society. It is a matter of survival.

Somewhere in the apartment building a TV blasted, advertising everything from Jesus to Jeeps.

I groped along the top of the bureau until my hand wrapped around the .44 Magnum. I watched the clock as the second hand drifted past the three. If it reached the three again—and the TV was still screaming about breakfast cereals, cars, athletic shoes, tampons, detergents, deodorants—I was going to walk out into the hall, find the offending apartment, kick in the door, and shoot everyone in sight.

You are such well-trained consumers, such obedient buyers. You listen, read, see images, digest the spin, allow reality to be created for you, then go out and buy—even when it is a product that will kill you. I have had only one victim who was as compliant as you, and even she did not pay me to end her life.

The second hand swept by the six.

Yeast infections. Beer. Basketball shoes. More cars.

The blasts of TV noise were probably some kids' mother plopped like Jabba the Hutt in front of Ricki Lake while they were out in the alley shooting dope.

Nine.

America's number-one-selling minivan.

Twelve.

I pushed myself off the bed and walked through the combination living-dining-kitchen area, a rectangular space demarcated by a sofa, a red Formica-topped, aluminum table, and the roach-ridden sink.

Barefoot, wearing a rumpled T-shirt and stained boxers, I stepped into the hall and listened.

There was laughter from the TV. "So you didn't know he was in the next room sleeping with your sister."

"No. And I didn't know he was seeing my mother, either."

More laughter.

I walked down the stairs and turned to my right. A black man carrying a lunch pail came out of a silent apartment and froze when he looked at me. His eyes drifted down to the Magnum. "Go to work," I said.

He slipped past me and ran down the stairs. I walked farther down the hall and stopped at apartment four. Listening.

"What was the final toll?"

"He slept with my mother first, then with me, both of my sisters."

I pulled back the hammer on the gun.

"Two weeks ago he called me in my dorm at college and had the nerve to say he wanted to see me again."

"But you did see him, didn't you?"

There were groans from the audience as I raised the .44, preparing to kick in the door.

The TV in the apartment went silent just as my sister's final gift, the pills, kicked in. My head cleared.

I lowered the hammer and dropped my arm to my side. Whoever lived behind the door had just won the lottery and didn't know it.

I walked back to my apartment.

Everything is part of the design.

What is meant to be, will be.

I TURNED THE TAP IN THE SHOWER AND WAITED for the hot water. Wildlife scattered for shelter in their cracks in the grout. The place was disgusting—even worse than Echo's trailer, which was at least clean. But the apartment was serving its purpose. There was one more act to be played out here. The rest of the show was set for other stages.

As water splashed into my face, I thought about my plan, my design—its exquisite detail, the way it repeated itself in multiple forms, like a kaleidoscope. The first time I saw an Escher print, I was fascinated by the figures—monks taking their measured steps for eternity, but achieving only a finite depth and height. No more, no less. Forever.

I toweled off, slipped into my Valley Carpet coveralls, and doffed my ball cap. I grabbed the keys to the van, took the freight elevator to the basement, and slipped into the alley.

I had emerged from beneath the earth, but I still had far greater heights to achieve.

AS I DROVE SOUTH ON I-95, I REMEMBERED reading a case report that Lucas Frank had written for a professional journal fifteen years ago. His subject was Norman Elgar, a man I knew well. Despite the enormous risk, I had visited Elgar at the Massachusetts State Prison in Walpole, the same facility that had housed Albert DeSalvo, but failed to protect him. DeSalvo had been stabbed to death.

My conversation with Elgar had been far more revealing and informative than the bullshit that Lucas Frank, M.D., had sold to his peers.

The short, wiry, blond killer and I sat at a table in the prison cafeteria, the rattle and chatter of other voices a constant annoyance. The diminutive but proud man grasped my hand and looked into my eyes. He saw a kindred soul.

"Dreams are better than the real world," he said. "When I understand a dream, its meaning, I never forget it. It's like a taste that stays in my mouth, something that can be savored for a long time. Sometimes the real world blinks out on me, fades, even disappears. Dreams never do that."

I remember that I nodded, and continued to allow him to grasp my hand. "Just like a murder done well," I said.

Elgar smiled.

In Lucas Frank's article, Elgar had greeted the doctor in much the same manner. Lucas Frank had broken the hand grasp, and the words he had attributed to this man were quite different.

I had not visited Norman Elgar because his artwork was good. It was not. He raped, sliced, and tossed. I went to see him because all the gurus of the criminal mind had been there. The FBI, with their cameras and questionnaires, had completed their work when Lucas Frank arrived.

"When I die," Elgar said, "they're going to cut into my brain. They want to examine the limbic area. They seem to think I might have a lesion or some other abnormality. They have to explain me. They can't diagnose those things until after you're dead. They did the same thing to the aliens who landed in New Mexico in the 1950s. Maybe they think I'm from Mars. It's strange. They harnessed the energy in an atom and blew up thousands of people, but they say they don't understand the drive to destroy."

He stared into my eyes, and then told me about the most triumphant experience in his long career. "Her name was filled with hard sounds. Cutting sounds. Biting sounds. It was like her face in profile—the sharp features. She had a piercing nose. She had a snotty attitude to go with it."

Elgar giggled.

"She walked stiff-legged in tight skirts so that her buttocks hiked up and down like the pistons in a big Dodge. I liked that. The way she clipped off her words, snapped them out into the air—I didn't like that. I never spoke to her. I was always there, and I listened. I watched her. I followed her. If she rode a bicycle, I stole one so that I could keep up with her. I looked at her through her windows. She never knew how close I was. She had blue eyes and poise. Confidence. When she smiled, she hesitated—just a fraction of a second before the smile—like she was teasing her audience with the mystery of whether there would be a smile. She was so clever. She made everyone wait and guess and want her. God, she was perfect."

He leaned back in his chair, his hands clasped behind his neck. "She was always on display. It was her own fault."

"She invited you."

"What else would you call it?"

This man was disgusting, transparent, reactive. But he had information that I wanted. "Lucas Frank described you as arrogant," I said, remembering the psychiatrist's comments to his favorite reporter.

Frank remarked about how devious and elaborate a psychopath's self-analysis was, how polished, sincere, and reasonable his "excuses" for his violence seemed. "Human predators succeed," Frank said, "because they are so believable. Norman Elgar is persuasive, especially when he talks about his own pain."

Frank cited the case of Jack Henry Abbott, the convict-author whose "maundering volume of self-pity" over a life lived in prisons convinced the New York literary world's heavy hitters to publish Abbott's *In the Belly of the Beast,* and to support his release from prison. "Jack Abbott made his audience feel compassion and guilt," Frank said. "They wanted to believe that they could succeed where others had failed. They were going to rescue him, change him. Abbott didn't last two months on the street before he killed again."

I had enjoyed the book. Lucas Frank spoiled it for me. His attack on Abbott was an attack on me.

"I've never seen the article that he wrote about me," Elgar said, "or any of the interviews that he gave to Anthony Michaels. I'm not arrogant. I trust myself. I know that I'll make the right choices at the right times. I'm content with who I am, and I don't regret anything. I cherish all eighteen of my special women."

I knew that the concept of trusting one's own mind was something that the famous psychiatrist would understand, but never report in any article for other shrinks, or discuss in any interview with a newspaper reporter. How could he expect anyone to seriously think he was just like us? They would laugh him out of his profession.

I do not operate on impulse. It is a matter of design, patience, intelligence, and self-trust. I would never react to provocation, which is a method that Frank has used with success.

Frank had wanted to tip Norman Elgar over, to see his rage, to see him in "the mind that allowed him to rip into human flesh," as he described it to the press. The interview was a move in the psychiatrist's game. He wanted Elgar's final stats, the details, so family members could be informed that their missing loved ones weren't missing anymore. I wanted to know about the doctor and his technique.

"Lucas Frank saw me as a smug sonofabitch," Elgar said. "He was pissed because I wouldn't give him details. He wanted me to crumble. I can still hear his words. He said, 'You achieved notoriety for a compulsion. It's like someone who can't stop washing his hands.' Is that a provocation, or what? Washing my hands, my ass. I reacted."

In his interview with Anthony Michaels, Frank described the reaction. Elgar didn't move, but his eyes were different. "He stared at me in disbelief," Frank told his favorite reporter.

Why wouldn't he? The egocentric shrink had made a diagnosis, then acted as if there could be no doubt about its veracity. The aspect of all of this that irked me the most was that Dr. Frank had been right. He knew exactly what to say to Norman and how to say it. How could he know? How could he understand? I had gone in search of answers to those question.

"The fantasy never gave me life," Norman told me. "I gave life to the fantasy. It was a matter of genuine superiority. I nurtured it."

The mental health industry does not understand the etiology of this system of thought, although they try to sound as if they do. I don't care what Lucas Frank says. You can look at a painting by Bosch or Magritte for as long as you want, but don't expect to read the artist's thoughts in his brush strokes.

Elgar told me that Frank had shrugged, looked down, leaned forward on the table, then snapped his eyes up to lock with Elgar's. "Did the others swallow that bullshit?" he asked.

Elgar's palms were flat on the table, his arms tense. He breathed heavily, but his eyes never wavered. "Police from eight states have been here," Norman told the psychiatrist. "FBI agents have been here four times. They know who I am."

Lucas Frank shook his head. "They don't know shit," he said. "Never have. Never will. You're obviously of average intelligence, and your wits served you well for a while. But you were coming unraveled, Normie."

That was what Elgar's mother had called him, and it had brought Elgar up out of his chair, backing away from the table, spittle on his chin, his eyes rolling around in their sockets like billiard balls after a split. He was yelling, and guards charged in from every direction.

The only thing that Frank had not done was to plunge a knife down through Elgar's hand, pinning him to the table. The range of behavior available to the doctor did not include the technique that I had used when dealing with Oliver. Apparently, he recognized some constraints.

Frank had elicited exactly what he was after.

"That just wasn't fair," Elgar told me.

Lucas Frank had slipped into his jacket, straightened his tie. "Totally unraveled," he said. "Psychotic."

And Elgar, all five and a half feet and 135 pounds of him, threw the guards aside.

"I'll get out of this fucking place," he screamed. "I'll do it all over again."

They Maced him, and he waded through it. "Rip you to fuckin' pieces," he told Lucas Frank as one of the guards nailed him with a stun gun.

Now, as I guided my car south on the interstate, I thought about symmetry, and about all the years that I have been close to Lucas Frank.

I have followed his career. I have read everything he has written. I have pursued the same people he has talked with, conducted my own intimate interviews.

I have learned more from them than he or the feds ever will.

Balance. Order. Justice.

Symmetry.

I know more about Lucas Frank than he will ever know about himself.

POP

A PSYCHOTIC PATIENT OF MINE FROM YEARS AGO would not use the phone. He both feared and detested the phone, and he adamantly refused to tell people his name.

"I don't want anyone to know that I haven't been murdered," he said.

I doubt that I'm psychotic, but I do hate phones. I don't like people much, either, especially when I have to observe complicated rules of etiquette like those that the phone requires.

"What if they remember that they didn't kill me?" my patient asked.

His logic was internal, and unassailable.

He complained about the noises in his head. "Can't hear myself think. Mostly because of the elevators whizzing up and down, and the doors that whoosh open and click shut."

"What about voices?" I asked him.

"Just Winston Churchill. He resembles J. Edgar Hoover, and he recites T. S. Eliot's *Murder in the*

Cathedral. Have you ever noticed how the past and present have a way of converging? I think it's a warning."

He had been a successful accountant in Boston. One day, he returned home from work and entered the lobby of his apartment building just as a man threw himself off the top of the stairs with a rope around his neck. The snap of the man's neck as it broke—"like a bomb going off"—was a sound he could not forget.

His first symptoms were blinding migraines. His family doctor prescribed painkillers. All he had to do was step on a cockroach, and the migraines would start again. It was the cracking sound that did it. Every time he heard it, he saw the man hanging in the stairwell.

He responded to psychotropic medication—Thorazine, I think—and made sufficient progress to be released from the hospital. Within two weeks, he stopped taking his medication. A month later he was dead. A priest found him hanging in the vestry of a nearby cathedral, a copy of Eliot's play in his pocket. He had been true to his voices.

While I did not share most of my patient's aversions, I remained a staunch opponent of the telephone and all the demands it placed on me. But a call to Vermont was necessary.

Wolf had survived the explosion, and had moved on somewhere to recuperate. If I could track him—discover where he had been, what he had done, who he had talked to, what he had said—I should be able to determine what payoff he had in mind for himself, and that might help me to find him. I figured that the first step was to inquire about homicides, Wolf's favorite activity. I had spoken to a Vermont police captain when I was checking to see if any cars had been stolen in Saxtons River on the day of the explosion. I phoned the same man.

"You don't have that many murders up there," I began.

"More than we'd like," he said. "Six, maybe seven a year."

"What about the past year?"

"Well, there was the double murder up in Swanton."

"I don't know about it. What happened?"

"I can't give you a whole lot of details. Just that a woman and her brother were shot to death in her trailer. Two bodies, killed with different guns, but only one of the weapons was found at the scene. We didn't get great cooperation on that one because they're Indians. The woman's daughter can't talk, and even if she could, she probably wouldn't tell us anything. A neighbor said there'd been a guy staying with them, but he was long gone by the time we got there."

"In his forties. Hair going gray. Maybe a mustache. Six feet tall. Medium build."

"That describes a lot of people, but yeah. That's basically what we got. He'd been injured somehow, and the woman was taking care of him. Look, Dr. Frank, if you can help us with this one . . ."

"John Wolf," I said.

"The guy who died in the explosion?"

"He didn't die."

"I don't know how anybody could have walked away from that. Of course, the feds locked us right out of there. We didn't get a real close look."

"Wolf was brought up by his stepfather. His biological father was a man named Pease, a logger who lived in Bellows Falls."

"I think there's still a few of that clan around. They're Abenakis."

"There was a tunnel," I began, then lost the rest of whatever it was I had intended to say.

The captain asked me questions, and I answered—but my mind was drifting far from the conversation. When I put down the phone, I stared straight ahead, thinking about Wolf.

The man's tenacity and cunning fascinated me. So did his tunnel, and what it represented. It demonstrated his ability to see into the future, and to plan for any eventuality. For me to have any hope of catching up with him, I had to backtrack. I had to know as much about his life after death as I could.

Again, I grabbed the phone and dialed—this time a familiar number in Lake Albert.

"Thought you never used these things," Buck Semple said.

I was amused, but wished that my eccentricities were not such common knowledge. "It's giving me hives," I told him, "but I think I'll be okay."

The chief laughed. "Where the hell are you?"

"Still in D.C."

"Don't know why you'd want to hang out in a place like that. What about the holes in your hide?"

"Good as new. I just wanted to touch base with you on that Charles Weathers ID. How far did you go checking that out?"

"Far as I could. The address in Lincoln was a fake. Driver's license is still valid. He paid cash for the gun, even though he had a MasterCard and a checking account in Boston. I've got an eighteen-month history so far."

"What about dates on the charge card, bank deposits, checks cashed? Is there any way to track him?"

"The card is what goes back the eighteen months," Buck said. "He opened the bank account early last September, then closed it about two months ago."

Wolf had closed his account on the day that Alan Chadwick was murdered. These was also a charge on his MasterCard that day—a one-way ticket to Fort Lauderdale.

"The police down there have been real helpful," Buck said. "Weathers rented a car from Avis. It was a month's lease, so they had a local address on him—a waterfront condo."

The sonofabitch heals, gets his cash together, knocks off Chadwick, then goes on vacation. Jesus.

"They're still checking for anyone who had dealings with him while he was in Fort Lauderdale," Buck said. "I don't have the paperwork yet, but he had a rental while he was here, too. Picked it up in Detroit and returned it at the airport there the day he took his shots at you."

"I'm going to need passenger lists for flights from Detroit to D.C."

"The feds could get those for you faster than I could."

I thanked Buck, said that I would keep in touch, and warned him to stay away from my largemouth bass. For years, we had been chasing that same fish.

"I'll make a deal with you," Buck said. "I'll leave your fish alone. You leave Mr. Weathers alone. That's the one I want to reel in."

We made the pact, both of us lying.

· · ·

AS I WORKED TO UNDERSTAND WOLF'S THINKING,
I knew that he would be doing the same—working to
get inside my head. He was the only man on earth who
could pull it off.

The knock on my door was Hiram Jackson. I had
been expecting him to return, but not so soon. I was
glad to see him.

"I should have them put a cot in here for you," I
told him.

Jackson smiled, settled into a chair, and leaned forward. "Maybe I'm too old and too tired for all this."

I could see that he meant it. His tan suit was rumpled, his brown tie loosened at the neck. The dark bags
under his eyes attested to a lack of sleep.

I sat opposite him.

"Tell me more about this guy," Jackson said.

"Which one? Wolf, or his fan?"

"The lupine fellow."

"He is the thoroughbred of human predators. Until
last year, most of us had never encountered anything
like him. What do you want to know that I can sum up
in five minutes? What do you *need* to know?"

"We've learned that Willoughby was called out,"
Jackson said, sighing. "We know why. We don't know by
whom. He took ten thousand dollars in cash with him
when he left his office. He was going out to buy information. The money was still in its envelope in his pocket
when we found him."

Jackson was working the case, and he had been
open-minded enough to brief me on his progress. Still,
I had no idea how my next suggestion would go over.

"Take Walker off the investigation," I said, up on
my feet and pacing the room. "House her at Quantico
until this is over."

"She will be one annoyed agent."

"She'll be alive."

Jackson nodded.

"Wolf isn't going to move on until he has cleared the way for himself," I said. "It's not that he couldn't create another identity and disappear. It's vengeance. Anyone who conspired to bring him down a year ago, and anyone who represents a current threat to him, will be eliminated. That doesn't include recreational killing."

I told the agent about the double murder in Swanton, Vermont, and about the possible connection between Wolf and the Abenaki community. "Those people helped him," I said. "They brought the sonofabitch back to life, and he killed them."

Jackson walked to the door. "I'll catch up with Susan Walker," he said.

WOLF

I SAT IN THE VAN, WATCHING AS THE YOUNG woman walked briskly across the parking lot to her apartment building. She was small, another miniature person for me to lift with one hand and break with the other.

The fenceless complex was a collection of rectangular atrocities in brick fronted by fake, white colonial columns. Dozens of these places dotted the landscape like bird droppings around the Beltway.

She wore tailored chinos, a white turtleneck, and a blue blazer. She always returned home for lunch at the same time. There was direction in her steps, determination. This woman had authority. She wielded power, made decisions that cut into others' lives—that had sliced into *my* life. With her keys in her hand, she was fully prepared for the next, and maybe the final chore in her mundane life.

When I was in her apartment earlier, I noted the sparse decor—in black and white—and the few magazines and books, her collection of new age Muzak. Her stride was like her abode, reflecting efficiency and an absolute lack of grace. She epitomized this nation of transient clerks, and like all the rest of them, she was vapid, empty, commenting on events and people that she knew absolutely nothing about. Her one attempt at taste and color in her home was a six-by-eight, imitation Persian rug, the pattern probably stained in place by illegal aliens using Magic Markers.

After taking a brief inventory of her possessions, I relaxed on her white sofa, sliding my hand across its rough fabric, thinking about all that I had accomplished since leaving Swanton. In Boston, I had obtained an additional ID, and visited two banks. I bought a suitcase, a duffel bag, and clothing at Jordan Marsh. Then I made my visit to City Hospital.

Alan Chadwick had looked up from his coffee and newspaper.

"Yes?" he said.

I sat opposite him, sliding the Magnum onto the desk between us, gazing around at his dingy office— barely more that a closet in shades of gray, off-white, black. Chadwick's only concession to color was the red of a corpse's blood on his lab coat.

"What do you want?" he asked, staring down at the gun. "Who are you?"

I stared at the pathologist's gnarled hands—the twisted, grotesque fingers that I had created for him with a baseball bat so many years ago. Chadwick had been enamored of a young woman in Cambridge. I doubt that she had even noticed him. She had made a pass at me in a bar, a place that I had used several times to select human projects. She and I had walked the cold streets. I showed her the birds that flew up among the city's office buildings. I think I had even started to tell her that sometimes the birds collide and fall, broken, dead.

Later, I helped her to fly like the swallows she had so admired. I launched her from the roof of her dorm. Chadwick had correctly doubted the medical examiner's ruling of suicide. He followed me. His mangled hands were the reward for his tenacity.

I stared at the doctor, watching as his blood drained from his face. He could easily have blended with his pallid walls.

"Oh, my God. You're dead."

"You should have let it go, Alan. I told you a long time ago that your adventures in vigilante law were over. When you thought that the police had me on the ropes last year, you assisted them. You conspired to cause my death, and you caused me a great deal of inconvenience."

I stood, and leveled the Magnum at him.

He stumbled on the stairs, begged, prayed. He fell in a heap on the roof's gravel, covering his head with his arms as if he expected me to hit him. I watched a traffic helicopter in the distance, took a deep breath of Boston's sulfurous air, then reached down and assisted the doctor to his feet. In seconds, Alan Chadwick flew out into space over Columbus Avenue, his white lab coat flapping crazily behind him.

He never screamed; he was almost graceful.

Two hours later, I was on an L-1011 out of Logan Airport, bound for Fort Lauderdale. I opened a book— *The Alienist,* by Caleb Carr—and relaxed for the three-hour flight.

Carr had done his research well—but, of course, he was describing antiquity. Killers like me have adapted to their times, become more sophisticated in the practice of their art. The criminologists and mental health people who seek to understand what they call "the criminal mind" fumble about like modern versions of Laszlo Kreizler—relying on nineteenth-century thought to survive in the twentieth century. There is no "criminal mentality," unless you include the work of the drones who carve up the population with chain saws and meat cleavers.

Against the true artist—the trickster without peer—the world doesn't have a chance.

Now, after the young woman had disappeared through the front door of her building, I continued to sit in the van. I waited another five minutes to be certain that no one was following her, then walked across the lot and entered the building.

My coveralls bore a name tag that said "Nick," and a business logo for Valley Carpet. I carried white, yellow, and pink copies of a work order. I doubted that Nick would miss any of these props.

I stood in the vestibule, between the outside door and the door to the building's lobby—studying the names on the dozens of mailboxes. A young man walked in behind me. "Too many damned boxes," I muttered.

He opened the door. "Who you looking for?"

"Work order says Bristol," I said. "Doc tells me I need glasses. I can't read the little print on the boxes."

He held the door for me. He was so fucking gullible that I had to suppress a laugh.

"They're on the top floor, I think," he said. "Let me see your paperwork."

I handed it to him. "Maybe I should just get some of those cheap reading glasses they sell at Kmart."

"Yeah. Bristol. Four-eleven," he said.

I thanked him and walked in. We shared the elevator.

He exited on the second floor. I rode up to four, then walked down to three, found her door, and knocked. She opened it as far as the chain would allow.

"Ms. Bristol?" I inquired.

"No," she said. "I think they're *four*-eleven."

"Nobody there. I thought maybe I had the floor number wrong," I said, scratching the back of my head below my Washington Redskins cap. "Well, they'll have to bring in the carpet themselves."

"Is their phone number on that order?" she asked, extending her right arm through the narrow gap.

I grabbed it, yanking her forward so that her head hit the side of the door, then I forced the door open with my shoulder—ripping the chain out of the woodwork.

The initial physical contact—her jacket's fabric, the skin on her forearm—and the fragrance of her hair, snapped something inside me. I wanted only to tear into her.

"You're going to sleep," I growled.

She went down, but I kept a firm grip on her right wrist, kicking the door closed behind me. I flipped her onto her stomach and removed the oversized gun from its holster at her back. Her mouth was open but, like Chadwick, she was silent. I'd seen it so many times before—that dazed, paralyzed moment of shock.

Just as she seemed to be emerging from it, I stabbed her in the ass with a syringe of Librium. "Nap time," I muttered.

I held her by the neck, twisting her wrist high on her back until her squirming subsided and she lost consciousness.

She weighed about ninety-five pounds. Rolling her up in the carpet and tying it off with heavy twine posed no problem. I tested the bundle on my shoulder—

perhaps 150 pounds—then walked out of the building the way I came in.

As I drove out of the complex, the black man I had seen in front of the Willard drove his government car in.

The feds are always late.

I CARRIED THE BUNDLE INTO MY BUILDING AND walked to the ancient freight elevator. It cranked its way to my floor. As I stepped into the hall and around the corner, I saw a D.C. cop standing at my door.

I had been preoccupied, anticipating the entertainment that my large package was going to provide me. I had not expected to encounter the police. It was time to quickly shift gears, not allow the cop to put me on the defensive.

"Excuse me, Officer," I said, slipping the key into the lock.

"You live here?"

"You kiddin'? I wouldn't live in a dump like this."

"What's the occupant's name?"

He helped me balance the load on my shoulder while I fished out another work order. "What's that say? Something Dexter, isn't it?"

"Wilbur Dexter," the cop read. "When did you see him last?"

"Never saw him. He left the key with my boss. My boss says make the delivery. That's what I'm trying to do here."

I turned the key and kicked open the door. "You comin' in, or what?"

"No," the cop said, glancing in at the apartment. "I got a different name here anyway."

He pulled a notebook from his pocket and opened it. "Wilbur Dexter, you say?"

I nodded as I deposited the carpet on the floor. "What name you got?"

"Alan Chadwick."

"Beats the shit out of me."

He was still writing Wilbur Dexter's name in his notebook as I closed the door and locked it.

The cop would be back, but not soon. In a city like this, he had to have more pressing complaints. I had successfully drawn attention to the apartment, probably thanks to my wandering the halls in my underwear with a Magnum in my hand. Now there would be a record of it. Wilbur Dexter and Alan Chadwick.

I wouldn't bother with such details if I didn't know that Lucas Frank would be an appreciative audience. I wanted that bastard reacting to every bit of information that came his way. I wanted him worrying over symbols and their complicated meanings—birds and resurrections and pages from books. He would tie himself in knots with that shit, while I made my few, simple preparations for the end.

The light is faint, but it is there.

Emerging.

POP

I HAD LOST TRACK OF TIME.

It seemed as if Jackson had just left, but that had been hours before. I was still immersed in Wolf's journals and sifting through the information I had gathered when Lane arrived at the door.

"We need to talk," she said. "A lot's been happening. As soon as we got the package of composites from Swartz, Detective Williams made copies. We faxed them around to area departments, distributed them to cab companies, car rental agencies, hotels and motels—you name it. I didn't know whether you wanted the feds to have them, but I faxed a set to Jackson's office."

"Good."

"We've had three hits so far."

Lane handed me a copy of a police report. "I'll summarize," she said. "Aggravated assault case. The victim's a guy, a hippie type who sells trinkets at neighborhood fairs. A white, middle-aged male, well dressed, put a knife through the victim's hand, pinned it to the ground. The whole time, the assailant is talking crazy—something about justice. Get this, Pop. The victim's name is Oliver Wendblat."

Lane had my full attention. The name, Oliver, had been stuck to the bottom of the brass phoenix delivered to my door.

"Go on," I said.

"Same location, same date, same basic description. Guy put a knife to seventeen-year-old Susan Parker's throat. Didn't cut her. Traded her a carved, wooden bird for a brass one that she had bought from Oliver Wendblat. Then he tossed her off a foot bridge. She's in D.C. General with multiple injuries."

"He didn't kill either one," I muttered, thinking that Wolf was making sure that messages continued to come.

"This one's a homicide," she said, handing me another police report. "Victim is Nicholas Wesley, black male, forty years old. Somebody cut his throat last night in an alley off Pennsylvania Avenue. A white guy sat with him in a bar, then followed him out. Witnesses saw the man drive off in Wesley's van. He also took Wesley's coveralls. Left him in his underwear and work shoes in the parking lot. Made no effort at concealment. We've got three positives that it was Wolf."

He had maimed two, murdered one. "What the hell is going on?"

"This one's the kicker, Pop. We don't have the paperwork on it yet, but a uniformed officer saw the homicide sheet on Wesley. The cop had responded to a complaint in Northeast D.C., a report of a guy walking the halls in his underwear, carrying a gun. When the officer got to the apartment where this man was supposed to live, he walked into a guy delivering a carpet.

Had a key to the apartment, and even invited the cop in. White guy, could fit the composite, but the uniform isn't certain. Wesley worked for an outfit called Valley Carpet. The apartment address is scribbled at the top of that report. The officer is tracking down his notes to see if there are any details that he missed. He thinks the coveralls might have had a Valley Carpet logo on them. The rest of those sheets are your copies of the composites, and the flight information and passenger lists that you wanted. Detroit to D.C."

"Has anyone been to this address?" I asked, tapping the report's cover sheet.

"Not yet. This is all breaking right now. They're waiting to see what the uniform comes up with. He was just out there a couple of hours ago."

Even as Lane paced the room, telling me how Detective Williams was nearly convinced that they were chasing Wolf, and speculating about how the FBI's involvement in the case would probably change, I was moving away.

Eventually, Lane dropped the reports on my table, saying that she was going to grab a quick shower and head back to the DCPD. She stopped at the door. "I almost forgot. Wolf told Oliver Wendblat that there would be no more acts of kindness."

"What?"

"He said Oliver should be sure to tell that to the police."

With that, Lane left.

No more acts of kindness. Wolf had not killed Susan Parker, Oliver, the complainant in the apartment building, the responding officer. He wanted them to tell their stories, for connections to be made. Wolf *had* killed

Nicholas Wesley, but then made certain that he was seen driving away, just as he had done at his sister's in Florida.

Why wouldn't he just steal a van? I wondered, then instantly answered my own question.

"Because he felt like killing," I said.

I sat, allowing my thoughts to go where they would. I knew how the formula worked, that it had to do with my own idiosyncratic notion of retribution—what the German killer, Peter Kurten, had called "compensatory justice."

Less than a year ago, I had explained to Lane how fine a line there was between "us" and "them." She couldn't stand to think of me as a murderer. As much as I might have wanted to tell her something different, I could not.

Justice is simply too abstract and personal a notion to ever exist as an absolute. The wild man who attacked Oliver the street vendor had mumbled something about justice.

I glanced at the address scrawled across the top of the police report on Nicholas Wesley's murder. I was about to leave when the phone rang.

"Walker's disappeared," Jackson said. "I couldn't find her through her office, so I went out to her place. Her door had been smashed open. Looks like there was a struggle. We figure he rolled her up in the carpet and carried her out. The carpet's gone, the mat is there. There was a guy seen in the building . . ."

Valley Carpet.

"I don't have time to explain," I interrupted, then gave him the address of the man who wandered halls with a gun, wearing nothing but his underwear.

"Meet me there. Now."

WOLF

I HAD PLACED SUSAN WALKER IN A CHAIR FACING the door. She was unable to see through the strips of tape that covered her eyes. I stood behind her, listening as she moaned through the gag and duct tape securing her mouth. She was trying to move her head, but the bindings and the chair's high back restricted her.

"Nothing would give me greater pleasure than to break your fucking neck like I did Willoughby's."

She stopped moving. The steady plink-plinking of a leaky faucet was the only sound in the room.

"You insulted me. I read the papers. 'FBI profiler says Wolf was a madman.' That's asinine. If I were a madman, I would have carved you into pieces by now. Fed you to the Maryland crabs. You said that I thought very little of myself, that I suffered from a poor self-image, that I was fixated. You people scoff at psychiatric terminology, but you flee into it whenever you can't explain something in simple English, or you want to make it sound repulsive."

Her head started to move again.

"You said that I was very much like other serial

killers. Am I? You'd better think about that one. You said that when I was a teenager, I enjoyed an incestuous relationship with my sister. That's not true. I didn't fuck her until she was dead. I *am* an insatiable beast, but I'm not the one that you described. You also said that my behavior was predictable."

I watched as she struggled to free herself.

"Predict, Ms. Walker. What am I going to do next?"

I placed my hands across the back of her neck, feeling the bristles of her short hair where it had been razor-cut. A woman's neck is so fragile. She cringed, as if I had hit her.

I leaned close to her ear and whispered, "Will I slit your throat?"

She pulled back as far as she could.

I turned my attention to the project I had begun earlier—tinkering with the necessary wires, switches, and batteries. This was a simple assembly, a small device— just enough to level the building.

"Many years ago," I said to the back of her head, "I picked up a young woman who was hitchhiking. She was about your age, similar in appearance. The same build, eyes, hair color. Her voice wasn't as shrill as yours, and she wasn't quite so full of herself. She was a graduate student. Her worst flaw was that she talked incessantly. Where did I work? Did I like Lou Reed and the 'Velvet Underground'? Had I ever been to Europe? Endless chatter. Tell me what you think, Special Agent Walker. Predict. Use your Quantico training. Did I fuck her and kill her?"

The agent remained still. Listening. The faucet continued its erratic drip.

"I picked her up in Santa Cruz, California, at the

same time that Edmund Kemper was beheading coeds. One would think that she would have had more sense than to be out there asking for it. What is your prediction, Ms. Walker?"

Silence.

"I dropped her at a theater entrance," I said. "An old Frank Sinatra film was showing. I continued on my way. I create my own opportunities. I don't wait for luck to hand them to me."

My mechanical work was complete. It was time for a change of clothes, and of appearance.

I turned the tap on the kitchen sink, splashed water into my face, then applied shaving cream.

"Your former partner used my death to advance his career. He offended me. Just as the profile that you wrote offended me."

Walker sat as still as a corpse, listening.

"The name of the car dealer—Featherstone Ford— was serendipitous. It was one of those things meant to be. Was that a detail that escaped you? I'm sure it wasn't wasted on Lucas Frank. He is superior to you people, you know. That's hardly a recommendation, but you really should heed whatever advice he has to offer. Otherwise, you may as well forfeit the game. As it is, there's very little time remaining."

The mustache was gone. I rinsed my face, then twisted the taps closed.

"I didn't spend much time with Willoughby. It was simply one of those menial chores we all have to do."

Hair color was next, but I hesitated, my attention drawn to the immobilized special agent. Behind her mask of tape, she had to be thinking. This woman would have doubted my ability to rise from the dead.

"When Alan Chadwick plummeted to the pavement, did you or your people at Quantico even think about me?"

I looked at the tendons on her neck, like cords strung vertically, taut against her throat.

"When they found what was left of my sister on the floor of the trailer, did you wonder?"

Scrubbed, distinct blue veins decorated the spaces between her neck tendons.

"What the fuck does it take for Quantico to start seeing a pattern? Should I have called it in?"

Stupidity angers me. I could feel my rage building, and knew that I had to guard against it. Rage is always counterproductive, a threat to the successful completion of any design. I had to stay focused, on track. I took a deep breath. The sink began to drip again.

"Have you ever been to San Francisco? I was there recently. I wonder why they call California 'the golden state.' The hills are brown."

I remember crossing the Bay Bridge and driving north on I-80. I was headed for Fourth Street in Berkeley where Spenger's Fish Grotto is tucked down beside a highway overpass. The restaurant started as a seafood market in the 1800s, and has been there ever since. It was at Spenger's that I tasted the finest French-style bouillabaisse in the world.

"Have you ever read the transcripts of Theodore Bundy sparring with his interrogators during the early eighties?" I asked Walker. "I remember when they were discussing memory. Bundy feigned an attempt to recall individual victims and the details of their deaths. He used an analogy to bouillabaisse, saying that some people remember the taste of clams, others the taste of mullet. Bundy was a vulgar person. The whole is always greater than the sum of its parts. You understand that when you have bouillabaisse at Spenger's in Berkeley. The experience stays with you, whole, to be savored forever. There is no breaking it into pieces. And Spenger's puts neither clams nor mullet in their bouillabaisse."

That early evening in Berkeley, I had lingered over my meal—sipping a glass of red wine and absorbing the atmosphere. As I left, I bought a carnation from a street vendor, stuck it in my lapel, then drove up Telegraph Avenue to Rasputin's, where I surveyed the two floors of music.

Experiences have always returned to me in their entirety. Sometimes there's a sense of distance, a fugue-like haze around them. I feel as if the memory belongs to someone else. My recollection of the trip to Berkeley is mixed. The early hours are clear, an experience that I can summon forth at will. Those later hours have lost shape and drifted just beyond my grasp. I'm not sure how long I stayed, or how the evening ended. I don't know whether anyone died.

I do know that the next morning I drove south to San Jose. My contact was a short, heavy, dark-haired woman who walked her dog in a park. She placed a shopping bag on a concrete bench, then reached down to release her dog from its leash and allow it to run. I did as she had always instructed: I stood ten feet away and waited. And as always, I imagined myself a child waiting for teacher's permission to go take a leak.

"I have to admit that I am more curious about you," the woman said, "than about any of my other clients."

"Curiosity is not a healthy trait," I said.

She shrugged. "I always read the newspapers. I try to guess which of the world's explosions originate here. I'm never sure."

She looked at me for the first time. "With you, I haven't a clue."

I said nothing.

"This one must be big," she continued. "So many sheets of plasticized cyclonite."

She turned away and whistled for the dog. "Leave the money on the bench," she said. "Take the bag and go."

Now, I tightened the kitchen taps, and looked at my reflection in the mirror. Reddish brown hair and eyebrows. Tinted contact lenses. Horn-rimmed glasses. A gray suit.

"This has been a perfect dress rehearsal," I said.

She did not seem to be breathing.

"I'm happy that you could attend."

I moved through the room, arranging wires, a timer, a toggle switch. I had completed my work.

"Listen," I said.

There was a click—louder than the dripping faucet—when I threw the switch.

"Did you hear that? You know how fond I am of explosive devices. You do have a chance, however—which is more than Lucas Frank gave me. I've drawn attention to myself in the time that I've been here. A police officer visited a while ago. It's possible that he'll return. I'll leave the door unlocked. Make all the noise you wish. No one will pay attention. People are woefully indifferent. Nobody seems to care about the welfare of others anymore."

I gathered up my briefcase and keys. "You're probably wondering why I'm allowing you to live at all, even for a few brief tickings of the clock. Should you survive, Ms. Walker—should a miracle occur, and you walk out of here—please sit down and have a long heart-to-heart with Dr. Frank. Someone needs to tell him that he's dealing with the perfect assassin. I can't be stopped. Everyone falls this time."

I slipped into the hall, my hand on the doorknob behind me. I stood there for a moment, wondering why I didn't just kill the woman. Then I heard the door click shut in the front hallway downstairs. I had no wish to compromise my new appearance.

Anyway, it really didn't matter. I knew that if she survived, I would be seeing Susan Walker again.

POP

THE APARTMENT BUILDING, A BLACKENED STONE structure, was a relic, something from more prosperous ages past. It squatted three blocks from where police had gunned down a man named Billy, and Senator Harry Storrs had picked me up in his Lincoln.

I stepped inside, onto a foot-worn landing. The heavy wooden door clicked shut behind me. As the street noises died, the building fell strangely silent.

Then I heard the clanking of an elevator somewhere in the rear of the building. It was on its way down.

A freight lift.

A man delivering a carpet—especially one with a woman rolled up in it—would not have carried his load up these stairs. I wondered if he would descend the same way, with or without the load.

I removed the nine-millimeter from my pocket, walked to the stairwell, and listened. The elevator rumbled past the first floor on its way to the basement.

I walked down the single flight into a dark, dank corridor and followed the noise to my left. When I engaged the action on my gun, the snapping noise echoed, pinging off the walls ahead where a single light illuminated the junction of two passages.

The elevator whooshed to a halt around the corner on the right, but the gate failed to crank open.

What the hell?

Adrenaline pumping, I flattened myself against the cracked plaster wall and moved slowly toward the hallways' intersection. I could feel my heart thudding as I stole a quick glance around the corner.

The freight lift was empty.

I heard footsteps overhead—someone moving fast toward the rear. I ran the length of the corridor, expecting to find a rear door. Instead, I came to a dead end. There was only a casement window that allowed a dim view of the building's back parking lot.

I caught a glimpse of a man walking rapidly away from the light, past a van that bore the logo: Valley Carpet. He disappeared into the alley's darkness.

Once again, there was silence.

As I began to climb up the steel-framed, concrete stairs, my gun still in hand, the place seemed vacant. Now, the only evidence of human occupancy was the mélange of smells—onions frying, urine, the musky aroma of sweat. This housing for semitransients was a structure removed from the air and light of day.

As I entered the top-floor corridor, I had no idea what I was going to find. I approached the door to the apartment and listened. There was a muffled noise and a scraping sound from behind the door.

I tried the knob, and the door slipped open a crack. I leveled the gun toward the room as I poked the bottom of the door with my foot. It creaked open, revealing a young woman taped and bound to a chair in the middle of the room.

"Is anyone else in there?" I asked.

The woman shook her head.

I checked out the bedroom and the bathroom, then used my pocketknife to cut away the bindings on the woman's wrists and arms. She immediately yanked the tape and a gag from her mouth.

"There's a bomb," Special Agent Susan Walker said. "I've got to call nine-one-one. We have to clear the building and get a bomb squad over here."

She struggled with the tape covering her eyes as I cut through the rope that held her to the chair. Together, we disentangled duct tape from her hair and eased it away from her skin.

Walker was stiff but quick as she moved through the door into the hall.

There's a bomb.

Reflexively, I looked up at the framing above the door. In the cellar of the house in Vermont, Wolf had placed the switch for his bomb on top of an arch. Now, I found a toggle switch where I expected to, then followed the wires down the side of the door, and across the floor under the sink where they ended, attached to nothing.

It was a dummy.

I took a deep breath and slowly exhaled as I walked back into the apartment to a table behind the chair where Walker had been restrained. There were bits of green and red wire on the floor and table, needle-nose pliers, wire cutters. The sadistic prick had terrorized the young agent.

I heard sirens in the distance. Walker was back in the doorway. "Clear the building, Dr. Frank," she said, then disappeared again before I could say anything.

When I walked into the hall, I could hear voices below as the building's few tenants were evacuated.

Why would Wolf arrange a fake bomb? He wanted Walker dead. She was another player in his Vermont demise. He had killed a man for a van and a pair of coveralls, then kidnapped a federal agent and staged a hoax. What the hell was he doing?

I began a slow descent of the stairs. It was a setup. The whole thing was a ruse. An elaborate stage setting. Why hadn't he killed Walker?

I turned on the landing to the last flight of stairs, picturing—

the black and red wires extending down from the toggle switch, the green and red fragments of wire on the table—

The wires didn't match. There was a bomb.

Wolf had concealed a real bomb somewhere else in the apartment, or even in another part of the building.

I ran the last flight, plunging into the street that had filled with emergency vehicles. Hiram Jackson was moving away from Susan Walker toward me, as space-suited members of the D.C. bomb squad began their approach to the building.

The pavement seemed to buckle even before I heard the blast, felt the thrust of hot air and debris blowing into my back. The explosion forced me against Jackson and slammed the two of us down.

THREE

WOLF

I SAT IN THE DINER, DIAGONALLY ACROSS THE avenue from my former apartment building, sipping the warm brown water that the management sold as coffee. I glanced at my watch, then at the street—where police cars, firetrucks, TV vans, and numerous unidentifiable vehicles congregated.

Obviously, someone had found Agent Walker. They would not find the bomb.

I was amused by the frantic activity, the collection of high-tech toys, the ludicrous outfits with shoulder-patch flags and designations of rank. They were Boy Scouts who had brought their badges with them into adulthood, never thinking for a second how childlike and irrelevant they continue to be.

I wondered if Special Agent Hiram Jackson was out there. He was my contact at Quantico—the man who would allow me to enter the inner sanctum of violent human behavior.

Jackson wasn't at Quantico when I visited as Alan Chadwick four years ago. I lectured there—weapon selection and its relationship to personality in cases of multiple homicide. My tenure as consultant was something Agent Willoughby may have discovered, but could not possibly have revealed. That would have been too embarrassing for the Bureau.

I also wondered whether any of them would make the connection—realize that they were the glue that held my design together. All of my players swung like planets in nonintersecting orbits around a small star. They were visitors to the homicidal mind, rescued from the task of cleaning up after a kill because they described and predicted with authority, if not accuracy.

He will kill again. He drives an old car. He is disorganized. He masturbates with his left hand, while turning the pages of Hustler with his right. He resides with an elderly female relative. He works as a menial laborer.

On a couple of occasions, the FBI had surged past me in their mad charge to nowhere. Lucas Frank was always right there. Even in the early days, he sensed a presence, but he could not give it a name or a face. I was the only one who moved freely from one orbit to another.

Now I wanted all of these parallel worlds to smash together and fall, so I had shaped events to set them on a collision course. None of my players would make any connections as they careened through space toward their last convergence.

Seventy-two hours remained.

ALAN CHADWICK HAD BEEN STEP ONE. THERE WAS another with whom I'd had an even longer history.

When I was in Florida, I spent a month listening to parrots cavort in the Fort Lauderdale morning. I walked on Dania Beach, where I couldn't distinguish the plastic-foam from the coral. For weeks, I didn't know whether I was hearing mockingbirds or car alarms.

Then, as Charles S. Weathers, I returned my Avis rental at the airport. Professor John Krogh, frugal as always, picked up an Alamo compact and drove to Orlando.

I doubted that any of these machinations were necessary, but I knew that someone would piss away a couple of weeks tracking the cars and identities—if they were able to.

I followed State Road 436 north, all the way to Winter Park Drive. Finding the turn for the trailer park was no trouble, although I was surprised to see that it had been paved since my last visit.

There was another new addition. On the patch of crabgrass that passed for a lawn, a sign declared: HUM-PHREY. It was one of those rectangular, wooden signs with jagged edges—the kind of thing a junior high student had to cut out with a jigsaw to pass woodworking for the term. Maybe her kids *were* that old. The sign was slopped with white enamel and had raised red letters.

One summer night in the old house in Saxtons River, I left my bedroom and walked to Sarah's. I was deter-mined to do it that night.

She was asleep. I could hear the soft intake and out-flow of her breath. I watched the thin blanket rise and fall. This was to be the end of all the longing, all the nights spent staining my own sheets.

I drove to the end of the cul-de-sac, turned around, then parked facing the exit. The kids would be at school. Her husband would be at whatever passed for work.

I grabbed my duffel bag, then walked the half-dozen steps to the door. It was unlocked.

I moved to the foot of her bed and slipped out of my pajama bottoms.

I stepped into the kitchen, listening to the silence. The trailer was stifling—no air-conditioning—and smelled of eggs fried in butter. Next to a half cup of coffee, the Orlando *Sentinel* was open on the table—a story about a man on Florida's death row. I dropped my bag, then sat down, facing the kitchen door.

Her eyes were open, staring, but she said nothing.

Her glasses covered the story. I pushed them aside and read. The key witness at the trial of "Crazy Joe" Spaziano had recanted, but Spaziano was still scheduled to die in Florida's electric chair. He had been convicted of killing a young woman, then disposing of her body at a dump where it would decompose along with all the other trash. There was another body in the dump—an unidentified young woman—and Spaziano had not been charged with her murder. The proximity of these two meant nothing to the authorities. The stupidity of the law and its practitioners were evident in the story.

Laws are collections of prohibitions and procedures that you feel passionate about today. They change when the fad passes.

The legal minds who represent you allow great variance when it comes to the taking of a human life. Whether you are black, white, rich, poor, hunting for deer when you shoot the woman at her clothesline, or hunting for humans when you shoot the buck out of season—you are entitled to a trial by a jury of your peers.

If the state followed procedure in the Spaziano case, despite doubt about the man's guilt, Spaziano would die. I wondered how Sarah felt about this.

"I want to fuck you," I told her.

"Go away," she said. "Go back to your room."

"I promise not to kill you."

She sat up. I could see the outline of her breasts through the thin fabric of her nightgown. I felt myself growing harder, erect.

"Ma wouldn't let me do it to her," I said.

"Oh, Jesus. Go back to your room."

"She was the one who wanted the bolt on their bedroom door."

Sarah treated me like a child. "Just jerk off on the blanket," she said. "Then go back to bed."

The key witness in the Spaziano case had found the Lord. He had gone to the authorities because he wanted to make things right. He had been hypnotized, he said. A different reality had been created for him.

I walked to the kitchen counter, tossed the duffel up there, and opened it. I slipped the Buck knife into my hip pocket, the .44 Magnum into my belt. I stood in the corner and waited.

"Touch it," I said.

"No."

"I won't leave until you do."

I couldn't wait. It came in long, throbbing, pulsing waves—warm and wet—all over my hand and down onto her blanket.

She sagged back on the bed, pulling the cover up to her chin.

I stood there for what seemed a long time—the sweat cooling my body as it dried.

And then I left.

When she walked through the door of her trailer in Florida, my half sister was shocked to see me. She, too, had been informed of my death.

With her, I created the stage props of an atrocity. I

wanted Dexter Willoughby to know, and Lucas Frank to believe, that I had slipped into a dimension inhabited only by wilding psychotics who drift unpredictably between madness and moments of lucidity.

Sarah was compliant. Needing only gentle assistance, she accommodated me.

And she never made a sound.

AS I SAT IN THE DINER, I SIPPED MORE OF THE muddy brew and glanced again at my watch. In less than a minute, the building would erupt into ashes and dust. I dropped two dollars on the table and left by the side door.

As I arrived at my car and slipped the key into the lock, I heard the rumbling in the distance. Dust and smoke spewed into the air, blotting out the sky. I drove off.

I had a quick stop to make, simply to satisfy my curiosity. I was anonymous again—just like being invisible—and I could go anywhere.

I am not like anyone else. I am not a nightmare. I am real, and there is no way to stop me.

The media would have you believe that all people like me are monsters—crazed and maniacal. I have read the sparse professional literature dealing with psychopathy. I wanted to know what the self-appointed experts were saying about me. It was ludicrous. Even the bible of psychiatry, the *Diagnostic and Statistical Manual*, has no description of me. This tome has only one available label, the antisocial personality disorder—the primitive, impulse-ridden character depicted in films like *Kalifornia*.

Life and art become blurred, but art remains more

informative than the labels and categories of the mental health industry. Watch Keaton in *Pacific Heights*, De Niro in the remake of *Cape Fear*.

You also won't find it in any of the journals, but there is an intimacy that exists between killer and victim. It is not in the walks, the talks, the lingering over coffee, the parody of courtship. It cannot be dismissed merely as a projection from the mind of the murderer. There is an intimacy, however fleeting, unlike any other, when we are inseparable in our terror and anticipation.

Sarah Sinclair knew that.

I PARKED, THEN WALKED INTO THE WILLARD'S lobby.

When Lane Frank strode around the corner toward the exit, I could see that she was as tall or taller than most of the men standing with their briefcases and newspapers. I saw her in profile as she passed me—auburn hair, skin the color of light coffee. I could have extended my arm, stroked her hair with my hand, or plunged a knife into her rib cage. Instead, I studied her for a moment, holding the image that I wanted to remember.

It was a strange feeling. I thought that I would have remembered her from a year ago, but she had faded in my memory. If it were simply a matter of killing her, I'd had plenty of opportunities.

I had imagined conversing with her—telling her the truth about how a man like me comes to be, and how I came to know her father's methods and every little wrinkle in his life. There was a time long past when I had wanted her to have the privilege of sitting with me over a glass of wine. We could have watched together as candlelight bent through our crystal glasses of carmine liquid—as the light shattered and cast streaks, like comet trails of blood across our white linen tablecloth.

I even imagined approaching honesty with her, before I killed her father, before I killed her.

As much as I might enjoy contemplating and acting on the surreal—a killer of dozens sitting in quiet conversation with a woman whose father is the one man who knows how the killer thinks, and who also wants him dead, serendipity always provides and should never be ignored. My design has changed everything.

I will tell someone about my youth, that my stepfather and his liberal use of the coal bin were not causal. He didn't make me what I am. I made myself. Mine was my own becoming. I have a flawless mask of sanity. I will tell my story. But not to Lane Frank.

Then, all our worlds will collide, and time will collapse. This, too, was meant to be.

I like to tease myself with the notion that I might want to stop killing. Perhaps it is a matter of aging, mellowing. I also like to think that I am achieving a new level of wisdom, that I have defeated my own demons.

But the wolf is like the coyote—a trickster.

I know that I am just deceiving myself.

There really isn't any way for anyone to stop me.

POP

I SAT WITH JACKSON IN HIS CAR, EXAMINING MY torn clothing, my scrapes and bruises. Emergency personnel worked to contain the blaze and help the injured.

"Somebody was leaving when I got here," I said. "I think it was Wolf. I didn't get a good look at him."

"Walker never saw him."

"What did he say to her?"

"They're debriefing her now. I talked with her for a few minutes. He put the screws to her about the personality study she did of him, and he dumped on the whole support unit. Told her she was attending a dress rehearsal. The real show is yet to come. It's what you were saying."

"When there's time, I'd like to talk with Walker," I said. "If the building didn't fall on it, you'll find Nicholas Wesley's van parked out back. He worked for an outfit called Valley Carpet."

"Homicide victim."

"Right."

Jackson looked more rumpled and sleep-deprived than he had the last time I saw him. His face was clouded with worry. "I've requested that the Bureau officially reopen the Wolf case," he said. "Walker was convinced."

I had mixed feelings about Jackson's announcement. I welcomed his help, and the resources that his agency could bring to the investigation. Jackson, however, was not representative of the rest of his group, and the Bureau moved more slowly than any state highway department.

Also, the agent had never told me the details of the scene at Willoughby's. He was every bit as cautious as I was, and I could never completely trust anyone that much like me. A man would have to be a fool.

Besides, I already knew what this was going to come down to—and it did not involve a third party.

"Lucas, what the hell is he doing? After a while, we see patterns to what these guys do. Not him."

"We're supposed to sift through the shit he leaves for us," I said. "He wants us to get hopelessly mired, while he takes care of business."

"Vengeance," Jackson said. "That's his business, and that's common enough with a serial killer. Only, he's doing things I've never seen one of these guys do before."

"No one knows how many times he's killed," I said. "He enjoys it, the way you or I might enjoy chocolate mousse. We shouldn't eat it. Cholesterol, calories, fat. We know it's wrong, but we shovel it in. Wolf knows the difference between right and wrong. He couldn't care less. He just demonstrated his skill with explosives. He's also a demon with a knife, a gun, a length of twine, or his bare hands. He told Walker this was a dress rehearsal. Think about that, Jackson. What did he rehearse?"

Before Jackson could answer, Rexford Landry poked his crimson face through the open car door. "You could've gotten everybody killed here, Doc. Who the fuck do you think you are?"

"Take it easy, Landry," Jackson said.

"We could've been here a hell of a lot faster if he'd called this in."

"And done what?" Jackson asked.

Landry was silent.

"The District had the case. They hadn't moved on it yet."

Landry pushed himself away from the side of the car and strode down the sidewalk.

"Keep that man away from me," I said. "If I can get my car out of here, I'm going back to the hotel."

"Lucas, we'd like you and Lane to join us in Quantico for a status meeting on our Mr. Wolf."

"So, he's really not just mine anymore."

Jackson shook his head.

In other circumstances, I would object to having my life dictated to me, but a brainstorming session couldn't do any harm, and might help.

"When is the meeting?"

"Friday morning, if I can get it signed off."

Well, there you have it. I nodded. "Okay, we'll talk before then."

AS I DROVE SOUTH ON PENNSYLVANIA AVENUE, I wondered again why Wolf hadn't killed Susan Walker. I could think of only one reason: he knew that he would have another opportunity. When? And who was next on his list?

Since his resurrection in Vermont, Wolf's bag of tricks had become more varied. Because of his treatment of his sister, I had concluded that he was caught up in the wild behavioral swings so typical of the personality disordered. I assumed that he was cycling down and out of control when he was in Florida, up and tightly controlled when he was in Michigan.

What if I was wrong? What if Wolf's design included leading me by the nose in the wrong direction? Perhaps he wanted me to think that he was fluttering all over the mania scale when he was totally focused, in absolute control.

I DID NOT RETURN DIRECTLY TO THE WILLARD. After a few wrong turns, I found the alley where Wolf had killed Nicholas Wesley.

A blue light was on over the door of the bar. A few of the patrons looked at me when I walked in; most were content with their drinking and conversation.

I sat at the bar. A woman in a wheelchair rolled over, and I slid the Wolf composites across the polished mahogany. I figured that Wolf might have been in the bar since the murder. He enjoyed savoring the events he set in motion.

"Don't look much like Harrison Ford," the woman said, starting to roll away.

"The night that Nicholas Wesley was murdered," I began.

"You come in here to drink?"

"I want to know if he's been back since the killing."

She banged on the wall. "Delta. White man to see you."

The woman who parted the curtains beside the bar was heavyset, dressed in a metallic blue evening gown. "What's the ruckus?" she asked.

She had a muted conversation with the bartender, then walked over.

"Has anyone seen him around since the murder?" I asked, indicating the composites.

"What you drink?"

"I prefer ale, but . . ."

"Wheels," she said. "Dredge a couple of them Bass pales from the bottom of the cooler."

The woman turned back to me. "That suit you?"

"Couldn't be better," I said.

"Things could be a lot better, but they ain't. C'mon. We can sit over there."

She led me to a table against a far wall, where I slid my hand over the damp rocks of the building's foundation. Another underground wall of stones, just like the cellar in Vermont.

"Who are you?"

"My name is Lucas Frank."

"You ain't a cop."

"No. I'm a psychiatrist. I track killers. Usually I do it for the police."

"Not this time?"

I shook my head.

"Personal?" she asked.

"Yes."

"He's a different animal. You won't take him alive."

"That doesn't matter to me."

"Didn't think it did," she said, drinking from her bottle of ale. "He's been in since. Ran his hand over them rocks just like you done. He didn't look like none of the pictures this time. We didn't say nothin'. We didn't do nothin'. He already killed once. We just waited 'til the man left."

"Did he talk to anyone?"

"Wheels. Said he wanted a Bud. She got him a Bud. He drank it, and he left."

"You said he didn't look like this," I reminded her.

She gazed down at the composite. "No mustache," she said. "Hair's not that dark, and there's no gray in it. Brown eyes. Big plastic glasses. I knew it was him. I got a damn good look at him driving Nick's van out of the alley."

"When was he in?"

"You just missed him."

WOLF

I HAD MET SPECIAL AGENT HERB COOPER ONCE, in an elevator in San Francisco.

The meeting was not fortuitous.

He was there for a session with the Unabomber Task Force. I was there, I said, to address a gathering of academic types on computer-enhanced anatomical reconstruction from bone fragments. The truth was that I had been doing some anatomical pillaging on the north coast, not far from Ukiah.

"No kidding," he said. "I've got this case in Oklahoma."

"The burial grounds thing? I had a meeting at Interior last week. Someone mentioned that case. You've got your hands full."

"Tell me about it," he said, grateful for the sympathy and impressed with my connections in government.

We had dinner at the Stinking Rose. By the end of the evening, we had agreed that on my return to D.C. I would contact Special Agent Hiram Jackson in Quantico, and arrange to review photographs and soil samples from the Oklahoma sites. It was too easy.

"After that, I can give you a preliminary idea of what you're dealing with," I told him, "but it doesn't sound good. You're probably going to need some DNA work if you expect to make any identifications."

I gave him a number in D.C. where I would be picking up messages. He gave me his office number in Oklahoma City.

"I don't know where I'll be staying," he said, "but I'll be checking with the office on a daily basis."

I ordered another round of wine. "It must be difficult, always hopping around the country."

"I enjoy it," Cooper said. "I joined the Navy to see the world, and the Bureau to see this country. Never thought much about settling down. You married?"

I smiled for the asshole who still sported his Navy brush cut. "Two teenagers. We have a place on Mount Auburn Street in Cambridge. Lynn, my wife, is in the education department at the university. I've always tried to confine my traveling to this time of year. The kids are at camp, and when Lynn isn't busy with summer session, she often goes with me."

"I've never even gotten close to that kind of life," he said. "Work always gets in the way—mine or hers. I've been dating a woman in D.C. Nothing serious, but this time it's her work that's getting in the way. Her name's Samantha Becker. She's divorced. Two kids who live with their father. She's attractive, intelligent, knows what she wants out of life. It's the first time I've actually thought about marriage. But right now, it just couldn't happen. We both know that."

All that I had wanted from my time with Agent Cooper was a connection to Quantico. Samantha was an unanticipated bonus.

.   .   .

I CALLED SAMANTHA BECKER'S OFFICE AT FORD'S Theater, where she was extremely busy in her position as an assistant program director, she said. Still, she invited me to stop by her place in Georgetown.

Later that afternoon, I found her town house, rang the bell, and suffered through the chatter of greetings. She left me in the living room while she went off to the kitchen.

I looked at her walls. They were covered with posters advertising upcoming events at Ford's. The posters dwarfed a family photograph of a blond mom and two blond kids.

Mom was Samantha, my victim.

More precisely, she was going to offer me the use of her town house as a stage. Samantha, of course, would be the central figure in my montage. She was a prop, an object to be placed and aligned in its proper position.

"What's in the package?" she asked as she entered the room carrying a tray with two glasses and a bottle of Van der Heyden Chardonnay.

She nodded her head toward the sleeve of brown paper that I had left on her glass coffee table.

Samantha's blond hair spilled down over her shoulders—uncommonly long hair for a middle-aged woman of the nineties. She was dressed in tailored jeans, a white turtleneck, and a cotton print shirt in muted shades of blue.

"It's the feather of a golden eagle."

"An eagle feather? Really? Why on earth? Aren't these illegal or something?"

She unwrapped the small parcel and glanced at the feather. "It's pretty, I guess, but hardly seems worth spending time in jail. Where did you get it?"

I wanted to slit her throat. I detest shallow prattle.

She guessed this fragment of a bird that had soared above the Sierra Nevadas was "pretty."

Lucas Frank had written a profile after one of my kills.

"He is reclusive, lives alone, does not socialize. He has never 'fit' in any social group. But as strange as others will consider his behavior, they would not think him impolite. He can smile, nod hello, but he does not waste time in frivolous chatter. He cannot tolerate others' perceptions of the world if they contradict his own. He is intelligent, above average, but far from superior."

"It is not a superior specimen," I said.

"It doesn't have mites or anything, does it?"

"If he completed any degree it was a bachelor's, no graduate degrees, with a major in biology or chemistry (a basic pre-med curriculum). He studies only what interests him, when he feels like it, and his resistance to authority rendered him a mediocre student."

She placed the feather on the table, brushed her hands on her jeans, and opened the wine.

"He could have accomplished more academically and professionally had he not been such a misfit. When he chooses to study, he does so exhaustively, perhaps in some esoteric fields, and works overtime at it."

Samantha leaned over the tray and poured two glasses of the Van der Heyden.

"What's it like dating an FBI agent?" I asked. "Herb seems to have to move around a great deal."

She brought my glass of Chardonnay. "Difficult," she said.

"He is meticulous, considers himself perfect, and he is proud of the creation that he has left for your examination. He has moved around, left jobs at his convenience. Any military career will be undistinguished because of

his inability to deal with authority. He did not live up to his own expectations for himself, so he has redefined them and rewritten the past."

"Well," Samantha said, "I'm glad you called, and I'm glad we could get together."

"So am I."

"Clinically, he is personality disordered—paranoid, narcissistic, obsessive compulsive. Also, he is dissociative. Despite the professional community's reluctance to accept the diagnostic nomenclature, the most accurate label for him is 'psychopath.' He can play any role he needs to, and be convincing. He sees himself as the most powerful and brilliant person on earth—godlike. 'Law and order' are intellectual abstractions that he considers himself above. He believes that he is witnessing a breakdown of morality, justice, social and economic systems—otherwise he would have been recognized for his brilliance. He uses no drugs, doesn't smoke. If he drinks, it is only the occasional glass of wine."

"What exactly is it that Herb wants you to do? Is it the Unabomber?"

I shook my head. "Samantha . . ."

"Then it must be the Oklahoma murders. You said on the phone that you were going to do some forensic work for him. What kind?"

"He is motivated by vengeance and the desire to have his superiority recognized, but he must maintain his anonymity. He is a game player, loves to taunt authority. All the clues he offers are spurious and will lead nowhere."

She had put down her glass and folded her arms across her chest. Her mouth was a thin line. Her eyes were narrow, questioning, skeptical. Samantha's face seemed to twist and mold and shape itself into a mask. This woman wanted an answer to her question, and she pushed like someone accustomed to getting her own way.

"The control he seeks is personal. The recognition he requires is public. This is frustrating to him because he cannot reveal his identity. He has dedicated his life to a single mission: murder. He sees himself as totally justified in everything he does."

As I explained the work that I would pretend to be doing for Agent Cooper, I reached behind my back and gripped the handle of my knife.

"Tell me what you do when the government doesn't have its fangs in you," she said.

"The feather has no mites."

"What?"

Lucas Frank had written his "profile of an unknown subject" in 1976. He completed it based on a single Massachusetts case, and submitted the document to the appropriate law enforcement agency. Of course, nothing happened, and the case remained open.

In 1985, with Quantico operational, I returned to that same community and committed an identical murder. I lingered in the small town, staying at a local motel, reading the newspapers, watching the TV news, and observing state and federal officials come and go from the police station diagonally across the street.

After a week of this, just as I was growing bored with my game, Special Agent Dexter Willoughby participated in a televised press conference dealing with the case. A Boston reporter asked him about the possibility of a connection to the unsolved case from 1976.

"We see no reason to assume linkage between those cases," Willoughby said. "To begin with, the 1976 homicide is remote in time, about nine years, and other than the type of weapon used, there really are no similarities."

At first I thought it was a trick.

It was not. The gurus of crime were just as daft as any other teachers.

I was in Houston several months later, skimming through the day's *Chronicle*, when I found an article describing the work of Quantico's "psychological detectives." A diplomatic Lucas Frank, M.D., was quoted in the article. He said that he envied the agency's resources, and anticipated that these highly trained agents would be at the forefront in dealing with the growing epidemic of serial murder. A new addition to the BSU staff, Special Agent Herb Cooper, mentioned the unsolved case from 1985. "We're constantly checking new cases," Cooper told the reporter, "looking for similar MOs, anything that would allow us to go back and close out some of these older cases."

Rubbish.

It was time to leave something for all the super sleuths—a replication of a brilliant work of art, signed by the artist.

Samantha Becker's head snapped back as I slashed my blade against her throat.

POP

LANE MET ME IN THE WILLARD'S LOBBY.

"Jackson's on his way to pick us up," she said. "He's taking us to a homicide scene in Georgetown. He didn't say much. Somebody called it in to the District police. They called the feds. Jackson wants us to see it."

She pointed to the door. "He just pulled up."

As I got into Jackson's car, he handed me a manila envelope. "I know Lane saw this in person," he said. "You might want to review the photos."

"What's going on?"

Jackson didn't answer. He pulled back into traffic and drove as I slipped a set of crime-scene photographs out of the envelope.

"That's Sarah Sinclair," Lane said, looking over my shoulder.

"Our victim's name is Samantha Becker," Jackson said. "She was an assistant program director at Ford's Theater, organizing events, booking guests. The crime scene is her home in Georgetown. I walked in there, took one look around, and bells started going off."

"Why are you giving me Sarah Sinclair?"

Jackson's expression was hard to read, but I did notice a tightening of his facial muscles. "The crime scenes are almost identical," he said.

We crossed the P Street bridge into Georgetown. Jackson made a couple of turns, then stopped in front of a private home, a narrow, Federal-style town house. The place was crawling with District cops and feds, including Rexford Landry.

As we got out of the car, Jackson said, "Looks like it happened sometime last night."

We walked up the steps and crossed the foyer. I hesitated for a moment beneath the churchlike, vaulted ceilings, then dropped into a crouch beside the blond corpse. Her long hair was matted with blood.

"Oh, God," Lane said, looking around the apartment. "This is exactly how Sarah Sinclair's apartment looked when we found her."

I shuffled through the photographs, stepped back, and looked at the room from a variety of angles. Everything matched the Sinclair scene. Candles burned down to puddles of wax. Wineglasses. A tray of crackers and cheese. Her dress was white, like a wedding gown, with birds embroidered on the neck, flying in the same direction as the slice through both carotid arteries.

"Samantha Becker wasn't wearing that dress," I said, stating the obvious. "He stripped her and put that on her after he killed her."

All the display was after the fact of murder. He had killed her on the sofa—there was a large bloodstain there—rolled her onto the floor, stripped and redressed her, then dragged her into position near the coffee table.

"What about the clothes she was wearing?" I asked.

"He must have removed them from the scene," Jackson said.

"She's divorced," Landry said from behind us. "Mother of two. Doesn't look like the kids live here. Ex-husband's a banker in Delaware. We're trying to locate him. We're also running a background on him. Couple of guys are up at Ford's finding out what they can about her."

"Waste of time," I muttered.

"There's the feather," Jackson said, indicating the glass coffee table.

I stood up, walked around the white, oversized sofa, and looked down at a large, brown and yellow feather. "Have somebody at the Smithsonian take a look at it. I think you'll find that it's a neck feather from a golden eagle. He didn't want us to miss it."

At the Sinclair scene, just beyond Sarah's outstretched fingers, Wolf had dropped a blue jay plume. With Samantha Becker, he had replicated the Sinclair homicide, and added another dimension to it.

"He's rubbing our faces in our inability to catch him," I said.

Wolf was working the city like a skilled politician, operating a step ahead of everyone else, making his moves, and leaving us to suck up his wake.

"Sarah Sinclair's murder was the reason that we caught on to Wolf," I said. "VICAP was filled with his escapades, but no one had ever connected them."

"I worked a serial case in Richmond years ago," Jackson said. "We didn't know what we were dealing with. Turned out that we had a burglar who graduated to sexual assault, then sexual homicide. The computers weren't much help on that one either."

"Someone should reprogram them. Danny Rolling

started out as a voyeuristic adolescent in Shreveport, Louisiana. He graduated from looking in windows to going through them. Sometimes he took something. Sometimes he just moved things around. Eventually he raped and murdered college students in Gainesville. It's the need for a higher level of excitement, a bigger payoff. If you looked only at the official record of his arrests, you would dismiss him as an armed robber."

"Anybody could've copied this," Landry said. "You'd be amazed at the crime-scene details that leak out all over the Internet."

"Lane, was anything about Sarah Sinclair's dress ever released?"

"No. The media picked up that she had been entertaining Wolf, that they'd had drinks. I remember a few other details, but nothing about the dress."

"He won't be ignored," I said to Landry. "He's going to have his recognition, even if he has to bring you and your agency to its knees to get it."

"You make this guy sound like some kind of fucking genius," Landry said. "Even if the asshole was alive, which he is not, he'd be just like the rest of 'em. You two are like girls at a slumber party, freaking each other out with ghost stories."

Landry turned away and stomped back through the foyer.

"Pop, why an eagle feather?"

"The first thing that comes to mind is power," I told her. "The eagle is a predator. It's also a significant motif in Native American lore. Wolf's biological father was Abenaki."

"Samantha Becker was dating one of our agents," Jackson said. "Herb Cooper. He's handling that Oklahoma case I told you about. He and Samantha went out a few times earlier this summer. She was wrapped up in her work, so was he. Then Herb was assigned to Oklahoma City."

"Maybe that's the connection," I said. "Cooper ever work with Willoughby?"

"One case. An unsolved in 1985. Massachusetts, I think. We've got someone pulling the records now. Will it connect to you?"

Wolf had spent time in Samantha Becker's home. He knew he could not perfectly duplicate the Sinclair crime scene, but he had come close.

He would also know that he had made a believer of me back in Lake Albert. Why take such pains to simulate this murder from a year ago?

To the FBI, Wolf was still officially dead. The bureaucratic wheels that Jackson had set in motion hadn't completed their rotation. Then there was Rexford Landry.

You want to be officially resurrected, don't you, lad?

"The Massachusetts case has to be connected to me," I told Jackson, "but I think Ms. Becker might be for the Bureau's benefit."

"Do you know what happened to that old house in Vermont after our people were finished with it?" Jackson asked.

"No."

"Willoughby bought it. He paid off the tax lien, then erected a ten-foot chain-link fence topped with razor wire. Apparently it looks like there should be a jail there, sitting out in the middle of the woods."

"If Willoughby thought there was more to find, why not Wolf's office—the loft over the barn up near Brownsville?"

"Our people took everything out of there. They removed wall paneling, floorboards, you name it. Willoughby's wife says the case was an obsession with him. He went over every object, skimmed through every book, read every piece of paper. At first she thought he was going to write his own book. All he'd say was that there was something missing and he had to find it. He had flown up there four times in the last six months."

Willoughby had more than doubts. His purchase of the Vermont property was obviously the information that he didn't want me to have. He was certain that Wolf had walked away from the explosion. The senior agent required something tangible, some physical thing that he could place on a table at a meeting.

"There's a young girl who may know what happened in Swanton. I want to show her the composites that we have of Wolf. Then I'd like to go back to the old house. Is there a way onto the land?"

Jackson handed me a key. "Willoughby's wife gave me that. It fits the gate. I didn't give it to you. Please check in with me when you get back."

WOLF

WITH THE SLATE ALMOST WIPED CLEAN, I EX-
perienced a wave of weariness. If it hadn't been for the
intricacy and bold scope of my script's final scenes, the
final thirty-six hours, I would have had difficulty dragging myself out of bed.

I knew it would pass. These periodic bouts of
lethargy have always lifted.

In college, I had been intrigued by the idea of en-
nui, especially the existential variety. I didn't think that
I had ever suffered from it. Sartre was a bore. Camus
was more to my taste—entertaining, as he did, both
homicide and suicide as philosophical statements.

As I drove south on I-95 through the rolling Virginia hills, I realized that as satisfying as my design was,
I was entering its most challenging phase. I should
have been feeling excitation, as I did in my youth.

Instead, as I left I-95 at the exit for the Marine base
at Quantico, I was thinking about theories of the absurd, and about how you tend to disregard the role of
legend in your lives. *I* am the stuff of legend. Samantha

Becker, in her role as the dead Sarah Sinclair, is the stuff of legend.

You have allowed statisticians to assign the label of legend to athletes, racehorses, politicians, serial killers. You are a nation that knows batting averages, elapsed times, trends, whether DeSalvo or the Manson family claimed more victims. The FBI allows the same number crunchers to determine the probabilities that are the life blood of a place like their cave at Quantico.

Even the cooperative international efforts of the English and the Russians rely on computer-generated models. Charts and bar graphs. They have discovered an approach that impresses the masses. The drunken Sunday football fan knows what to expect from Thurmon Thomas or Emmitt Smith in yards per carry, and believes that all numbers are scientific. Even those who flunked basic math have been drugged with this *Guinness Book* mentality.

This is part of the reason that I want to bring it all to their doorstep—to provide them with the ultimate experience in humiliation, laced with a dash of cataclysm.

Your numbers are meaningless. You cannot measure what you cannot comprehend.

The "mind hunters" ask their incarcerated serial killers whether they believe in God, and whether they believe they'll have to answer to God for what they've done. Why? Is it a reminder? A projection? An exercise in a socialized variety of sadism?

"Maybe we couldn't juice you, but God's gonna burn your ass."

This exercise is similar to the way they shove crime-scene photos in front of visiting members of Congress or media people. The civilians recoil in disgust. The federal cop nods his head sagely and says, "This is what people are capable of doing to one another. These are the cases we look at every day."

Who would dare cut their funding after a display like that?

Your experts are floundering—laboring to cling to some system of beliefs, some structure of biblical justice. An eye for an eye—something to keep them going when they realize that we are multiplying exponentially, and are far more intelligent than they could ever dream of being.

When they ask about the quality of a life lived within walls of concrete and steel, are they establishing rapport? After removing the suit jacket and loosening the tie to appear casual, just one of the guys, do they believe that they are approximating compatibility with the man in chains and orange coveralls?

I've read many of the interviews. I've seen the photographs—Ressler and Douglas posed like midgets on either side of Edmund Kemper. They went to obtain their own trophies. Is the motivation to collect souvenirs any different for them than it was for Joel Rifkin, the Long Island killer?

I found the unmarked road that I was seeking, made my turn, and began the long drive to the gatehouse.

Profilers are amateurs, racing around the country speaking authoritatively because they have a collection of numbers—probabilities. They drop names. They have talked to Charles Manson, John Gacy, Ted Bundy, Arthur Shawcross. The caged killers kept them running in circles—telling them partial truths and total bullshit—but the agents didn't care. Their audiences on the workshop circuit looked up at them in awe.

I stopped at the small enclosure, handing the renta-guard my identification, my instructions from Agent Cooper, and the name of my contact—Special Agent Hiram Jackson.

"Straight ahead, then to the right, Dr. Krogh," he said.

"Thank you."

Of course, I had no trouble finding the large gray building with the sign in front—FBI Academy. The offices of the Behavioral Science Unit, Investigative Support Services, were underground.

The site of the carnage to come.

At the entrance to the building, I presented the same materials that I had at the gatehouse. A middle-aged woman with a soft southern accent informed me that Special Agent Jackson was "in the field."

"I'm not certain when he'll be back, Doctor," she said.

"That's a shame. I have only today and part of to-morrow to complete the preliminary work that Special Agent Cooper wanted. He seemed so sure that Agent Jackson would be available."

"Let me see if there's another agent who can help you," she said, then, after a moment on the phone, asked, "How much time will you need?"

"I won't know that until I've seen the site photographs and the soil samples. I just need a corner somewhere. Space isn't a problem, but I don't know about the time."

She repeated that information into the phone, listened, then hung up. "It'll just be a minute."

I didn't recognize the agent who opened the door. "Sam Draper," he said, extending his hand. "Sorry about the inconvenience. You're here on the Oklahoma case, right?"

"For Herb Cooper, yes."

"Let me just ask you to walk through the metal detector. Any keys you have, pocket change."

I smiled. "I know the routine. You'd better take this, too," I said, handing him my briefcase.

"What's in this thing?" he asked, hefting the case.

I walked through the metal detector, setting off no alarms. "Magnifying glasses, small hammers, picks, tweezers, a microscope. Open it. It's not locked."

He slipped the two latches and gazed at the trays of tools resting in velvet compartments. He snapped it shut and handed it back, returning a .44 Magnum, two knives, and my strips of plasticized cyclonite.

"Follow me, Dr. Krogh," he said.

I stepped through the door behind the agent, glancing at the institutional decor, then began my descent into the catacombs that housed those who most wanted me.

POP

LANE WAS AT THE DISTRICT PD. SHE AND DETEC-
tive Williams were reviewing more of the lead sheets
they had generated when they distributed the Wolf
composites.

I scribbled a note explaining where I was going and
why, then left for the airport.

I couldn't shake the feeling that answers awaited
me in the mountains. I just wished that I had a better
grasp on what the questions were.

I HAD PHONED AHEAD AND ARRANGED TO MEET
Corporal Lucy Travis of the Vermont State Police at the
airport in Burlington. Travis had eight years in with the
VSP, had worked the double homicide in Swanton, and
she could communicate in sign language.

"I appreciate your meeting me on such short notice," I said.

She was tall, and seemed to be a slender woman,
but she was bulked out by the uniform and equipment
she carried. I was reminded what my daughter looked

like before she moved to Homicide and was permitted to wear her own clothes.

As we drove north on I-89, Travis said, "I remember reading about the Wolf case. The house blew up with him in it. I thought that was the end."

"So did I. Events seem to be proving me wrong."

We left the city limits of Burlington and Winooski, driving through countryside that glowed with the dying traces of autumn.

"How early do you get your first frost?" I asked.

"We've had a couple," she said. "We had snow this time last year."

Of course they had snow at this time last year. I was here for it.

After a few moments of silence, Travis said, "You think Wolf is responsible for our Swanton cases."

"Those two, and at least four since."

She didn't say anything more, just nodded.

TRAVIS AND I SAT IN THE POLICE STATION IN Swanton. I looked into the dark eyes of a young Abenaki woman named Terry.

She was not the homeless waif that I had expected. Terry was a poised sixteen-year-old dressed in blue jeans and a black T-shirt bearing the logo of a rock band, "BugJack." She wore a silver nose ring.

Her inability to speak did nothing to conceal a streak of defiance to rival any other teenager's.

I explained who I was and what I wanted.

Terry stared at me.

When I placed the composites in front of her, she pushed through them with one hand, found the picture she wanted, and shoved it across the table at me. Then she signed briefly.

I looked up at Lucy Travis. "Terry said, 'He told us he was like us, of the wolf. He lied. He is a jackal.' "

"What happened at the trailer?" I asked.

I listened to Travis as Terry stared into my eyes and signed. She had seen Wolf shoot her uncle.

During the time that Wolf stayed at the trailer, Terry avoided going home. She stayed with her boy-friend or relatives because of the meanness, the evil that she sensed in the man. It was in his eyes, in the way he moved, the few gestures that he made. He was too relaxed, like someone who believed that he had the answers to all the questions in the world. Whenever she returned to the trailer, Terry looked through a win-dow before entering. If Wolf was there, she went away.

On the night of the shootings, Terry approached the trailer and peered in through a front window just as Wolf fired his handgun. Her uncle fell. Terry ran to the diner where her mother worked, hoping to catch her, to warn her before her mother went home. Another wait-ress told her that Echo had gone to the local library.

" 'I ran into town,' " Corporal Travis translated, " 'but my mother was gone. Everywhere I went, I missed her. When I got back to our road, it was dark. I went into the woods. My mother was lying on the walk. I could see her blood. He came outside, stepped over her, and drove away in my uncle's pickup.' "

"I'm sorry, Terry," I said.

She shrugged, then signed.

"She wants to know if you're the Frank who haunted the jackal's dreams," Travis said.

I raised an eyebrow and nodded. "Perhaps."

" 'When he first got there, some nights I watched him sleep,' " Travis continued. " 'I sat near the couch and listened to him talk in his sleep. He said that Frank shot him. He was buried as dead, and it was Frank's fault. My mother helped him to heal and he killed her. I wish you were a better shot. You should have killed him, Frank.' "

I gazed down at the computer-enhanced drawing that Terry had selected.

Death had not changed John Wolf.

CORPORAL TRAVIS DROPPED ME AT A CAR RENTAL agency.

"Thanks for all your help," I said.

"I'm wondering how I explain to my captain that John Wolf is our suspect in the Swanton double murder."

"If there's anything I can do to help, of course I will. You're welcome to the material we have. I don't know how cooperative the FBI will be, but Hiram Jackson would be the agent to contact."

Travis gave me her business card, and I gave her the number at the Willard.

WHEN I SWITCHED ON THE IGNITION IN THE RENTAL car, the radio came on. On my trip south on I-89 toward Saxtons River, I was saddened to learn that Wal-Mart had conquered Vermont. Even the Green Mountain State—declared the most liberal state in the nation after the last election—had allowed the monster chain store and corporate censor to open up shop.

The bad news got worse.

The same elected officials who seemed hell-bent

on leveling the population's taste and destroying old downtown areas now had focused their acumen on the mind-body relationship. What thousands of years of theology, medicine, philosophy, and psychology had been unable to understand, the Vermont legislature would decide by fiat. They were debating a "parity bill," an action that would require insurance carriers to offer equal coverage for emotional and medical disorders. There was no mention of the soul.

At the same time, a separate government committee was investigating whether HMOs were sacrificing quality in health care to increase profits, exactly what some prognosticators had predicted years ago. Now, of course, managed care horror stories were being told nationwide.

With insurance money weighing more than Wal-Mart's fortune, and "Boomers" entering their arthritic, menopausal, depressed, bowel-clogged, and prostatic years, there was more money to be made. Since the politicians had rolled over for Sam Walton's empire, there was little justification to hope for reasonable access to health care for the body or the mind.

Somewhere near Bethel, I switched off the radio. Vermont's few remaining non-plywood cows were far more enjoyable to see than the state's surplus of simpleton politicians were to hear.

I had no idea what I would find at the old place. I was guessing, just as Dexter Willoughby had guessed. I figured that Willoughby probably had spent most of his time around the foundation and whatever else remained of the house. I wasn't going to have much daylight, so as I drove, I thought about how to narrow my search.

I had disliked Dexter Willoughby, but I knew that

he was not a stupid man. He had been searching for something more than evidence of Wolf's death—souvenirs, trophies—a cache of special things that the killer had collected. Joel Rifkin had kept his victims' jewelry on his bureau. Jeffrey Dahmer had kept his victims in his freezer.

Jesus, what were we coming to?

I remembered the apple trees where Wolf, as a child, had built a town. He took scraps of wood and other building materials that his stepfather had left around and designed a miniature village on the hill behind their house.

He built his perfect world. No people.

When I turned onto the road that led to Wolf's old house, I knew immediately where I was, and remembered my last trip there. I had gone away thinking that I had ended a killer's life.

Terry said that I should have been a better shot. She was right.

It was odd. As I pulled off the road and parked, I felt fear bubbling somewhere inside of me. Willoughby had intended that his fence keep out intruders. What if he had locked something in?

The place had been leveled by the explosion and fire, then excavated like an archaeological dig. The sweet scent of honeysuckle was in sharp contrast to the stench of charred wood and paint. Separate piles of foundation stones, dirt, and ashes were scattered on the house lot. The entire place looked like Willoughby had gone over it with a backhoe. Even the tunnel—winding its way from the building site, up through the field and onto a slope beside the orchard—had been opened up and lay like a jagged wound upon the earth.

The agent fervently believed that Wolf had concealed something there.

Clumps of beech and birch leaned like gray and white sentinels over an open grave. A soft breeze through the grass and leaves whispered like mourners, or the ghosts of the dead.

Wolf had buried victims here. It had been my intent that this mass grave receive its creator, but I had failed.

I unlocked the gate, then walked around the foundation hole toward the hill in back. I wandered out among the apple trees, looking at what had once been a clearing, long since reclaimed by nightshade and sumac.

In the 1920s, Carl Panzram kept a journal that documented his years in a brutal reform school, his twenty-one murders, and his thousands of other crimes. John Wolf, a Proustian obsessive, had kept a meticulous computer record of his own savagery. His was a rigid and self-serving attention to detail.

When police searched Rifkin's bedroom in his modest Long Island home, they found his collection—photographs of his victims, their jewelry, credit cards, clothing. Wolf, too, was a collector, and a meticulous labeler of whatever he accumulated.

Wolf's words were logged in his computer, or jotted on scraps of paper and filed alphabetically. He had altered crime scenes by adding objects to some, removing items from others. No one had ever found the cache of materials that were most important to him, that gave him the greatest pleasure when he fingered through them. These items—possibly a lock of a victim's hair, a photo, a piece of clothing—would have anchored him to the reality he had created for himself, and allowed him to relive his conquests.

I wandered through the clearing into the surrounding brush, kicking at the clumped grass, occasionally gazing back at the cellar hole where Wolf and I had struggled.

I had nearly died here.

On that day a year ago, I had told Wolf to get into the coal bin.

I asked him, "What about your trophies?"

He said that most of "them"—his victims—were less than memorable.

Bullshit. He knew all the details. He recorded every last bit of information.

I turned to look at the sun disappearing behind the hill.

What was most important to you, lad?

I imagined Wolf answering, "To defeat fear."

He had returned again and again to the one place that frightened him most, the house where fear resided. I remembered the taped music that played as he killed Sarah Sinclair—Julian Cope's "Fear Loves This Place."

His stash contains objects that he loves.

"Where the hell would he put it?" I muttered.

The apple trees marked the boundaries of your sanctuary, didn't they, lad?

I walked to the middle of the triangle formed by the three gnarled trees. Willoughby had not dug here. I kicked at the dirt, unearthing fragments of ancient lath and plaster, metal wire casing—the remnants of Wolf's town.

If you could defy the night, survive your stepfather's cellar, you believed that you would emerge stronger and more powerful. You had to do it over and over. Taste your fear, then spit it out.

I was preoccupied, drifting, and didn't hear the footsteps until the last possible second. I swung around, my hand on my gun.

"Just leave it be," the young man said, leveling a long-barreled .38 at me.

He was tall and muscular, in his twenties, and wore a knapsack over his red flannel hunting shirt. His John Deere cap held his scraggly blond hair captive, and he gripped a Budweiser in his left hand. He also had a deer rifle strapped over his shoulder.

"You another fed? Jesus. All you fuckin' assholes carry."

"I'm not a fed," I told him.

His eyes were glazed. I figured the beer probably wasn't his first of the day.

"The other dipshit chased me out of here with a nine," he said. "You Lucas Frank?"

I hesitated, then nodded. "How did you know that?"

"I'm gonna want to see some ID. I got something for you, and I'm gonna be fuckin' glad to get rid of it."

"I have to reach into my pocket to get my wallet."

"Go ahead and do it. You come up with something besides a wallet, you ain't gonna have no balls left. Maybe a guy your age don't care about that."

He drained his beer can and tossed it. "I've taken all the shit I'm gonna take over this fuckin' thing."

I reached for my wallet, and held it up so that he could see my photo ID. He glanced at it, then slipped the knapsack off and tossed it at my feet.

"What I'm supposed to tell you is that a guy came here a couple of months ago and left that for you. He said his name was Charles Weathers. I don't fuckin' believe him. He paid me a thousand bucks to make sure you got that. Said if I didn't give it to you when you came, he'd come back and stick a Buck knife in my chest. *That* I believed. You got your shit. Now I'm leaving."

"Wait. The man who owns this land . . ."

"The fed? First time he came was way before Weathers did, not long after the old house blew up. That's when he put up the fence. After Weathers gave me the money, I seen a car parked where yours is and came up here to see if it was you. I got as far as the gate, and the asshole chased me off. Other times, I saw it was him and I didn't bother. Weathers told me the little prick would keep coming back. He was right. He also called you a killer. That true?"

"I'm a doctor," I said.

His laugh was a short, derisive bark. "I don't fuckin' believe any of you," he said as he backed down the slope.

"Look, I need your help," I said. "Just a few questions."

"I done what I got paid to do. That's it."

I watched as he walked out through the gate and headed up the dirt road.

John Wolf had known that Willoughby would come here to search. Two months ago, Wolf had also anticipated my visit to the land, and made his arrangements. The man was uncanny.

I crouched over the knapsack and lifted out a rusty, dirt-encrusted lockbox that had obviously spent some time beneath the earth. Using my pocketknife, I jimmied it open.

I imagined that I could hear Wolf's voice whisper, "What have you got?"

I fell back on the ground, lifting out musty, yellowed papers and photographs. I know what I had expected—

a collection of artifacts related to Wolf, the moments of his special kills. I expected his whole life.

"My whole life," I said into the emptiness. "My whole fucking life."

It was a collection of clippings, photos, and articles on *me*, kept by a man obsessed. There were copies of professional papers that I had written, both of my books, newspaper clippings—most of them under Anthony Michaels's byline—covering many of the cases that I had worked. Wolf had critiqued all of them with slashing red strokes.

I felt a rush of nausea and dizziness. Wolf had prowled through my trash, digging out personal letters, even greeting cards. The bastard had stalked me.

It was monstrous. He had been at it for so long that at first he snapped his photographs with an old Polaroid—the kind that you had to peel the photo apart from its built-in negative. In a fading black-and-white, Ray Bolton and I stood in front of Cora Riordan's Huntington Avenue apartment building.

Eight-year-old Lanie and I walked out of our house on Beacon Hill. Ten-year-old Lanie and I sat in the sand at Winthrop Beach.

"Jesus Christ."

I could feel tears welling up in my eyes. As I lifted the various papers out of the box, the world was spinning, my hands shaking. I hadn't eaten since USAir, but my stomach surged as if it wanted to empty itself.

The quality of Wolf's pictures improved. Color, some thirty-five-millimeter telephotos. Me with Lane in her cap and gown at her graduation from college. Me participating in a forum at Harvard's Sanders Theater.

"I don't fucking believe this."

There were shots of the aging killer, Norman Elgar. All of these were photographs that Wolf had taken. He had visited Elgar, talked with him, just as I had.

"His whole life has been about me," I whispered.

At any moment during the last two decades, Wolf could have stepped from the shadows and annihilated my entire family.

The flawless predator. Once he has selected his prey, he is locked on. Nothing distracts him, moves him away, especially not time. There are no time limits in a reptilian mind. But why did he lock on?

I remember walking along a dike in the Loxahatchee National Wildlife Refuge in Florida. I had looked down over the bank into the murky waters of the canal and saw the snout and hooded eyes of an alligator. The rest of the beast was under the water. I watched him for a while. He seemed to be just basking there. Then I noticed the broad, black wings of an anhinga, drying itself in a bush overhanging the canal, perhaps five feet away from the reptile. The bird, too, was motionless. I was wondering whether these were simply the parallel lives lived by two of the swamp's inhabitants, when, after nearly half an hour, the anhinga moved its head, poking its beak at some irritation.

The water exploded as ten feet of alligator, jaws agape, snapped the bird from its perch and disappeared beneath the surface of the canal.

The eruption was sudden, startling, and final.

I remember that I was impressed with the beast's patience. I knew that it would not have mattered how long he had to wait for that momentary distraction, and the bit of motion that identified his target. Time was not a limiting factor.

The flawless predator.

What was I? A meal, or a threat?

As I pawed through the contents of Wolf's metal box, I understood everything that had happened a year ago. Wolf had wanted me involved in the investigation into Sarah Sinclair's death. He knew that to get me involved, all he had to do was threaten Lane.

He had been waiting.

This time, he had sent his invitation with three shots from a Remington 30.06. Once again, I accepted. I had gone seeking Willoughby.

Wolf was waiting.

For two decades, I had been guilty of the worst possible sin that one can commit against the narcissistic psychopath. I had failed to notice him. Wolf had haunted my life, and I had not heard the floorboards creaking in the night.

And always, Wolf waited.

He wanted me to see him, to be aware of him, to know that he was there. He positioned himself at the edge of my vision, slightly away from the corner of my eye. He baited me, waiting for me to snap a glance in his direction. That never happened.

"Why me?" I said into the evening air.

He was an enduring shadow, but I didn't know that he was there.

He kept his obsession separate, split away. None of it appeared in any of his files.

It was no wonder that Wolf knew how I thought, how to anticipate what I might do. He had paid more attention to me and my work than I had.

Why was I the one?

His collection contained a brochure from a workshop I had attended—The Expert Witness: Presenting Forensic Evidence in the Courtroom. A Polaroid photograph was tucked inside the brochure. In the picture, I stood outside the conference room talking with Teddy Morgan.

I remembered that moment. Teddy and two of her associates had organized the workshop, and I was complaining that their presenter, despite his sterling credentials, had an accent that was incomprehensible.

"People are taking notes," Teddy said defensively.

"They're writing letters home," I told her. " 'Send money and explosives.' "

I remember the camera flashes. Teddy and I had ignored them. We were both involved in high-publicity cases at the time, and reporters had been plaguing us.

I stared at the photo. Wolf couldn't have been more than ten feet away when he snapped it.

Obsession.

As I became more well known, Wolf had wallowed in enforced anonymity. When a detective, reporter, lawyer, or polygrapher wanted to talk murder, she or he called me. As one who killed, Wolf knew more about the subject than I, but was denied his place in the sun.

I remember other cases that spanned years, and most of those involved emotional attachment. Predation occurred, but only following a period of subconscious incubation. An Oregon man's twenty-five-year fixation with his ex-wife ended in her murder and his suicide in North Carolina. He hated her, blamed her for everything unpleasant that had befallen him, but his compost pile of passionate detritus had required a quarter century to percolate.

The case of Donovan Kane had been more prominent. Kane was an attorney who had negotiated with a former Louisiana cop to have Kane's wife murdered.

The woman had the good fortune to develop appendicitis on the night that she was supposed to die. Having collected most of his fee, the cop could afford a spasm of conscience, and assisted the state with their case against Kane.

A plea agreement would have required that Kane serve no jail time and pay a substantial fine. His license to practice law would be revoked. The judge in the case, Martin Lockworth, rejected the negotiated plea. Kane stood trial, was convicted, and served seven years before being released on parole.

Each Christmas during his incarceration, and for a decade after that, Kane sent Christmas cards to Lockworth. He also sent birthday notes, and congratulatory scribbles for each of Lockworth's publicized professional accomplishments.

As Lockworth's reputation grew, Kane wallowed first in jail, then in obscurity.

Nearly eighteen years after his appearance in Lockworth's courtroom, Donovan Kane, a passable realtor, emerged from the shadows of the parking lot at a fashionable local restaurant, fired nine rounds from a semi-automatic pistol into the judge's body, and vanished.

Obsession.

When Kane, as "Donald Kahn," was arrested in Toledo, Ohio, where he worked as a legal adviser to city government, he refused to speak to anyone. The shrinks called him paranoid, but competent.

Donovan Kane was not paranoid, and he was more than competent. With the assistance of his attorneys and a psychiatrist from Columbus, Kane convinced the court that he suffered from Multiple Personality Disorder as a result of childhood abuse. He was found not guilty by reason of insanity, and confined in a state institution for the criminally insane. He promptly escaped.

Kane then murdered his ex-wife. He also killed the cop who had betrayed him. This ghost of a man was implicated in a dozen other murders, apparently random killings that had no connection to his past. His fingerprints turned up at homicide scenes in Illinois, Iowa, Tennessee, Florida, Texas.

Once he had killed, it seemed as if Kane had developed a taste for it. He enjoyed the act of murder, tripped on the rush of power. Like D. B. Cooper, who leaped with his bag of money from a jet somewhere over the rugged mountains of the American Northwest, Donovan Kane had his own cult following. There were clubs, discussion groups on the Internet exchanging bits of information, possible sightings. Instead of seeing Elvis at Burger King, it was "DK at the BK."

For all I knew, Donovan Kane, now in his middle fifties, could still be plying the trade that had begun as a single directed obsession—the judge who had rejected the plea agreement in Kane's case.

I had been John Wolf's Judge Lockworth.

The past is a scrap heap of myths and realities, confused dreams and nightmares, bits of illusion and shards of evanescent truth. That was never enough for you, was it, lad? I came along and read your mind without committing murder, without ever knowing you. You immediately saw the similarities. Later, you recognized the threat.

There was an audiotape at the bottom of Wolf's metal box. It reminded me of the many messages that Wolf had left with his victims—the music that played over and over in Sarah Sinclair's house when her ex-husband found her body.

This tape had its own message, a single sheet of paper. "Where will you celebrate the anniversary of my death?" Wolf had written. "It is only fitting that I return to the underground to observe the holiday. Perhaps you will join me for the fireworks."

On our way to Swanton, Lucy Travis said that it had snowed in Vermont at this time last year. I knew that because I was here, tracking Wolf. I'm not good with dates, but the "anniversary" had to be within days, perhaps even hours. There was nothing left of Wolf's tunnel. What the hell was he talking about?

I walked down the slope, closed and locked Willoughby's gate behind me. I sat in the car and slipped the tape into the cassette player. It was Jacques Brel's "Le Moribond," "The Dying Man," a song about the death of a long-time friend. There was nothing homicidal in the song, but it didn't require a great deal of imagination for me to get the message.

I was a threat, an irritation that you were compelled to tease like an aching tooth. You had to be there— watching, waiting. I just might have snapped my head around. But since I did not react, you allowed us to live parallel lives until you decided otherwise. Now, of course, it was my turn to fade into dust.

I was John Wolf's "dying man," and had been for twenty years.

WOLF

THE CEMETERY IS AN ART FORM.

Angles, lines, shadows, and at night, the purest darkness—all are part of the geometry and stage setting of death.

We are linear in life, then we lay each other down in straight lines on strict planes when life has ended—all according to a grid that resembles a map of city streets. Of course, the place of the dead is more symmetrical, and extends deep into the earth. It stays that way until someone detonates a charge that dislocates both the living and the dead.

Special Agent Herb Cooper's burial ground was a slice of prairie wasteland. Sand and bones—no flowers—a cactus here and there. I sat in his cramped, subterranean office, skimming through the photos. Vials of dirt and decomposed human tissue were arrayed on the desk. I opened my wooden case, removed a few tools, and created the appearance of a forensic consultant at work.

When Hiram Jackson stopped by to introduce himself, I recognized him. He was the fed who was driving into Susan Walker's apartment complex as I was leaving.

"Sorry I couldn't be here yesterday," he said. "Looks like they've got you pretty well set up. Is there anything else you're going to need?"

"I have what I need for a preliminary read on this material," I told him. "There's more sophisticated testing required, of course, but your lab will have to do that. I do have to stop back briefly. I hadn't expected to, but it's unavoidable. The dead seem to require so much more than the living."

Jackson's forehead wrinkled. "Oh?"

"People are seldom gratefully dead. Sorry. Anthropological humor."

Jackson smiled. "Hang on to your security tag, Dr. Krogh. I'll let them know upstairs. How long have you and Cooper worked together?"

"This is the first time, actually," I said. "We shared an elevator in San Francisco last month. I was familiar with the Oklahoma case from my work at Interior. They think you might as well give it up, by the way, that there's no way you can get what you need out of those burial grounds. I didn't know that Herb was the case agent. I was out there to deliver a lecture. One participant wanted to know what made my work most difficult, and what helped me the most. Cyclonite and Elmer's glue, I told her."

Jackson laughed. "Well, in the event that you do need anything, Dr. Krogh, just let me know. I'll check with you again tomorrow."

I thanked him and he left.

IN SO MANY WAYS, MY WORK HAS BEEN TOO EASY.

I heard some of the agents talking in the hall, making sure the conference room was available for their

Friday morning "status meeting." I was disappointed
that no one mentioned me by name, but I was pleased
with their choice of date and time. Of course, Samantha Becker and I had assisted them with that decision.

Something will end when Lucas Frank walks
through the doors sixty feet above my head, then passes
through these long corridors. Perhaps then I will finally
claim a permanent place aboveground.

There have been many times that I've tried to see
beyond murder, to understand what is required by intimacy. As a young man, I watched the faces of couples
engrossed in conversation over coffee at the Hayes-
Bickford Cafeteria. I saw them talk and touch and
smile and agonize, communicating privately with only
their eyes. I studied them.

Theirs was a drama that they played out for themselves while fucking their way through school. The play
was a titillating mystery—the excitement of curling
into a dormitory bed intended for one. The late night
phone calls made to microscopically examine the details of a life together were an essential aspect of the
mystery.

I decided that all relationships were self-referential.
They turned back upon themselves and stayed that way
until one or both participants grew bored. For me, murder remained the simpler and more satisfying endeavor.

One night during those years, a group of students
gathered at a warehouse fire in East Cambridge. They
gazed at the fire from a distance, fearful, while I inched
closer to the flames, wondering what fear was, wanting
to know if what I had tasted in my stepfather's cellar
was fear. The building crashed in upon itself, smashed
down and blew up a shower of flaming chunks of debris.

I heard shrieks from the group behind me.

"Aren't you frightened?" a young woman asked.

I shook my head.

"You should move back," she said, standing at my shoulder.

We walked together, back to Central Square, but the subway had shut down for the night.

"Ever walk the tracks?" I asked Annie.

"Through the tunnels? What about rats?"

"There's a world underground."

I remember the red and yellow caution lights blending into their own colors of fire, and casting over-sized shadows on the walls. We became giants in the underground maze.

We ended up at her place, talked, and drank.

"I think we're too drunk to fuck," Annie said. "But I'd really like to."

She fell asleep on the floor, her hair spread in a fan around her head, her hands clenched into small fists like a child. I got down on my knees and touched her face, ran my fingers across her lips, and, finally, touched her lips with mine. She never moved.

The next day she slipped into a seat beside me in the lecture hall and handed me a note. "Did you do anything to me last night?" the note said. "If you didn't, I'm gonna be pissed."

She had scribbled her phone number across the bottom. We both stared forward as a graduate teaching assistant tore into *The Winter's Tale*. "Shakespeare's message is simple," he said. "Sin must be paid for before it can be forgiven."

When he finished, she leaned over.

"I think I had a good time last night," she said. "But I think all the heat was at the fire."

The second night, she opened two beers, handed

me one, and said, "I want to know you. You don't want that, do you?"

"If you drink faster, I won't have to answer that question."

"Then I'll pass out and you'll take advantage of me again. Or would it be the first time? I don't remember."

"You have no idea of the risks that you're taking."

"That's what makes it so exciting. You could be a murderer. You could be the one who killed that girl last spring, strangled her with her own sock."

She pushed a bowl of nuts across the table. "Have some," she said. "I bet you snuck up there while she was sleeping, broke into her apartment . . ."

"How did I break into her apartment?"

"With a crow bar? No. A screwdriver. You pried the door so the lock slid open. Then you went in, found her in the bedroom. You probably didn't mean to kill her, but she said she was going to tell the cops that you raped her. So then you had to kill her."

"Annie, I'm in pre-med. I study martial arts. I know the pressure points on the neck. Why would I bother with the sock?"

"Aha," she said. "Just like the Boston Strangler. You killed her with your bare hands, then tied the sock around her neck in a bow like he used to do."

"Let me tell you exactly how I did it."

"Great. Let me get more beers first."

She returned with a six-pack. "I want all the details, and don't let me pass out."

"I climbed up the fire escape," I began.

"So that's why nobody saw anything."

"Are you going to keep interrupting?"

"No. I can't help it, though. This is exciting."

She was playing a game, and having a wonderful

time. She had no idea that what I was telling her was precisely what I had done.

"The bathroom window was open about two inches. I pushed it up and stepped inside."

"Was there any light?" Annie asked, her eyes opened wide. "I'm sorry. I interrupted again."

"No light," I said softly. "It's much better that way. Your eyes adjust to the darkness, and the darkness becomes your friend. It was a one-bedroom apartment, so it wasn't hard to figure out where to go. I didn't rape her."

"That's it?"

"Oh. She wore her socks to bed. During the brief struggle, she pulled off one sock. I don't know why. Maybe panic. She grabbed at my hands, and the sock ended up draped across her throat. It wasn't tied there."

"You didn't even rape her? Then why'd you kill her?"

"I wanted to spend time in her apartment, with her things, without her being there."

Annie took a long drink from her beer. "Well, shit. Why didn't you just break in and sniff her underwear when she was at class? I like my version better."

Eventually, Annie married a guy from the business school. They moved to Connecticut and raised three children. Thirteen years after the warehouse fire, she sent me a gift—a copy of Loren Eiseley's *The Unexpected Universe*. She had circled the author's inscription: "To Wolf, who sleeps forever with an ice age bone across his heart, the last gift of one who loved him."

A month later, I killed her in a horse stall.

POP

I DOZED FITFULLY ON THE RETURN FLIGHT, thinking about Wolf's extended stay in Vermont. He'd had plenty of time to plan what was happening now. It was mere detail work. The man's design for himself spanned a lifetime.

I also heard my father's voice.

Trust your own mind, lad.

My father had thirteen "heart attacks." Most of them were trips to one drunk tank or another. The South View at least once, the Pines more than once. Sometimes, as I discovered much later, it was the less posh Charles Street Jail. They didn't have a coronary care unit there.

Then he did die. Number fourteen was for real.

I remembered standing on a hill as he was lowered into the ground, and thinking about how we inhabit both the surface and the depths of the earth—wondering how long it would be before there were more people beneath the ground than above. Maybe there already were.

Because the living can be as blind as the dead, chance continues to rule the universe. There are no absolutes—not even in quantum physics. We exist for the blink of an

*eye in the lifetimes of the galaxies. We have no choice but
to trust our own minds.*

I stood in that cemetery on the hill, and I watched a
bird on a phone wire. It flew out from its perch, snapped
an insect out of the air, then returned to the wire.

"It's a kingbird," I had told my sister. "See the white
band across the bottom of its tail?"

She squeezed my hand and whispered, "Listen to
what the minister is saying."

I didn't understand a word of what the man in
black went on about, but I was fascinated with the
bird's darting movements, its abrupt changes of direction, how it seemed almost to stop dead in midair.

*Wolf had given Janet Orr a page from Peterson—the
kingbird.*

Dexter Willoughby's words about Wolf's note in
The Collector echoed in my mind: "It was dated and he
wrote down the time."

I had received a mockingbird.

All of Wolf's entries in his computer journal were
numbered.

Coots and old squaws.

"Jesus Christ," I said, sitting up and grabbing the
back of the seat in front of me.

The woman in the seat beside me glared and
pulled away.

The first characteristic of Wolf's that I had identified a year ago had been his rigidity. The man was methodical to a fault.

*You have owned your world, lad, but you had to give
it balance and order, didn't you?*

"Sorry, ma'am," I said to my flight companion. "I
left my duffel in a locker back in Hartford."

The birds had nothing to do with Wolf's messages.

It was the fucking page numbers. What had Jackson said? Coots, page sixty-one. Wolf had killed Chadwick about two months ago. I needed a calender, but I was willing to bet that sixty-one was the start of a count-down, the number of days remaining until Wolf's grand finale. He had killed his sister about a month ago. Old squaws, thirty-four.

"Shit," I muttered.

Again, the woman's head snapped around.

"My wallet's in the duffel," I explained, wondering how far I could go with that particular charade.

Kingbirds, eight. Mockingbirds, one-twenty-four. Only the final digit mattered. Wolf had delivered the phoenix four days after he had killed Janet. What did that leave?

Less than two days.

Thirty-six hours.

IT WAS LATE WHEN I ARRIVED BACK AT THE Willard. I wanted to sleep for an hour, but my mind wouldn't stop. I settled back on the bed with a bottle of ale, and drifted.

Suddenly, I was working in a restaurant on Nantasket Beach. It was the sixties. I wore jeans, a T-shirt, a white apron.

I was closing the restaurant—Amanda's—while Leo, the owner, counted the night's receipts.

The kid was carrying a knife when he walked in through the kitchen at the back. He held the blade at Leo's chin and said he wanted the money.

I felt a familiar stirring inside me. I grabbed the kid by his greasy black hair.

He brought the knife up and sliced my arm. For an

instant, I gazed into his eyes, at the wild panic there, then slammed his face down through the glass candy counter. Then I did it again. His blood spurted up, spattering my white apron.

The cops questioned me. They said I might have killed the kid. They made it sound like I was the one who had done something wrong.

Even Leo said, "Something like that happens, you just give 'em the money."

But I couldn't. I had been cursed with my very own beast. A beast not unlike Wolf's. I feared him. I loved him. I knew that if he ever escaped, ever took over, I would never be able to bring him back under control.

After that incident—seeing the blade pressed into Leo's flesh and feeling its edge myself—my beast was agitated for days, glaring at me with his black eyes, moving about, refusing to sit with his back to me.

My sister had said, "It happened again, didn't it?"

I nodded.

"Can't you stop it?"

"I don't want to."

"But . . ."

"He's part of me," I explained. "He scares me, but he'll never let me down."

"He always finds a way to get out," I muttered.

I lit a cigarette and watched the smoke spiral upward, remembering the fog as it moved in and hugged the Massachusetts shoreline. I thought about the worlds that lay beyond the fog. An ocean. A continent. Another continent. If I let my thoughts fly free enough and far enough, they circled the world, working their way home to me again.

I couldn't remember how old I was the first time I knew that I had lost my way. Too young to cross the street without holding my sister's hand. Too young to walk down to the pier without her. But I could remember the sound of the waves crashing against the wall— the feel of the air and the smell of the sea. Even then I knew that people kill each other—a piece at a time, or in an orgasm of homicidal rage.

A man like Wolf fits smoothly into the scheme of things. Just as I do.

The line between us has blurred.

It has to, if I am to stop him.

LANE AND I WERE GETTING TOGETHER FOR A late dinner.

I had my hand on the doorknob, prepared to step into the hall, then realized that I was distracted. I was about to walk out without my gun.

I retrieved my nine-millimeter and headed for the lobby.

When I begin to drift, when my beast begins to stir, the breaking away becomes involuntary. My thoughts assume lives of their own.

Of all things, I was thinking about a family trip we had taken years ago to Franconia Notch State Park in New Hampshire. After a picnic lunch, Lanie and Savvy and I had crossed Route 3 to the Flume, a series of underground caverns, rivers, waterfalls. Savvy said the place made her feel claustrophobic, so she had stayed behind in one of the larger caves while Lanie and I forged through the tunnels worn into the rocks over millions of years.

"Pop?"

I looked across the table at Lane.

"Where are you?" she asked.

"What?"

"You haven't touched your food."

I looked down at the slivers of chicken breast adrift in a sea of maple syrup and slices of Mandarin orange. "Smells good," I said.

"It's probably cold."

I tasted it. "Warm."

Lane's plate was empty. I winked and smiled. "You eat too fast," I told her.

She shook her head. "You're impossible."

I had decided to leave the matter of Wolf's metal box and his obsession with me for a later conversation, preferably after the bastard was dead. Lane knew that I was the focus of Wolf's rage, and I could see nothing to be gained by alarming her even more.

The chicken was excellent, the wild rice cooked to perfection. I wished that I had eaten when it was still hot.

"So, what do you think of the Knicks this year?" Lane said, laughing.

"Watch out for the Miami Heat," I said.

I sipped my ale.

"Pop?"

"What, Lanie?"

"When did you start paying any attention to basketball? I said something about Michael Jordan the other day, and you didn't even know who he was."

"Is that what we were talking about?"

"You glanced at a sports page."

Lane was well aware of my propensity for eidetic recall. While skimming through a book or newspaper, I might catch a glimpse of a page, then later reproduce it as a visual image in my memory.

"Guilty," I said.

"You know, sometimes I wish I'd gotten that particular gene. Then, other times, I'm glad that I didn't."

"What you only see can often get in the way," I said.

I was ready to give Lane my standard lecture on experience—the appreciation of all the senses—but I had distracted myself.

What you only see can get in the way. What happens when your eyes adjust to the darkness? What about what you don't see—or hear, or smell, or feel? Wolf's reference to the underground had triggered my association to the Flume.

What was John Wolf leaving for me to see? What was I seeing that was getting in the way? I had been so visually oriented that I thought I was missing something. It had nothing to do with what I wasn't visualizing.

The pages from Peterson. I had locked on their content.

"Pop?"

"Let's walk," I said, getting up from the table.

"What is it?"

"I want to walk," I said. "Initial the check."

I headed for the door.

"Was everything satisfactory, Dr. Frank?"

I stopped. I had heard. I could still taste the maple syrup. I looked at the maître d' and had no trouble managing a smile. Sometimes these automatic behaviors can be a problem. "Most enjoyable," I said.

I shoved the door open and stepped out onto the sidewalk. I fumbled through my pockets looking for a cigarette, lit it, and sucked down the hot, soothing drug.

Lane came through the door. "I wish you wouldn't do that," she said.

I handed her the package. "You can trash that."

"You've said that before."

"Until the next time," I said. "Come on."

I started walking—threw the cigarette into the street—walked faster.

Lane was almost trotting to keep up. "You've got him, haven't you," she said from behind.

"Hell, no. I've just recognized my own stupidity. You out of shape?"

She caught up. "God, you can be a royal pain."

"I do my best."

"Where are we going?"

"For a walk. Tell me what you see."

"I'd rather hear about your trip," she said. "Okay. I see buildings. Hotels, government offices, restaurants."

"Look closer."

"I see glass, bricks, steel, people . . ."

"Closer."

"Cracks in the glass," she said, struggling to keep up with me. "Posters on the walls."

I took the left onto Tenth Street and stopped. I pointed across Pennsylvania Avenue. "The Justice Department," I said. "Law and order. Be nice if we ever had it. Big crook used to hang out there. John Mitchell."

I pointed to my left.

"Ford's Theater," Lane said, "where Samantha Becker worked."

"Piece of history, isn't it," I said, gazing up. "Do you remember the play?"

"*Our American Cousin.* April 14, 1865."

"The audience was laughing. Most of them never heard the sound of the shot."

"Booth got away on horseback. Later, they shot him. They said he was resisting arrest."

"Down there," I said, pointing to my left. "Peterson

House. They carried the president there. He died in the back bedroom. They still have the pillow that his head rested on. Bloodstained. Under glass. Like pheasant."

What you see can get in the way.

"What do you hear, Lane?"

"Pop . . ."

"Do it," I said, looking up at the building that a southern fanatic had rendered memorable.

"Traffic. Voices. A plane going over."

"Listen," I said. "Nighthawks. They spend most of their time on the wing, snapping insects out of the evening sky. They're common in urban areas."

Lane looked up into the blackness. "I can't see them."

"That's the point," I said.

When everything is black, effectively we are blind and must rely on our other senses.

Wolf knew that I would get hung up on feathers and birds and his ascension from the dead. I would look up, even into the blackest sky. What I should have known was that I had to look back to where he had come from, beneath the earth.

Underground.

"I've been looking in the wrong direction," I said. "He's not soaring through the evening sky. His game has something to do with tunnels."

"You confronted him in the cellar."

"His home. He went deeper before rising up from his own ashes."

"Pop, this city is laced with tunnels. The subway, all the government buildings."

It wasn't enough for Wolf that I was in Washington. He wanted me to join him for his fireworks underground. A year ago, I had been the hunter and had tracked Wolf to his lair. Now, I was the hunted. Would he come to my lair?

"What about the Willard?" I asked.

"Oh, Jesus, Pop."

"There has to be a basement of some sort. Maybe there's something below that. Wolf has already demonstrated that he knows the building."

A cool breeze whirled dust up around us. "Let's go back," I said. "I'll call Jackson."

For the first time since our arrival in the capital, I felt as if I was beginning to get a grasp on my phantom. I imagined the sketch of the nighthawk in Peterson's *Field Guide*. Eidetic recall: page 101.

Only the last digit mattered.

THAT NIGHT, AS I SAT SILENTLY ALONE IN MY room, Hiram Jackson returned my call to his pager. After I had explained my thinking, he said, "I'll get a team of specialists down in that cellar tonight."

"How long will it take?"

"There are probably foreign delegations staying there. We'll have to be discreet, get the Secret Service involved, work with the hotel's management. With an old building like that, there's no way to tell how much area they'll have to cover. I don't know how long this will take. We'll move as fast as we can. We don't want an international incident."

"Hiram, Wolf's messages were in the page numbers from the bird book. It's a countdown."

"How much time?"

"I figure we've got about thirty hours."

Jackson said he would get back to me.

I did what I knew I would eventually have to do. I

began to stroke the back of the beast who lived so deep within me. He shifted uncomfortably, jerking his head from side to side.

I remembered that night so many years ago, after the attempted robbery at Amanda's, after the police had questioned me. I sat in my small room listening to the sound of the waves lapping across the sand. I took pencil and paper, and wrote down the few words that rattled around in my mind.

> *it's almost time, they say—*
> *they say, and walk away,*
> *leaving me with the night*
> *and the sea,*
> *and no handle on my soul—*

I had slipped out the window that night, and climbed down through the branches of the old lilac. I walked on the beach, then sat in the deep sand, shivering, watching as the sky grew lighter in the east. The blood on my T-shirt looked black.

I was afraid that I had shattered along with the face that I had plunged through the glass counter. There was the restlessness inside then, too—the glaring eyes, the muscular, hunched shoulders. My African lowlands gorilla refused to be quieted.

I AWAKENED IN THE CHAIR WITH THE FIRST LIGHT of the D.C. morning. My eyes felt as if they were filled with beach sand.

I called room service for coffee, then retrieved the newspaper from the hall.

John Wolf's face was on page one.

WOLF

OVER COFFEE IN THE FBI ACADEMY'S CAFETERIA, I gazed at my image on the front page of the Washington *Blade*. It was not a bad rendition of a former life. Amazing what a skilled artist and a computer can do.

I glanced around the room at agents and students carrying their trays of eggs, toast, and juice. A few carried newspapers.

Two young men in jumpsuits sat across from me. One of them immediately unfolded his copy of the *Blade*. "You see this, Red?" he asked his partner.

Red glanced at the composite, skimmed the first paragraphs of the story, nodded, then went about the business of inhaling his omelet. "We got twenty minutes, Louie," he said.

And I had twenty-four hours until my final scene—the purest form of justice.

The Quantico people—the few who paid any attention at all—seemed to be growing accustomed to my presence.

When all other drives and desires have passed,

burned themselves out on the dying embers of age and impotence, the one pure motivation remains.

Vengeance.

It has always been there. Not just for me, although I have nurtured it properly, sheltered it, forced it to blossom like white narcissus in winter. Rocks, water, bulbs, and an explosion into bloom.

Vengeance.

The affluent residents of Greenwich, not far from my former home in Hasty Hills, Connecticut, summoned their Hispanic servants to wipe their kids' asses, clean the stains off the sheets they stole from hotels in Palm Springs or Aruba. They paid no taxes for their ass wipers and sheet washers.

The Lord said vengeance was his. Fuck him if he can't take a joke.

In New Hampshire, a school board refused to allow the movie *Platoon* to be shown to a class on American affairs. Too much violence, too many murders. It was their war that I had attended. They owned the murders. How did they want it portrayed? As a barbecue under the fronds?

Vengeance.

Anything else is impure, dishonest.

Today I can feel the rolling waves of Sibelius's second symphony. The cellos, the violins, the horns, the timpani, vibrate on the surface of my skin. I have the spirit, the soul of the assassin. It is all that I have ever wanted.

I reached across the table and tapped my photo in Red's newspaper. "Interesting man," I said.

"Yes, sir. Sick. If he's even alive."

"I had some minor involvement with that case," I continued. "I'm John Krogh, by the way. I'm a visiting anthropology consultant. I think it would be possible to survive an explosion like that. Not terribly likely, though."

"What was your involvement, sir?" Red asked.

The cadet was not at all interested. He was humoring an old bone man while he filled his face with food.

"Two cases that remain on the books as unsolved, although I was convinced that they were Wolf's work. The victims—the odd collection of bones that were left of the young women, at least—were found within a mile of one another. Rural area in Connecticut. Raccoons and coyotes had been at them. They'd eaten most of the flesh, of course."

He slowed his ingestion of eggs.

In Vermont, after Lucas Frank shot me, I had seen ghosts on the road. As I drove north, shapes and faces curled up like smoke from the snow-covered highway. White shapes with gray faces in the black night. I rolled down the window to keep myself conscious. Then I heard the ghosts howling in the night.

It is merely the wind, I told myself as hands reached out and grabbed at me, then were blown aside by the snarling, whining wind, winding itself up in cyclonelike coils.

Vengeance.

In the subway station at Park Square, Boston, just after I came home from the war, an old drunk told me that I was why we were losing Vietnam.

"Fuckin' got no balls," he said, trying to burn his eyes into mine. "You're a loser. I fought in the big one."

He hated me, but as he continued to stare, the blaze faded from his eyes. It was replaced with confusion. His grip relaxed, and he stepped backward. He was afraid of what he saw in my eyes.

"You're fuckin' crazy," he said.

I moved toward him as he backed away.

He waved his arms. "Stay away from me."

He was moving away fast, but I would not let him go. I gripped his coat and spun him around.

"No," he pleaded.

When a subway cop grabbed me, the old man ran.

"What the fuck?" the cop said, and I plunged a knife deep into his gut.

Vengeance.

As a child, sometimes I was attacked in my dreams. I was never equipped to defend myself, so before I knew any better, I tried prayer. It was always after hours at the church, and prayer is an unpredictable effort at best, so I was left with what I could devise.

"Animal depredation is a real problem," I told Red. "I don't want to bore you with the intricacies of forensic anthropology, but . . ."

"Sorry, sir," Red said. "We're due on the range. Louie?"

As he walked away, I heard him mutter to his friend, "I gotta hit the head. My breakfast's comin' back up."

Solid recruits.

I glanced at the wall clock. By now, USAir had delivered Dr. Frank back to Washington. Perhaps his brief respite in the mountains taught him the true magnitude of his task, and provided him with a proper appreciation of *his* ghostly counterpart.

POP

DARLA MICHAELS, AN ENTERPRISING INVESTIGA-
tive reporter, had gotten her hands on the Wolf composites. She had also found a reliable source.

The story was mildly sensational, but accurate, and
contained information that I was finding out for the
first time. According to the article, John Wolf was the
most prolific serial killer in history. Thought to have
died in an explosion nearly a year ago, he was alive and
well, and terrorizing the nation's capital, blah, blah,
blah. Investigators had linked Wolf to three deaths in
the metropolitan area: FBI Special Agent Dexter
Willoughby, Nicholas Wesley, and Samantha Becker.

What fucking investigators? Neither Lane nor Jackson would talk to the media, and nobody else was conceding anything. I wondered whether Darla Michaels
believed in the Wolf angle, or was simply selling papers.

Rescue workers reported only minor injuries, the
story continued, following an explosion in the northeast
section of the city. The blast—a bomb—was also attributed to Wolf. The presence of a hostage in the building
moments before the explosion was unconfirmed.

The article provided some of Wolf's history, then quoted an anonymous source who placed NYPD Detective Lane Frank and her father, Dr. Lucas Frank, in the city working with local law enforcement and the FBI in the hunt for the elusive killer. "The father-daughter team tracked Wolf to Vermont last year, where the serial murderer was believed to have died," the article concluded.

What I had not known was that John Wolf, posing as Dr. Alan Chadwick, had lectured at Quantico four years ago. The sonofabitch was absolutely incredible.

When the phone rang, I expected it to be Lane. It was Hiram Jackson. "You saw the paper?" he asked.

"You didn't tell me that Wolf taught at Quantico."

"I didn't know that. I checked our records, and we did have an Alan Chadwick lecture at one of the homicide schools. I don't have all the information yet."

"You said you had Landry checking Willoughby's files."

Jackson said nothing.

"If Landry is responsible for putting our names on the front page, I'll break his fucking face. Look, we'd better get together. You have people in the cellar?"

"They got started before dawn. Nothing so far. It will be business as usual in the hotel. I'm in Quantico right now. Herb Cooper's consultant on that Oklahoma case is here."

Protocol.

"Hiram, we don't have much time. The Winklers and Parmenters have been dead for thirty years. They can wait a few more days. What about the 1985 case that Cooper worked with Willoughby?"

"I've got a fax on that. How about if I meet you at the Willard for lunch?"

I hung up.

The knock on the door was Lane. "You see this?" she asked, holding her own paper and walking in.

My coffee was right behind her. I poured for both of us and said, "There's been too much morning already. Either I get to drink this, or I go back to sleep."

"Wolf was teaching at Quantico. Jesus Christ. Didn't those assholes ever hear of doing a background? They must have zero security in that fucking fortress of theirs. I can't believe this."

"I hope they paid attention to Wolf," I said. "He would have had a thing or two to tell them."

Lane still had her head in the newspaper, but managed to accept her coffee. I settled into a chair across from her. Finally, she looked at me. "You slept in your clothes. Why didn't you go to bed? Were you out?"

"One at a time," I said. "I fell asleep in the chair."

The phone rang again. "Shit. That's the reason I won't have one of these fucking things. They ring all the time."

I was expecting the media. It was Detective Williams at the DCPD. "We just had two young women come in," Williams said. "They saw the newspaper. The two of them were in the bar there at the Willard the night that Nick Wesley was murdered. They sat with the guy in the composite, talked to him. One of them says he had blood on his shirt."

"He didn't clean up after Wesley," I said, thinking how careless that was for a man like Wolf.

"He explained it by saying there'd been an accident, and that he had pulled people out of the wreck. I checked with the traffic division. It's a bullshit story."

"What else do they remember about him? What more did he say?"

"Their names are Courtney Davenport and Jean Posner. Davenport did most of the talking. The Posner kid was freaked by the guy as soon as she laid eyes on him. Said he was acting friendly enough, but he was strange, like he was sizing them up the whole time they were sitting there. It finally got to her. She insisted on leaving, so they left. Davenport thinks he said he was an archaeologist. She can't remember anything else. Both of them are pretty shook."

"Are they still there?"

"Yeah. We're just getting their statements typed now."

"Any objection to my talking to them?"

"Not at all."

Lane was still reading the morning paper when I got off the phone. "How did the reporter get this stuff?" she asked. "How's it gonna affect Wolf? God, this pisses me off."

"Would you please limit yourself to one question at a time? Jesus. I need time to wake up. They'll probably assign a select committee to identify her source. Washington spends more time and money probing for leaks than dealing with the shit right under their noses. Wolf's going to do whatever he's going to do. It was planned a long time ago."

I grabbed my jacket. "That was your D.C. detective just now."

"Williams?"

"A couple of young women walked in. They think they might have spent part of an evening in The Nest with Wolf. I'm going over there to talk with them. They're the best direct link we have to Wolf right now."

"I was headed there anyway. Let's go."

As we walked through the Willard's lobby, the atmosphere had not changed, just as Jackson had said—"business as usual." I told Lane what was going on in the cellar of the building.

"If Detective Williams's two witnesses are right about seeing Wolf here," I said, "it would seem to support the idea that he's had time to familiarize himself with the place."

"You sound doubtful, Pop."

I shrugged. "Something isn't right."

LANE AND I TALKED WITH THE TWO YOUNG WOMen, but got nowhere. Courtney Davenport could not stop talking, but she had nothing to add to what she had already said. Jean Posner seemed to be traumatized. She was composed, but quiet, almost withdrawn. She reminded me of victims of violent crime that I had treated years before.

I asked to talk to Jean alone. She agreed. Williams directed us to an interrogation room that wasn't in use. The two chairs were beat-up, folding metal, and someone had abandoned a dust-covered polygraph machine on the table. It wasn't the best setting, but it would have to do.

"Is it okay if I call you Jean?"

She nodded.

"Jean, most people discover that talking about a frightening incident helps. It's unpleasant to recall all the details. Remembering can be almost as scary as the event itself. But it can be a way to put things to rest."

Jean nodded again.

"You've heard of hypnosis, Jean," I said.

Once more, she nodded. Jean Posner was in a positive response set.

"I don't mean the watch-dangling kind, but a deep and gentle relaxation—a quiet place where two people agree to go together. You and I could do that. I would be with you the whole time. No one could hurt you. We can remember together, just like we were watching a tape on TV. You will control the picture and the sound of the video about that night in the Willard. Okay?"

She tipped her head in a slight nod.

"If you allow our eyes to close," I continued, slowing the pace of my talking and lowering my tone of voice, "and allow your thoughts to drift freely through—effortlessly—and you take a deep breath, feeling the air fill your lungs, then, very slowly, let it out, as your eyelids . . . close . . . down."

Jean's eyelids fluttered, then closed. Her breathing, which had been shallow and irregular, settled into a comfortable rhythm. I waited a full minute, then said, "Deeper."

I watched as the tension disappeared from her face. Her hands rested on her knees.

"If you would take me back to that one particular night at the Willard," I said.

After a long pause, Jean said, "Our table is taken."

"What are you seeing?"

"A man. We're sitting across from him. Blood. He has blood on his shirt."

"What are you hearing, Jean?"

"Bones. John digs up dead people. John is an anthropologist at Harvard. He's looking at me. His eyes are dead."

The young woman began to tremble.

"He's a picture on a TV screen," I said. "Whenever that picture upsets you, you have the power to switch it off."

In seconds, she had relaxed again. I was satisfied that she had told me all she could. I offered her the posthypnotic suggestion that she would control her awareness of what had happened that night. She would remember only what she could handle, when she was ready to deal with it.

When I assisted her out of the trance, Jean smiled. "I haven't been sleeping well. Work has been hectic. But I feel rested."

"You'll allow yourself to sleep well tonight, I think."

Jean Posner went off to sign her statement, and I found Lane with Susan Walker.

"We watched through the mirror," Walker said. "Impressive. Jackson said you wanted to talk to me. I also wanted to thank you."

"Your appearance is a vast improvement over the last time we met. If I had paid more attention to you, I might not have been blown halfway across the street. I figured the bomb for a hoax."

"Jackson also told me it was your idea that I remain at Quantico. I appreciate your concern, but as you can see, I have refused. So, you have some questions? I hope you're not planning to try on me what you just did to Ms. Posner."

"Certainly not."

Out of the corner of my eye, I saw Lane wince at my lie. I watched as Susan Walker folded her arms across her chest, straightened her legs, and tensed them against the back wall of the cubicle.

"I'd never go along with hypnosis," Walker said. "I don't think it would work with me, anyway."

I needed the subtleties, the nuances that only her subconscious would have registered during her time with Wolf. The Bureau's debriefing wouldn't have addressed those. She had watched me with Jean Posner. This was the perfect opportunity for an indirect hypnotic induction.

"By your presence here," I said to Walker, "I'm assuming you have clearance to talk with me."

She nodded.

I turned to Lane. "Have you ever noticed, Lanie, that when people express their resistance to hypnosis, they tend to do it physically? They create tension in their own bodies—rigidity in the legs and arms. Even in their eyelids—working against their own desire to allow their eyes . . . slow now . . . to close . . . all the way . . . down. This resistance and tension seem to . . . go very deep."

Lane folded her own arms. "Someone should put a leash on you," she said.

When I looked back at Walker, her eyes were closed. She moved her legs away from the wall and dropped her arms to a comfortable position on her lap. I remembered the tape across her eyes when I found her in Wolf's apartment. "When we can't see," I began, "we sense things in other ways. We hear words that are spoken, the noise of people moving around us. We grow more sensitive to odors. We feel—tactile feelings, intuitive thoughts. We say that our minds race. It's up to us to slow down. We do have that power."

"Soap," Walker said. "I smell soap. No. Shaving cream. I hear water running."

She had also heard the clicking of Wolf's wire cutters, and had smelled what she thought was hair coloring. This fit with what the woman at the bar where Wesley was killed had told me. Wolf had changed his appearance.

Occasionally, a bit of mind manipulation is necessary. I spent the next hour listening as Walker traveled beyond cognition and beneath conscious thought. The details of Willoughby's death would pique her cohorts. I was more interested in the rage she heard in Wolf's voice when he complained that Quantico had not thought of him after Chadwick plunged to his death. His was the fury of the neglected narcissist. He was telling her that he was the superior man—that he created his own opportunities—that he was a sophisticated traveler with a taste for fine food, and that he had risen from beneath the earth.

He also described his time with Walker as a "dress rehearsal," and reminded her how fond he was of explosive devices.

What the hell was he going to do? Was his target the Willard? How was he planning to gather his cast of players?

When I felt that I had everything that I was going to get from Susan Walker, I turned back to Lane and terminated the trance in the same indirect manner that I had used for the induction.

Walker sat up in her chair, stretched, and asked, "So, what do you want to know, Dr. Frank?"

"I've got to run," I told her. "I'm meeting Agent Jackson at the Willard. Lane, perhaps you would explain."

Lane followed me, telling Walker she would be right back. "Are you getting anything out of all this?" my daughter asked.

"The question has always been, what is Wolf's notion of the ultimate act of power and humiliation? What would give him the greatest satisfaction? We need to view the world as he does, not attribute our perceptions to him. Wolf told Walker to talk to me. What I have is a notion about tunnels, something underground, something buried. Maybe the Willard. I don't know. I do know that it's set for tomorrow, the anniversary of our confrontation in the cellar in Vermont. We also have the distinct possibility that our killer is walking around posing as an anthropologist."

"What are you gonna do?" she asked.

"Meet Jackson," I said. "You check with the Smithsonian, the various universities. Put together a list of visiting anthropologists, consultants—that kind of thing. In the event that Wolf was flirting with the truth, include all Johns, regardless of their faculty status. And move fast."

As I walked through the corridor, I realized that I probably had all the pieces of the puzzle, but I was not comfortable with how they were fitting together. I'm never comfortable with a dilemma like that, but this one was gnawing at me. I felt like the answer was dangling tantalizingly nearby, but I could not get a grasp on it.

Was Wolf about to go underground and disappear forever? Is that what the bastard was telling me?

Or now that he'd had his dress rehearsal, was he planning something far worse.

WOLF

I FOLLOWED DARLA MICHAELS FROM HER OFFICE at the Washington *Blade* in D.C., to a country-western bar—Barb's Barbecue—in Quantico.

I enjoyed following the unsuspecting reporter. She was the intermediary who would bring my design to its completion, and she knew nothing of what was going on around her. Quite delightful, really. She was about to file the biggest story of her career, but now she scampered from her car into a ramshackle, barn-board watering hole just off the state road.

Barb's defined itself with antique neon beer signs, black cowboy hats, Confederate-flag-decorated denim jackets, and a jukebox that disgorged twangy, whiny, warbling blather about lost loves, last beers, dead dogs, and bright red pickup trucks with gun racks.

This was a strange land.

I sipped a beer and studied Darla Michaels. She was dressed casually in jeans and a shirt, and wore her light brown hair cut short. It was her profile that fascinated me. I stared at her face, searching for some hint, the slightest resemblance between her and her father,

Anthony Michaels, a Boston reporter from the past. The senior Michaels had been one of Boston's leading crime writers until his death from cancer six years ago. He had covered DeSalvo, the Cora Riordan murder and Jeremy Stoneham, Norman Elgar—all the big ones. He was a fan of Boston's own wizard, Lucas Frank, giving the psychiatrist unlimited credence and all the public exposure that he wanted. Now, his daughter was the final prop for my last act.

It was fitting that we all come together like this, necessary that time collapse upon itself. The temptation to rip all of these people to shreds was strong. I had to fight it off, and I had to remain patient.

Rexford Landry ambled through Barb's door. He seemed right at home in this non-English-speaking enclave. He waved to people, stopped and hugged a fat woman in a polka-dot dress, shook hands with a tall man wearing too-short jeans, white socks, and black shoes, and kissed a little girl whose face was covered with barbecue sauce.

Shit. He looked like Clinton campaigning.

He was still wiping sauce from his face when he sat with the reporter. "Hey, Darla," he said, sliding into the booth across from mine. "You hit page one. Some spread."

"This isn't exactly anonymous, Landry," she said. "I thought you were concerned about our being seen together."

"These folks know me. They don't know you."

She shrugged. "Your funeral."

"What I gave you was solid, huh?"

"No flat denials. Your superiors did some scurrying on Wolf-as-Chadwick teaching at the Academy."

Landry laughed. "Jackson called me at home."

"He has to suspect you of leaking the story."

"I am so fed up with sitting in a fucking office I could puke. What are they gonna do, reassign me? Anything's better than this shit. I want to go back on the street. I don't know why they pulled me off the street. We were taking down dopers all over Miami. Anyway, what are you drinking?"

"Scotch."

"Millie," Landry yelled, "a shot of what she's got and a draft."

He turned his attention back to Michaels, who seemed barely able to tolerate the boorish cop. "I told you I could deliver the Wolf angle," he said.

"I'm curious, Landry. Do you think he's still alive?"

"There is no fuckin' way that anything human walked out of that blast. Willoughby was obsessed, like he was tracking the Superman of serial killers. Establishing that Wolf was alive, then bringing him down— that was going to be the final feather in his distinguished cap. The Bureau's official position remains the same: Wolf died in Vermont. Jackson's getting mesmerized by Lucas Frank. He's trying to reopen the case. They're 'looking at possibilities.' It's all bullshit."

"Then, who is doing the killing?"

"Millie, you're a love," Landry said as the waitress deposited his drinks on the table. "We call them 'fans.' They're copycats. They devour everything they can find about a prick like Wolf. They read the tabloids, the paperbacks, watch *Inside Edition*, *America's Most Wanted*. They're fucking experts on these killers."

He slammed down the shot, then sipped his beer. "Listen. Check for a land transfer, a house and ten acres in Saxtons River, Vermont. Corrigan to Willoughby."

"He bought the fucking place?"

Landry laughed. "I told you he was obsessed. Talk about a fan. He put a big fence around the cellar hole, most of the land. Frank was in Vermont yesterday. He stopped in Swanton, then went to Saxtons River."

"What was he after?"

Landry swallowed. "He's staying at the Willard. Go ask him."

"You don't know?"

Landry shook his head. "But I can do better than that. You know the murder in Georgetown?"

"Samantha Becker. We attributed that to Wolf, just like you said."

"I never said Wolf was the perp. You decided to use that angle. It was set up to look exactly like a murder that Wolf committed in New York about a year ago. Victim's name was Sarah Sinclair. The lead investigator was Lane Frank. You fill out your story with that."

"Details on Becker," Michaels said, snapping open a steno pad.

"Throat cut with surgical precision. Dolled up in a fancy white dress which, we've been told, she didn't own and never would have owned. The place looked like she had been entertaining. Wineglasses, all that shit. The dress had birds embroidered on the collar. Feather left at the scene."

"I remember that," Michaels said, looking up from her writing. "The feathers. They found cases all over the East Coast. VICAP never spit them out."

"I'm not so sure they should've been spit out. These killers aren't that smart, for chrissake. You people make them sound that way. Shawcross? Dumber than shit. Didn't know enough to walk around puddles. Fuckin' Bundy went *pro se* right into the electric chair. I think Ted Bundy wanted people to think that he'd killed more than he did. Like that guy in Texas, Henry Lee Lucas. Every time the Rangers brought him a strawberry milkshake, he confessed to a couple more. Three hundred plus before somebody finally said, 'Wait a fuckin' minute, here.' Asshole was in jail for a bunch of 'em, or in Florida when they were getting whacked in Oklahoma."

"So, what we have here is a copycat?"

"Of course," the agent said, slamming his hand on the table. "That's what I've been saying. Maybe we cloned some fuckin' sheep, but ain't nobody come back from the dead in a while."

As Michaels prepared to leave, Landry's tone changed. "Hey, shit. Listen to me. You're the writer. You want to go with the magical maniac bit, sell a few papers, you do that. Millie?"

Darla Michaels left as Millie brought Landry his second round.

IT WAS NO SURPRISE TO ME THAT LUCAS FRANK had discovered the events in Swanton. Clever orchestration on my part.

For him to return to the old house to regain a mindset would have made sense only in some fiction writer's melodrama. He always had the mindset. It didn't matter whether he wanted it. It was as much a part of him as it was of me. The only difference between us was that he feared his love of murder, and I nurtured mine, cultivated it to a fine art form.

No, like Willoughby, he had gone to Saxtons River in search of something elusive, but definitive—something that would tell him everything he needed to know to catch a killer.

Did you receive my gift, Dr. Frank?

That rusted metal box is all that remains of his life. Those scraps of paper change everything. A few photos, a couple of articles—they alter events that happened twenty years ago, ten years ago, yesterday. Trees only seemed to be falling in the forest when no one was there. There was someone there. I sent ripples of sound and emotion and chaos into his world.

I had been no more than a whisper to Lucas Frank—a whisper that he could not hear above the din of his own life. Now, as he fingers through his past, all of time and space and what he has known as reality is different. Two decades of his life have been disturbed.

Do I have your attention now, Dr. Frank?

AS I DROVE TOWARD D.C., I REMEMBERED YEARS ago, moving from a basement apartment on Boston's Bay State Road to a brighter, first-floor unit on Fenwood. During my second week in the new place, I arrived home from my job at the hospital and found two detectives waiting for me.

The lead cop was a short Irish bulldog from South Boston—Tommy Sullivan. His partner was a tall, heavyset black man from Roxbury—Raymond Bolton. I wondered at the time if it had required a court order to bring these representatives of disparate sections of the city together.

They had some questions they wanted to ask me, Sullivan said.

I couldn't imagine what they wanted. I invited them in, then sat on the sofa. They stood in their overcoats and hats in the center of the room, ignoring my suggestion that they make themselves comfortable.

Sullivan verified that I had lived on Bay State Road, the date I moved, when I turned in my keys and to whom.

"Mr. Rayle, did you make the acquaintance of the subsequent occupant of that apartment?" Sullivan asked, in the police version of our language.

"No."

"You didn't go back there? You know, for something you forgot?"

"I didn't forget anything."

"Did you know the place had been rented?"

"No. May I ask what this is about?"

Sullivan raised a single finger. "I'll ask the questions. While you lived there, which entrance to the building did you use?"

I shrugged. "Both. Mostly the back one in the basement. The alley connected to Kenmore Square. Usually I use the bus or the subway. I don't own a car. The back door was faster."

"Your apartment key fit both doors?" Sullivan asked.

"It did," I said, realizing what they were getting at, "but I didn't need a key for the back door."

"The lock was broken?"

"I don't know. The door didn't close all the way. It was like it was swollen, didn't fit."

Sullivan nodded his head. "Can you account for your time from midnight Saturday until noon Sunday?"

"Midnight Saturday? I was asleep. Sunday morning I got up around nine, went running on the Riverway. When I got back, I had a late breakfast, read the paper. I got called in to work Sunday afternoon."

Bolton spoke up. "You lived in the Bay State Road apartment for eight months."

"Yes. It was a sublet."

"Ever have any trouble with people coming in through that back door?"

I thought about it. "Not enough that I ever complained. When I first moved in, it was still winter, and there was an old drunk who'd come in and sleep in the hallway. He seemed harmless enough, and it was cold. A couple of months ago, somebody jiggled my doorknob, but that's happened other places I've lived. Once on Marlborough Street, I remember. I yelled and he went away. That's about it."

Bolton pushed magazines on the coffee table aside, sat there with his knees almost touching mine, and stared intently into my eyes. "We figure that somebody came through that alley door early Sunday morning, let himself in to your old apartment, and raped and murdered a young woman."

"The new tenant?"

Bolton nodded.

"I don't know anything about it. Like I said, I haven't been back there. Sounds like Albert DeSalvo."

"It does, doesn't it?"

Bolton looked away. Sullivan continued taking notes.

I found all of this to be an amazing coincidence. I had not been back to the apartment. I had not killed the woman. Some kindred soul was working my city, and had found his way to my apartment after I had moved. Suddenly, I wanted to meet this man, to talk with him. There are so few opportunities.

I also found the situation ironic. There was Ray Bolton—Lucas Frank's partner in crime, Lane Frank's godfather—sitting with his pant legs brushing against my jeans. He was so close that I could smell his Old Spice.

The Boston detectives finally left, saying they would return if they'had further questions. They never came back.

Six weeks later, on a snowy Christmas Eve, I walked up Fenwood Road, crossed Huntington, and killed Cora Riordan. Late into the night, I stood in a small crowd across the avenue and watched as Dr. Frank arrived.

The reporter, Anthony Michaels, briefly walked among us, asked questions, got reactions. Then he crossed Huntington and locked himself in conversation with Bolton first, then Lucas Frank. Later, I continued to watch as Bolton led Jeremy Stoneham away.

Years after that, when I visited Norman Elgar at Walpole State Prison, he told me about the young woman whose name was hard and caustic like she was. Kira Kirkman. Elgar had followed her home, entered her building through a broken rear door, then strangled her.

He remembered all of his conquests. Ms. Kirkman had lived on Bay State Road.

Clearly, it was meant to be. I had worked long and hard to maintain us all as family.

POP

WHILE WAITING FOR JACKSON, I READ ANOTHER
entry in Wolf's journal.

FREDERICK LAW OLMSTEAD, THE ARTIST WHO DE-
signed New York's Central Park, also developed plans for
aesthetically pleasing cemeteries—garden cemeteries,
with their rows of gravestones demarcated by bending and
sloping paths, then adorned with thousands of tulips, daf-
fodils, peonies. My favorites, standing out among the yel-
lows and pinks and whites, are the bloodlike bursts of red.

Cemeteries are more sensuous than the places we inhabit in our time above the ground. In life, these mag-
nificent gardens allow us to leave the wasteland we have
created—a few short steps can be a transcendent experience, a chance to walk away from the wails of the living,
and spend time among the quiet dead. We're all going to
join them anyway, so why not become comfortable in
these grassy quarters.

·   ·   ·   ·

SO MUCH OF WOLF'S YOUTH WAS ASSOCIATED with the underground. His fascination with cemeteries, his time in the cellar of the old house, the tunnel that he had obsessively dug out from the coal bin.

Obsesssion.

I was the audience that not only never applauded, I never even noticed that a show was going on.

Tunnels under the ground.

I remembered when I had begun examining homicide cases for Lane a year ago, right after Sarah Sinclair's murder. One victim was a woman named Annie who had been found dead in a horse stall on a Connecticut farm. Wolf had written extensively about Annie in his computer journal.

She was a student in Cambridge when Wolf was there, and years later told her husband about a young man she had met at a warehouse fire. The night of the fire, she and her new friend walked the subway tracks from Central Square to Harvard Square.

He took her beneath the earth. He was comfortable there, she told her husband.

There was so much that I had not noticed, or had failed to appreciate. Wolf wanted me to feel haunted, and now I was feeling it—a twenty-year dose of it shoved down my throat for a single swallow.

I LOOKED DOWN AT THE PETITE WOMAN WHO HAD knocked on my door.

"My name is Darla Michaels," she said. "I'm a reporter with the Washington *Blade*."

"I know who you are. Despite your assurance at the desk downstairs, the gentlemen there knew that you were not expected. He also recognized you. I just got off the phone with him. Sounds like you must haunt this place. Come in."

"You'll talk to me?"

"Not standing in the hallway, and for only a minute. I'm in a bit of a rush. Come in."

She sat on the edge of a chair, and produced a notebook and pen from her bag. "I was the lead writer for the *Blade* on the original Wolf case. I had been working on a series about the Bureau when that broke. It made a perfect opening for the other articles."

I sat opposite the reporter. "I live in Michigan. I don't get your newspaper. I did see your current story, though. You were quite thorough."

"Thank you. Dr. Frank, you were in Vermont recently."

"Lovely state. It's going to make a nice national park, unless they sell it to Disney."

She laughed. "When I was little, my father and I used to ski at Mount Ascutney. It's such a beautiful area. Dr. Frank, did you go to Swanton because of the double murder they had there in March?"

"Yes. Look, let's speed things up. John Wolf is alive, and he killed those two people in Vermont. What has happened here in D.C. is not the work of a copycat."

She stared at me for a moment. "What about Willoughby?"

I nodded. "Wolf."

"Samantha Becker's murder was made to look like another homicide, Sarah Sinclair, the New York case that your daughter was lead investigator on. The killer arranged the scene."

I waited.

"Even the dress that Becker was wearing was identical to the one that Sinclair was wearing when she was killed."

Rexford Landry was responsible for feeding her information. Jackson had assigned the bitter, irascible agent to review Willoughby's records. Landry had been at both D.C. crime scenes and knew all the details.

"I'm running late," I said.

"Are you saying that Wolf is responsible for the Becker homicide, too?"

I led her to the door. "Absolutely. There's your confirmation, Ms. Michaels."

"I had hoped to get more detail, Dr. Frank," Michaels said as I gently pushed her into the hall. "I especially wanted to ask you your feelings about being hauled out of retirement twice by the same killer."

"Pissed off," I told her, and closed the door.

I DIDN'T FEEL LIKE EATING. JACKSON ORDERED SOUP.

"The basement is clear," he said. "Nothing. They even ran dogs through there."

If I was right, we were down to a matter of hours. Wolf would want things set, in place. If his target was not the Willard, what the hell was it?

"We're leaving a couple of agents down there in case he shows up."

"Did you discover anything more about Wolf's teaching at your place?"

Jackson shook his head. "Somebody pulled Chadwick's file. We figure Willoughby did that. He probably thought he was saving the Bureau embarrassment, and we know he was covering his own tracks. Wolf was his ticket to that corner office down the street."

"Also his ticket to the grave. What about Landry?"

Jackson put his hand up, palm out, as if he were directing traffic. "Internal matter," he said.

"An affliction of the bowels," I muttered. "I just had a visit from Darla Michaels."

Jackson hesitated, then said, "She'd never reveal a source."

I shrugged. "Not intentionally, perhaps."

Jackson shook his head. "I'll handle this my way. I told you that Samantha Becker was dating Herb Cooper for a while. I talked with Cooper this morning."

"Could Wolf have met Agent Cooper at the homicide school?"

"Cooper was working out of the Denver office then. That wouldn't make much sense anyway. It was four years ago."

"Decades don't mean anything to Wolf. What about the case that Cooper worked with Willoughby— the one from 1985?"

"I don't think it helps us much. It's an unsolved. A young woman was strangled, left in the foundation of a burned-out ranger's cabin in one of the parks on Cape Cod."

I remembered the case. It was identical to one that I had worked on in 1976. I had completed a profile in the earlier case.

A murderer with a mission—one who intends to make a career of killing.

"She was found fully dressed, but the clothing wasn't hers," I said. "The victim's fingernails had been done, her hair had been washed and combed out."

Jackson raised an eyebrow. "You worked that case?"

"There were two identical cases. The one I worked was in 1976. Clearly, Wolf killed both young women. I remember Willoughby saying that they weren't connected. At first, I thought it was an investigative ploy. Later, I realized that he meant it. Wolf was telling us that he was out there. None of us heard him."

Jackson handed me a sheet of paper. "This is an outline of the material he covered when he was here as Alan Chadwick."

Wolf had lectured on weapon selection in serial murder cases. He mentioned the cases from 1976 and 1985. Both were ligature strangulations with wire loops. In the later case, he had left his weapon with the body. He wanted the connection to be made.

"VICAP kicked out another wire loop case," Jackson said, leaning across the table and pointing to where I was reading. "It's an older one. Sanford, Maine. Female done with the wire. Male, beside her in bed, done with an ax. Looks like two assailants. They took her head. No changing her clothes in that one. Wolf would've been just a teenager then."

"He was in that private school the state put him in," I said. "When other kids that age were playing Legion baseball, Wolf was honing his skills as a killer."

I continued reading. Wolf had also discussed the Cora Riordan case, and another—Kira Kirkman—on Bay State Road in Boston. Ray Bolton and I had always believed that Norman Elgar had done that one.

Something about Wolf's case selection was bothering me, but I couldn't put my finger on it. They were New England cases, but that wasn't all of it.

"That stuff telling you anything?"

I shrugged. "Did Cooper ever talk to anyone about his relationship with Samantha Becker?"

"He says no. Was Walker any help?"

"She confirmed most of what we already know, added a few new items. Wolf likes bouillabaisse."

"What's that?"

"A French fisherman's stew. A few restaurants in Marseilles serve the finest bouillabaisse in the world. All of the fishy ingredients are supposed to come from the Mediterranean Sea. The closest we get to the genuine item would be Spenger's in Berkeley. Wolf mentioned Spenger's to Walker."

"Cooper was in San Francisco," Jackson said, putting down his spoon. "He spent a few days with the Unabomber task force."

"In the last month?"

"Three or four weeks ago. That's where he ran into the consultant he's using on the Oklahoma case."

Jean Posner's words from deep in her trance echoed in my mind.

Bones. John digs up dead people. John is an anthropologist at Harvard.

"What kind of consultant?"

"He's a forensic anthropologist," Jackson said. "From Harvard, I think. Dr. John Krogh."

I leaned back in my chair and relaxed for the first time since Wolf had cut me down at Lake Albert.

"Difficult work," I said.

"Krogh's at it night and day. I don't know when he sleeps. He's there until midnight, and he's back at dawn."

Wolf's underground was not the Willard Hotel. It was the BSU at Quantico. My God, what a mind.

He would spend time there before his anniversary, conditioning the personnel to become accustomed to his presence.

"Will he handle the DNA testing, too?"

Jackson shook his head. "We'll have our lab take care of that."

"You trust them?"

"Jesus. You don't let up, do you?"

"Well, they did fall from grace, didn't they? Maybe you should send your samples to L.A. I hear they handle evidence well. So, Cooper might have run into Wolf on the West Coast."

"I'll call him back, have him reconstruct every minute of his time out there."

There was no need.

The corridors of the FBI's Behavioral Science Unit, sixty feet beneath the earth.

To control and humiliate, walk into their lair. Kill right under their noses. Bring the whole shithouse down.

It was vintage Wolf.

The killer and I were more alike than I would ever want to admit. We are creatures of thought and impulse—like everyone else, I suppose—but there is a certain lethality that we collect around ourselves. A cop friend once sensed the surges that bounce inside my skull, and told me he was glad that I was on his side of the badge.

"Most of the time I am," I had told him.

This was one time that I knew he would disapprove. I had a clear choice. I could level with Jackson, turn the matter over to him and his army of agents, and allow them to invade their offices in search of their own consultant.

Yeah, right. I had no intention of delegating this task. Landry was unreliable. Jackson and the rest of his people would make every effort to take Wolf alive. I wanted him dead.

Lane's trip to Lake Albert had been prompted in part by the variance between her sense of justice and mine. However critical of the Bureau she might be, she had been trained in the enforcement of the law. Where this one man was involved—this killing machine who had made a special project of me and my life—I did not care about the law.

John Wolf had been my shadow for twenty years. I had been negligent a year ago; Wolf survived and others had died. Killing him was not a task that I would entrust to anyone.

Krogh is at it night and day, Jackson had said.

I preferred the night. Wolf would be making his preparations for morning, when Lane and I were to walk through the corridors to the status meeting. By going in at night, I would have the element of surprise, and there would be only the two of us.

WHEN I RETURNED TO MY ROOM, I FOUND THE flight lists that Lane had given me. I did not feel that checking them was necessary, but could offer a final validation. I opened a bottle of ale, sat on the sofa, and leafed through the sheets.

Two days before Lane and I flew from Detroit to Washington, John Krogh had made the same trip.

WOLF

DARLA MICHAELS SAT AT A METAL DESK IN THE
Blade's newsroom.

She wore the same black jeans and blue work shirt
she had worn to Barb's in Quantico. Her eyes were an
elegant green.

She was talking on the phone. I pulled over a chair
and sat a discreet distance from her, but close enough
to hear her conversation.

"This is going to take longer than I thought," she
said into the phone. "I found two more. A pathologist in
Boston and a woman in an Orlando suburb. I'm starting to believe. The woman was his sister."

She glanced at me during the pause at her end,
held up one finger, then snapped her attention back to
the phone. "I don't expect to have all the details for tomorrow's story, but I want to at least have confirmation
that Willoughby had tied them to Wolf. You'll have it."

Michaels slammed down the phone.

"Sorry about that," she said. "Editors. Sometimes
they just make it harder to pull a story together. Look,

I'm real busy here. I've got a deadline. Is this something that can wait?"

She turned away, not waiting for my answer.

"I was at Harvard in the sixties," I said. "For a year, the man you call John Wolf was my roommate."

She swung back in my direction, and I had her complete attention.

"Do you know anything about what's been happening here?" she asked.

"I read your article. A year ago, the FBI and the New York police interviewed me extensively. They seemed to think that was the end of it. You know, that he was dead. I knew he wasn't."

"What's your name, sir?"

"I'll tell you that, and I'll show you some identification, but I'd like to be a confidential source. Please don't refer to me as his college roommate."

"Agreed."

"My name is Roger Curlew," I said, flipping open my wallet and showing her a Maryland driver's license.

"I'll have to check with security," she said, dialing an extension, then spelling my name and reading my driver's license number.

After a moment, she said, "Clergy? Okay. Thanks."

"Without church," I said as she replaced her phone. "I'm a pastoral counselor."

"Is it Reverend Curlew?"

"Roger."

She nodded. "Roger, why are you so certain that he survived the explosion in Vermont? Do you mind if I tape this?"

I shrugged. She pulled a microcassette recorder from her lap drawer and clicked it on.

"Why do you think he's alive?"

My experience with reporters had taught me that they hear only key words, never complete sentences. Which is why they never spell a name correctly, and why they always know which of the victim's body parts police find.

"Ms. Michaels, I said I *know* that he's alive. He called me in January of this year, then again in June, and then two days ago. He and I had lunch today at the Willard. Yes, I know that's where this psychiatrist, Lucas Frank, is staying. Paul—I've always known him as Paul—thought that visiting the hotel where this man is staying was a delicious bit of irony. He's always been like that."

"You two stayed in touch after college."

"Not really. He left school before I did. I know nothing of his time in Vietnam. He got my name and address from an alumni directory, and started writing to me during the eighties. He called occasionally, too. I told the police all of this."

"Did you tell them you know he's alive? Did you tell them he called you after he was supposed to be dead?"

I nodded. "I tried to. They treated me as if I were crazy. Paul—excuse me, *John*—is a dangerous man. He would never hurt me. He's told me so. But he has hurt so many others. He understood that I would have to talk with someone. He's not crazy. He's not unreasonable. He just can't, or won't, stop killing."

"God," Michaels said, shaking her head. "What did you two talk about at lunch?"

I could have said anything at that point, and Darla Michaels would have believed. I decided to stick to my script. Only hours remained until its final scene.

"It was small talk at first, just catching-up kinds of things. He asked for my wife, my kids. He looks very different now, nothing like the drawing you had in your paper. He's blond. His hair has thinned. He told me about being a medical examiner in Connecticut. He laughed about that—how he'd become a doctor despite never having completed his undergraduate degree. Oh, dear. What else did we talk about? Oh, yes. He had spoken with an FBI agent. In order to prove who he was, he gave the agent details of that poor woman's death—the one in Georgetown."

"Samantha Becker."

"Yes. Details that only the killer, only *he* could have known. The agent hung up on him."

Michaels furrowed her brow. "Who was the agent? Did he say?"

I thought. "Landers, maybe?"

"Landry?"

"Yes. That's it. He had an unusual first name."

"That sonofabitch."

"John told me who he was going to kill next. The police won't even take my calls. They hung up on him, and they don't let me through. That's why I decided that I had to come to you."

"Mr. Curlew . . ."

"It's Roger."

"Right. Roger. He actually told you who his next victim will be?"

"Oh, dear. I thought you understood. That's why I came to you."

"What . . ."

"You are the next victim, Ms. Michaels."

POP

I EXAMINED MY NINE-MILLIMETER, THEN SLIPPED the gun into a belt-clip holster at the small of my back. I was pulling on my blue sports jacket when Lane arrived.

"Evening out?" she asked.

I handed her a slip of paper. "Pack. Go to National. There's a Lear waiting for us. Instructions are in the note."

"Wait a minute, Pop. Where are you going? What's this about?"

"I don't have time, Lane. Trust me. Do as I say. I've already sent my bag ahead. I'll join you in about three hours. Make sure there's some cold ale on the damn plane."

She dropped into a chair. "What about Wolf? Has he been caught, or are we conceding? I'm not leaving until you tell me what's going on."

I took one look at her face and knew that she was not about to budge. I also knew that I was not going to allow myself to be distracted by my concern for anyone else's safety.

"There's a metal lockbox with my stuff on the plane.

It's in my duffel bag. Everything you need to know is in that box. You'll have to work it open with your pocket-knife."

"Where are you going?"

"Quantico."

"The BSU?"

"Yes."

She cocked her head to one side. "We're supposed to have that status meeting there in the morning. Is that off? Why are you going down there tonight?"

"I need some time there alone."

"Is this legal?"

I shrugged. "I have my security pass from the other day."

"What about Wolf?"

"That's what I don't have time to go into with you. It's all in the box on the plane. After you go through that stuff, if there's anything that you don't understand, I'll explain as soon as I arrive."

"Are you in danger?"

The treasures in Wolf's metal box had erased all boundaries between the two of us. There were no souvenirs or trophies of his kills. Instead, there were fragments of a past that Wolf had rewritten. My past. His past. Knotted together.

He cared more about savoring his success at tricking me than he did about lingering over any of his more than fifty murders.

"I've always been in danger. Lane, the answers are where I said you'll find them. I have to do this my way. There isn't much time. Please get going."

Lane stared at me. Finally, she nodded, got up, and walked to the door. She glanced at her watch. "If you're not at the plane by two A.M., I'm coming after you."

"Deal," I said. "There are some other instructions in that note, two calls that I need you to make after you're on the plane. What I want you to say is sketched out there."

She glanced at the sheet of paper, then back at me. "Two A.M.," she said again, and walked out.

I SLIPPED INTO THE CAR AND SWITCHED ON THE ignition.

Just the two of us, lad. But then, it has always been this way, hasn't it?

When I was a kid and lived in Roxbury, my sister often wandered into my room to read my scribblings.

"Do you mind if I read this aloud?" she asked one time.

I shook my head.

Her voice slipped softly through the words.

> *Home*
> *what it's like to live here,*
> *the black old woman says,*
> *is different now*
> *because we shoot each other*
>
> *sweet jungle of cities,*
> *fire in the southern skies—*
> *no one taught us how to live*
> *and no one seems to know*
> *that you can't put the blood back in*
> *once it spills out on the snow*

"Living here is like that for you, isn't it?" my sister asked.

"Yes."

"Were you thinking about the boy who was struck by the el?"

I shook my head. "The boy they shot on Mission Hill."

"Does everything have to be about violence and death?"

"It just is."

Now, as I drove south on the interstate, I realized that the biggest part of my life—all of what was represented in Wolf's metal box—was violence and death.

Many of Wolf's killings had been designed to impress or confuse or taunt or frighten me. It hadn't worked because I never knew that his one-man show was going on. I even left the theater and retired. That's when Wolf made a few adjustments. He was no longer entertaining me; he was going to kill me.

That hasn't changed. He wants me dead.

Wolf's style of thinking hasn't changed any, either. The young man who carved marks in the wooden sides of the coal bin became an adult who did the same thing. Each slash in the wood represented an injustice, an atrocity done to him, for which he had licensed himself to get revenge.

On my first morning home from the hospital in Lake Albert, I had grabbed Margaret Wagner's book about Peter Kurten. Somewhere below the level of my consciousness I sensed a killer's message.

Compensatory justice.

Wolf had been fixated on me for years. He had directed all of his homicidal energy at me.

After the Cora Riordan murder, I had told Ray Bolton that her killer was another Albert DeSalvo.

The Bay State Road case, six weeks before Cora Riordan, was the product of another's lust for creating mayhem. It had not been Jeremy Stoneham, nor had it been his "wolfman." Norman Elgar had bloodied that basement apartment. I said as much to a reporter.

Then Wolf had visited Elgar.

Of the 1976 profile I had done in the Cape Cod case, I told the same reporter, "He'll kill again."

But I did not know who "he" was.

I had watched the 1985 case in the same Cape community with interest, then disbelief. The FBI hadn't connected the murder to the earlier, identical homicide. The press called again.

"Hey, Lucas. This is Anthony Michaels."

"Anthony. Good to hear your voice. Why do I have the feeling that we're going to be talking about murder?"

Anthony Michaels had died around the time I had left my practice and retreated to Michigan. Cancer, I thought.

"My name is Darla Michaels. I'm a reporter with the Washington Blade."

I remembered that Anthony had shown me a photograph of his daughter. She was Lane's age. The name Michaels was a common one, but as much as I wanted to dismiss it as coincidence, I couldn't.

"My father and I used to ski at Mount Ascutney."

Anthony Michaels had been an avid skier.

Lane and I were supposed to arrive for the status meeting in the morning. Wolf, as Krogh, would be waiting, prepared to kill us all in the bowels of the BSU. If Darla was Anthony's daughter, what did she have to do with it? It was clear that she had gotten her story from Landry.

"I was the lead writer for the Blade on the original Wolf case."

She had given Wolf a splash in the press, one that he desperately craved, but her father—if Anthony was her father—had given me all the newspaper attention I had ever wanted or needed.

A composite drawing and a day or two on page one could not feed Wolf's insatiable need for recognition. He had never experienced the luxury of being able to exert control over what cops and shrinks said about him, and what reporters wrote about him. His image was not his own. During his years in Boston, without knowing Wolf's identity, Ray Bolton and I had shaped what the public learned about the killer.

That pissed you off, lad, didn't it?

I pulled off the highway into a gas station, found a phone, and dialed information for Boston. The listing hadn't been changed since Anthony's death. I listened as the phone rang three, four, five times. Finally, a woman answered.

"Mrs. Michaels?" I asked, managing to keep any evidence of urgency from my voice.

"Yes."

"My name is Lucas Frank."

"Dr. Frank? Of course. My Anthony used to speak of you."

"I'm in Washington, D.C., Mrs. Michaels, and . . ."

"Our Darla is there. She's a reporter now, you know. Just like her father. Crime."

Mrs. Michaels sounded as if she could talk all night. I didn't have time. "I'm having trouble with this phone," I said. "Sorry I disturbed you. I'll call back another time."

When I called the Washington *Blade* and asked for Darla Michaels, I reached her voice mail.

I ran back to the car and continued driving south.

The past had already collided with the present. Wolf would go after Darla Michaels, but for what? Was she to be another victim? Was she supposed to pay for the sins of omission and distortion that Wolf would think her father had committed?

It made sense—Wolf's kind of sense.

I had to get to him before he had the chance to get to the young reporter.

A year ago, probably the only thing that John Wolf had not anticipated was my willingness to kill him. Now, of course, he knew that I, like him, would not hesitate to kill.

The only advantage I had was that Wolf did not expect to see me until morning.

WOLF

DARLA MICHAELS LOOKED AS IF I HAD HIT HER. Her eyes widened. Her pouty mouth fell open.

"He told you this?" she said.

I nodded.

She grabbed her phone and punched numbers. "Landry, where the hell are you? Call me. Fast."

She clicked off.

"Answering machine," she muttered.

She looked up, stared pleadingly into my eyes. "Why is Wolf after me?"

"He said that your article was inaccurate, and that he found it terribly offensive."

"I don't believe this. Jesus."

"When I spoke to the agent, he was in his office in Quantico. Can we go there?"

She chewed her nails.

"Well, perhaps for your own safety you'd rather just go to the local police," I suggested.

She slammed her palm on her desk. "They aren't worth a damn. You'll go with me to see Landry?"

"Of course. I feel an obligation."

"Are you armed?"

I gave her my best blank expression. "Good heavens, no."

She punched more numbers into her phone, waited, then said, "Landry, this is Darla Michaels. Meet me at your office as soon as possible. I'm on my way there with Roger Curlew. Remember him?"

My cast of characters continued to grow. I had anticipated that Landry would be among those that I incinerated. I had not expected the bonus of some private time with him.

Michaels grabbed a .32 from her desk, dropped it into her purse, then picked up her jacket.

"Let's go."

WE TOOK MY CAR. THE REPORTER WAS TOO SHAKEN to drive.

I had redefined her reality. How could she not trust a composed, nonthreatening, churchless pastor? She sat, leaned against the passenger door, and continued to chew her nails.

Only now could I feel the excitement that accompanies the anticipation of carnage. Odd. With other kills—even other multiple kills, other versions of the Apocalypse—the notion, the formation of a rudimentary plan, the initial preparations, catching sight of a victim, were enough to stimulate me. This time was different. Could I have doubted myself, questioned my ability to bring this off?

I had to smile at my self-analysis. It was so wrong.

"You strike me as someone who is always very tense," I said to Michaels. "I know this must be a terrible ordeal for you, but I don't mean just this situation right now. That was my first impression when I walked into your office and saw you on the phone. You seem like a nervous person."

"I say it's the job. I don't know. I guess I've always been a little wired. Maybe that's why I found my way into this kind of work. That and my father. He was a reporter. I've never had my life threatened before, though."

"Can you remember a time when you were truly relaxed?"

I glanced over at her. She stared straight ahead for the moment, then dropped her eyes down and to the right—to the back of her hand.

"Yeah," she said, sighing.

When I learned that the key to Lucas Frank's technique was hypnosis—that he was capable of self-inducing a dissociative state—I had researched and mastered that skill, as well as the talent to effect a hypnoid state in anyone I chose. For my entire life, I had been exiting my body involuntarily. It required little effort or training to harness that ability.

"Sometimes it can be relaxing to think about other times that you felt that way," I said.

"Just a few days ago, I had this strange but pleasant experience. It wasn't a feeling, really. It was like being able to see things around me that I always thought were unimportant. I could really *see* them."

"What were you seeing?"

"Oh, that was the strange part. One thing was a small brass frog."

"Its brass tongue sticks out, and there's a brass fly wrapped up in the tongue," I said.

She turned toward me, a hint of anxiety in her voice. "I thought it was an unusual piece. How did you know that?"

When I was in Michaels's apartment, I had placed the frog next to a carved wooden starfish on the top shelf of her bookcase. I fingered through her copies of *Primary Colors*, and *Rush Limbaugh Is a Big Fat Idiot*. She was not terribly eclectic. Hers were books that a Washington reporter would read.

"Just a guess. Seems like the sort of thing an artist would do. I may even have seen an object like that once, or maybe a picture of one."

I had also prowled through her more personal belongings and inhaled her scent, the same fragrance that I could smell now in the car. I am always prepared for any encounter.

"I had admired that frog when I found it," she said. "It just appeared there, on a shelf in my apartment a few days ago. I had a couple of dates with this guy, and I figured he put it there. He denied it, but I'm sure he put it there. I named it Oliver because of the artist's sticker on the bottom of it. I liked it, but I hadn't really seen it, absorbed all the details of it. Then, it was as if I were seeing it for the very first time, just for a moment."

"Then, for another small increment of time, there was a sense of loss," I said.

She hesitated, and agreed. "I couldn't see it again. Not the same way."

"As if in a dream."

"It was like that."

"It just happened. There was no effort involved."

She sighed. "You must be good at what you do. I don't feel nearly as freaked as I did."

"There is a sense of lightness that accompanies experiences like those. You feel as if you can rise up from your chair, or that you can soar out of your own body. Or that you're going to, regardless of whether you want to."

Darla nodded. "I thought it was just me."

"We don't pay enough attention to the subtle moments of our lives. We're trained not to. Public schools do that to us. I refused to give in. Fought 'em every inch of the way."

She laughed softly. "Tough talk for a minister."

"I remember a teacher," I said. "Miss Gossett. I wrote a poem about a flying squirrel. I had that little rodent soaring all over the place. Miss Gossett was very science-minded. She explained that squirrels don't fly. The ones that are called flying squirrels glide. I knew that, but I wanted my squirrel to travel all over the universe if he wanted. I believed that I was free—in poetry, at least—to do as I wished. She gave me a C. What was worse, when I argued about the grade, Miss Gossett told my mother that I was arrogant. I heard about it for weeks."

Marjorie Gossett never should have called me arrogant. It was ironic, really, because I always worked hard at not attracting attention to myself. There was no poem about a squirrel. Miss Gossett had walked in on me when I was using the faculty reading room adjacent to the library.

"What are you doing in here?" she demanded.

I started to explain that I had permission to be there. I got half a sentence out of my mouth when she told me that I was arrogant, then went off and reported me to the principal. He sent me home for the day, and that night my stepfather used me for a punching bag.

Later that year, Miss Gossett had a nervous breakdown. Someone had been calling her late at night. They were hang-up calls, heavy breathing, laughter.

Then, one by one, her several cats turned up on her doorstep with their throats cut. When all of her cats were gone, more dead cats arrived. Despite a police patrol in her neighborhood, the dead cats kept coming.

The last one graced her bed pillow.

Someone said that Miss Gossett began to scream then, and didn't stop screaming until doctors had pumped her full of Thorazine.

Years later I sent my former teacher a postcard, unsigned. It was a picture of a mother cat nursing its kittens.

"Do you like cats?" I asked Darla.

"I like them, but I'm allergic to them."

"So was Miss Gossett."

"Who?"

"That teacher I was telling you about."

"Oh."

"Eventually, her allergy killed her."

POP

I CONTINUED TO DRIVE SOUTH ON I-95, LEAV-
ing behind the city and suburban lights, and entering
the darkness.

I remembered another entry from Wolf's journal.

PEOPLE COLLIDE ALL THE TIME. WE NEVER CON-
*verge for more than an instant, but we do collide. If we
were up high, we would come together, I'm quite certain.
But I worry that there may be too many of us. When we soar
so near the limits of the universe, we go at our own risk.*

*Tomorrow always goes on as scheduled, but some of
us don't make it. And no one ever remembers for longer
than it takes to pronounce a name.*

THE BSU'S MAIN ENTRANCE WOULD BE LOCKED
at night, so I walked into the adjacent building. I went
up a flight of stairs, turned to my right, then walked
through the glass-walled corridor that connected to the
BSU offices.

I stepped into the stairwell, slipped out my gun, and listened. It was silent.

Staying close to the wall, I began a slow descent.

Cellars.

Tunnels. Caverns.

Places underground.

As it had on my first visit with Jackson, it seemed strange to enter a building and travel downward. I remember doing some research at Harvard, descending in a claustrophobia-inducing elevator into the underground stacks at Widener Library.

It was at Harvard in the sixties that Alan Chadwick had followed Wolf into the cavernous Peabody Museum. Chadwick watched as Wolf, in a hypnoid state, stared at the mounted birds and mumbled what might have been some parody of a prayer.

One flight down.

Wolf had told his sister how angry he was about the birds that are carried down into the coal mines as living gauges on deadly gases. That story had reminded me of a test for guilt or innocence in 1600s Salem, Massachusetts. Suspected witches were weighted with large rocks and thrown into a pond. If the women floated, they were declared possessed by supernatural forces, and the penalty was death. If the rocks carried the women down, they were not prosecuted, but there was an often lethal side effect: drowning.

John Wolf had studied and met the same people I had. While I was trying to achieve some understanding about what made them tick, he was making sure that he was nothing like them. He was also learning to think exactly like I did.

As I descended the stairs, I thought of the hanging man, and of murder in holy places.

The animals that reside in the lightless recesses of our minds achieve their full potential only when we nurture them, stroke them, allow them out from time to time and use them.

I had spent a lifetime struggling to maintain a balance with mine.

Wolf had set his free.

Two flights.

We project ourselves into everything we create. That fact is one of the foundation principles of effectively understanding the mind behind a crime scene, working backward from the carnage to its creator. Each of us leaves traces of our emotional self in everything we do. Even with our mouths shut, we are walking communicators.

Most of what I had read in Wolf's journals was thematically familiar. He wished to terrify, humiliate, and ultimately destroy anyone who demeaned him by failing to acknowledge his existence. Every ounce of Wolf's energy and intellect were devoted to the perfection of murder.

Sometime in his youth, Wolf had assembled a plan for his whole life. That's where his rigidity originated. He didn't know who he would kill, or when, or where. He trusted that one experience would lead him to another. His was a self-designed, closed system. He extolled the excitement that he associated with the anticipation of the kill. Waiting, titillating himself with his fantasies, knowing what he was going to do—these were his most exciting acts in his time on the stage. By remaining silent, scouting the environment in the safety of anonymity, isolating his prey, seizing a victim here, a victim there, the terror he set in motion soon developed a life of its own.

Three flights.

It was time to bring that life to an end.

I had reached the deepest level of the building, sixty feet down, and slipped into the corridor. With my back pressed to the wall, I moved through the dimly lighted hall toward the one bright room somewhere in the distance.

The offices were small, cramped burrows. I stepped into the room that Jackson had told me was Herb Cooper's office. From the glow of the lights in the hall, I could see that the desk was covered with small vials, plastic bags containing fragments of bone, and a wooden case with a brass strip that said, "Dr. John Krogh." I used my pocketknife to pry open the velvet-covered tray in the bottom of the case, then looked down at a folded Buck knife. There were also spaces for another knife—a straight blade—and a large caliber handgun. But the spaces were empty.

I picked up one of three identical paper wrappers that had been discarded in the bottom of the case. A single word had been block-printed on the paper: CYCLONITE.

"Jesus Christ," I whispered.

I had seen the plastic explosive only once in my life. I had seen the craters that well-placed cyclonite had created three times that I could remember. Wolf intended to blow the place off the face of the earth.

What the hell was I doing? I had the chance to hand this to Jackson. He had an army of specialists to deal with this shit. There was a phone on Cooper's desk. I could call Jackson, then sit tight with my gun aimed at the door until the troops arrived.

As fast as it hit me, all doubt vanished. Wolf had to be terminated. Now.

Rage had always served me as the perfect replacement for fear. I breathed deeply, then stepped back through Cooper's door, and slipped farther into the depths of the BSU.

I heard voices originating somewhere near the end of the hall.

> *it's almost time, they say—*
> *they say, and walk away . . .*

Wolf had someone with him.

> *leaving me with the night*
> *and the sea . . .*

It was a woman's voice.

> *and no handle on my soul—*

Darla Michaels.

I had violated every law and ethical constraint I could think of so that, at the end, there would be no one between Wolf and me. Once again, I felt as if the bastard had read my mind.

WOLF

"DO YOU HAVE SOMETHING TO WRITE WITH?" I asked Darla Michaels.

"What? Oh, sure."

She dropped her purse on the table and walked along the row of cubicles, glancing in at each one. I removed her .32 from the leather bag and placed it in my pocket. I had done my work well; she trusted me.

When she reached the last workstation, Michaels turned and started back. "Why do I need something to write with?"

"I'm going to give you the rest of your story."

She sat at the table and folded her hands. "Roger, why don't we just wait for Landry. He shouldn't be long."

"My name isn't Roger."

Darla looked up at me. As she stared at my eyes, her face clouded with confusion. Then her expression cleared and she dove for her purse.

"I have your weapon," I said.

She continued to dig through the leather bag, emitting a low-pitched whine. Her performance was undignified and annoying. Finally, she collapsed across the bag, her head resting against her arms.

After several moments she looked up at me and said, "John Wolf."

"Yes."

"You're going to kill me."

Her voice shook. Her green eyes were wide, and darted in wild sweeps of the room.

"No. You have to carry my words to the world. Your readers depend on you for their vicarious thrills. I need you, and you need me. I want the story done right. You want your Pulitzer. We have only a few hours, so let's get started. Sit in that chair."

Her face was a mess. "Landry's dead, isn't he?" she asked, falling back into the chair I had indicated.

"We're all going to die."

Silence. Too shocked to think.

"How will you die?" she asked, rallying, a hint of challenge in her voice.

"I was in Greenwich Village one time," I said as I peeled a length of duct tape from a roll and cut it with my knife. "I was still a student then. You probably should write this down."

She was slow to move, but did manage to find a pen and steno pad. "You're playing a game. Then you're going to kill me."

"I give you my word."

"What good is that?"

"It's all you have to believe in right now. There's no one else here. If I wanted you dead, you would be dead."

"What's the tape for?"

"To fix your ankles to the chair legs. As long as you behave, that will be the only restraint I use."

"What did you do to Landry? He should've been here by now."

"Nothing. Darla, do you *want* to die?"

"No. Of course not."

"Then listen, and write," I said, pointing at her pad. "How many reporters get an opportunity like this? Your father would have jumped at the chance to sit and talk with me."

"You knew my father?"

I taped her legs to the chair.

"He knew my work."

"Oh, Jesus. You've been killing that long?"

"Longer."

"I can't . . ."

"Greenwich Village," I said again as I removed my jacket, reached inside its lining, and retrieved the soft cloth that contained my tools, wires, timer, batteries, and wafer-thin, cream-colored sheets of plastic explosive.

"What's that?"

"I visited the White Horse Tavern," I said as I folded open the cloth. "That's the place where Dylan Thomas did most of his drinking when he was in New York. Then, I walked toward Washington Square. I saw a sign for a palm reader."

Darla's hands were trembling. "I can't concentrate. What is all that?"

"Remember your brass frog? The one that sits next to the wooden starfish on top of your bookcase."

Her head snapped up. "I said it was on a shelf. I didn't say anything about the starfish. You've been in my fucking apartment."

"Oliver—the artist—was an acquaintance of mine."

Again, she seemed confused. "You put it there? When? How . . . ?"

She was like a child searching the heavens for Orion, finding a star here, a star there, but never the constellation in its entirety.

"The palm reader," I interrupted, pointing again at her hands. "You don't need to concentrate, Darla. Just write."

Once more, she looked down at the pad. "I still want to know what you're doing."

"For two dollars the future could be mine," I continued. "It was already mine, but I walked up the narrow flight of stairs anyway, sat at a small, round table, and waited."

"Why are you telling me this?"

"I don't like it when people interrupt me."

"I'm a reporter."

"An old woman came in," I said as I began stripping half-inch bare ends on my wires. "She asked for the money, and told me to hold out my right hand. She gazed down at it, then folded up my fingers and pushed my hand away. She shook her head and said, 'You know too much.' The she returned my two dollars, got up, and walked back through the curtains the way she had come."

"If you know so much, you can answer the question."

"What question?"

"How will you die?"

"By violence."

There was a curious expression on her face. "What about me? How will I die?"

This young woman would travel to my Web site on the Internet. I was mildly impressed. I had made a good choice for the person I wanted to see me, to know and to record my accomplishments for others to finally appreciate.

"Let's finish with me first," I said. "Then maybe I'll tell you the story of the rest of your life."

I fixed the sealed battery case in its seat on the timer's back, then threaded wires through the clips that would brace them, and attached the bare copper ends to the appropriate poles.

Michaels watched. "What's the tan stuff?"

"Cyclonite."

She looked up from my hands. Her eyes widened. "You're going to blow up this place."

I smiled. "They've never been very nice to me."

POP

I COULD HEAR WOLF'S VOICE—THE DEEP, THROATY bass, and the tone, the inflections of a man who is absolutely sure of himself—the same voice I had heard a year ago in Vermont, and countless times in my mind.

I moved into the corridor on my right, my back against the wall, inching toward the lighted room thirty feet away, and remaining in the shadows.

My old friend's daughter said, "You can't do that. You'll never get away with it. If you thought you had cops after you before . . ."

"You just don't get it," Wolf said. "I'm the killer. You're the reporter. You write down all of this, and then you make a story out of it. I build the bombs and blow up whatever I want. Police are inept. They'll hint at nonexistent progress while waiting for the public outcry to subside. Case closed."

"What if your hand slips?"

"It won't."

It was no longer the simple matter of surprising Wolf and executing him. I was within twenty feet of the lighted doorway, listening as Darla Michaels con-

fronted John Wolf—pushed the killer, challenged him—
and Wolf grew increasingly restive as he assembled
his bomb.

Michaels was not applying school-of-journalism
technique. What I heard was the person she was. Her
demeanor could be enough to get her killed.

"You can't let me go. You have to kill me."

"You and I will leave here together. I'll drop you at
your office."

"Why would you risk coming here? Why blow up
this place?"

Darla, please don't push him.

"In a few hours, Lucas Frank and his daughter,
Agent Jackson, your friend Landry if he doesn't respond to your message, Agent Walker, some of the
other BSU experts—all of them plan to gather in the
conference room and debate my existence. I am flat-
tered to be the focus of so much attention and specula-
tion, but these cretins will not complete their meeting.
Within minutes of our departure, Ms. Michaels, this
place will cease to exist."

"Why a bomb? Jesus. I can't think. Which of those
people is the target?"

"The target is everyone," Wolf said. "Lucas Frank
thought he had killed me. He made a mistake. My message to the FBI is simple. They can't create their categories of homicidal behavior fast enough to keep up
with the killers. You should write that. After the Versace
murder in Florida last summer, agents bickered about
whether their suspect was a serial killer, a spree killer,
or a hybrid. They had no idea where he was, but they
knew who he was, and they were going to pigeonhole
him. What fucking difference did it make? The care-
taker for a houseboat stumbled onto him."

"What about Lucas Frank?" Michaels asked. "What's your message to him? Just that he made a mistake?"

"He's received a lifetime of messages from me," Wolf snapped. "He paid no attention. You are getting ahead of the orderly development of things, and you're wasting time. *I* am the news. I *make* the news. I *decide* what's news. What you do is write it down. Report the news. That's all. I will not caution you again."

I was close enough so that I could see Wolf's shadow fall across a table. Darla Michaels sat at the table. I needed Wolf to move from where he was pontificating, or I had to get close enough to the doorway so that I had a decent angle for a shot.

"I can't interview you? I can't ask any questions?" Michaels asked.

Wolf sighed.

Jesus, Darla, back off.

"One question. Ask. Don't waste time."

"Most of your victims were women. Was there ever a woman you cared about?"

There was a long silence.

"Her name was Annie. I met her in Cambridge at a warehouse fire."

"Did you kill her?"

"Many years later."

"Why did you kill her?"

Again, Wolf sighed, but he was granting Darla Michaels considerable latitude. She was his Boswell—his biographer. "She talked about her father often, but seldom with affection. He was a hard man, a wealthy breeder of world-class horses, and a drunk."

I knew what was coming. The story of Annie's father was an entry in Wolf's computer journal.

"One night when Annie was home for a weekend,"

Wolf continued, "something was bothering the horses. Her father went out to the stable. The horses were frightened, nervous, jittery. He didn't know why. Then he saw what he thought was a large dog—really just the shadow of the animal—moving away from the barn. It disappeared into the darkness, and eventually the horses settled down."

His account was verbatim. John Wolf could not exist without rehearsal. He was fact and he was fiction. I wondered if he knew which was which. The problem had always been that he was so fucking believable, so seductively real.

"When the same thing happened the next night," Wolf continued, "her father took their German shepherd with him. The dog was afraid, too. This was a trained attack dog, but he put his tail down and backed away toward the house. Annie's father got a better look at the animal, though. It was like a dog, but bigger than any dog he had ever seen. It wasn't afraid. It was almost casual as it drifted into the shadows. It had no fear, which intimidated her father. On the third night, he took his deer rifle with him. When he saw the profile of the animal moving away from the barn, he fired. Annie said that the animal went down. The game warden came and looked at it. He said it was a wolf, the first one on the south side of the mountains in fifty years."

The room was silent.

"Because she told you that story, you killed her?"

There was a sharp edge to Wolf's voice.

"I told her that it had to be a mixed breed. She was adamant. Her father couldn't be wrong about something like that. 'Pure wolf,' she said. No pure wolf would be that stupid. I told her that. Whatever it was, that animal just walked out there for her father to shoot him. One shot. It would never happen. A scavenger like a coyote, maybe, but not the purest predator of them all. Not a wolf. Not one shot."

"You identify with the animal?"

"He lives inside me. Always."

The elevator doors whooshed and clicked behind me in the corridor, followed by the sound of footsteps approaching fast.

I saw Wolf's arm reach across the table and grab Darla Michaels by the shirt. He skirted the table, a long knife in his hand, and started to move into position behind the young woman.

I raised my nine-millimeter and aimed at the space where I expected to see the side of his head.

As he brought the knife up against her throat, he came into view for the first time. He turned his head to look toward the doorway, his eyes glazed gray and empty. He was inches from Darla Michaels's face.

I had one chance, one shot to stop him.

"Freeze," Rexford Landry called from behind me.

The FBI agent could see me, but he could not see Wolf and Michaels.

Wolf held his grip on the reporter's shirt. I moved my head only slightly, but in that split second Wolf disappeared into the maze of cubicles.

"Place your weapon on the floor," Landry said. "Do it now."

Darla Michaels continued to sit at the table, staring straight ahead, slowly shaking her head.

"Landry, John Wolf is in this room," I shouted.

I heard the snap as Landry engaged the action on his gun. "Put it down, Dr. Frank."

Michaels slipped from her chair onto the floor and began to crawl toward me. The chair, taped to her ankles, slid along behind her, then wedged against the aluminum table, threatening to tip it.

"Okay, Landry," I said. "You want him? You go after him."

Landry approached slowly, directly behind me, still unable to see beyond the doorway, and unconcerned as he moved into the light that spilled from the room.

That was when I first saw the bomb. With each of Darla Michaels's attempts to move forward, the chair banged the folding table, and the explosive device slipped toward the edge. I had no idea how stable cyclonite was—whether the impact of a two-and-a-half-foot fall would set it off.

"Darla, don't crawl," I said.

Wolf was quick. The BSU's tunnels echoed with the large caliber handgun's explosion as the slug ripped into Landry's shoulder and spun him around. The agent bounced off the wall and went down, his weapon skidding back along the floor.

"Oh, God," Michaels said, again sliding forward, and again nudging the bomb toward the edge of the table.

I dove forward into the room, landing beside her.

"Stay put," I said to Michaels. "Stay flat on the floor and don't move."

"He set the timer," she said, her voice shaking. "He did it real fast. He snapped a red wire into place, then clicked something."

"Darla, I need you to stay as motionless as possible."

She nodded. "Just hurry up."

I crawled forward into the first cubicle, where I pulled myself to a crouching position and looked back at the table. The bomb had slid to the far side and rested at an angle, extending two inches out over the floor. I couldn't see the timer.

From my glimpse of Wolf, and the smoke from his gun when he shot Landry, I knew that he was near the back of the room on the right side. I figured there were thirty feet between Wolf and me, and I was between him and the exit.

I glanced around, searching for inspiration.

If I moved down one line of cubicles, Wolf could move up on the opposite side. If I dove up over the partition that separated the two rows, I would make an excellent target. If Wolf missed, me, all he had to do was disappear through the row that I had vacated.

Then, just as my calf muscles started to cramp, I saw it—a can of solvent and thinner for rubber cement. The cubicle's occupant was the person responsible for mounting crime-scene photographs. The agent's desk was also decorated with a dried wildflower arrangement in a narrow-necked glass bottle. A smock hanging from a hook was my final ingredient.

I yanked the weeds from the neck of the bottle, and emptied the solvent into it.

"I plan to have a glass of red wine when I leave here," Wolf's disembodied voice said. "What about you? Oh. I forgot. It's late. You're an old man. Probably right to bed, huh? You hadn't thought about it, had you? You were trying to figure out how to finish me off, so you gave no consideration to what you might do after that. There isn't much time, you know."

Wolf was moving. He had a forty-foot area that was his. As long as he remained there, I couldn't see him.

"Doesn't this piss you off?" he asked. "You already killed me once. Now you have to do it again. Well, it was your own stupidity. You thought to the end as you defined the end. That's never good enough. A killer must look beyond the end. Shit. I gave you every possible advantage. This episode proves what I've known from the beginning. No mere theorist will ever be as good as a man who plies the trade."

Using my pocketknife, I cut the smock into several foot-long strips, wound them tight, and pushed them through the neck of the bottle until only four inches remained exposed.

Wolf snorted in derision. "You are a theorist. Instead of a place like this filled with federal drones, or a college crawling with sociology types, you sit in your log house on the lake and create your own mythology of behavior. How does it feel to know that I watched you fabricate in Boston, feign expertise in New York, Miami, Dallas? I was there."

I reached for my cigarettes to get the book of matches I kept tucked inside the cellophane. They were gone. I had quit smoking again, and I had given Lane the package the night we had walked on Pennsylvania Avenue.

"You think you have me at a disadvantage," Wolf said. "In a few minutes, this place is going up."

I had no wish to indulge Wolf, nor did I want him to know exactly where I was. But he was winding down, and I needed time. I had to say something.

"We've been through this before," I said. "In Vermont."

There was a short laugh from the back of the room. "There's no coal bin here, no place for you to bury a bomb. Jesus. You're just as homicidal as I am. An empty, hollow player of games. We see the world the same way. Your invitation from the Bureau was for morning. Do you think that I wasn't expecting you?"

I dug into my pockets, finally finding a book of matches that I had picked up at Delta's Blues Bar, where Wolf had killed Nicholas Wesley.

I did not believe that Wolf had been expecting me. He was playing a game, a transparent attempt at conning another who had made a business of mastering manipulation.

A full minute passed. I heard no movement at the back of the room. Then, he spoke. "I think I've already explained this to you. Before I could begin to set something like this in motion, I had to resign myself to my own death. Having done that, I have nothing to lose, nothing to fear. You just don't learn. I learned a great deal from you. Through the years, you helped me to become a better artist. You were the inspiration. With your guidance, I matured into a creative killer. No one else can claim to have achieved what I have."

I climbed onto the desk, keeping my head below the top of the partition.

He believed that he was the embodiment of perfection, that there was no challenge he could not meet. "You have a world-class ego, Mr. Wolf," I said. "Tonight, you were more concerned with your press coverage than with properly assembling your device."

When he spoke, he sounded too relaxed, as if he hadn't a care in the world. "Think what you want."

John Wolf was the perfect psychopath. I wanted to grab the advantage.

"I think that one of us will die," I said, then lit a match and touched it to the rags that extended from my Molotov cocktail. The odor and the smoke would give me away, so I had to act fast.

The ceiling was low. I reached up and rifled a line

drive toward the back wall. The bottle shattered with a roar, a wall of flames, and billowing smoke.

I threw myself up onto the top of the cubicle's partition, precariously balancing on the junction supports, and aiming my nine-millimeter at the spot where I expected Wolf to appear.

Seconds passed. A minute.

What the hell was he doing? Black billows of smoke rolled from the rear corner toward the center of the room.

I lowered myself to the floor on the other side of the partition, remained in a crouch, and moved slowly toward the smoke. As I neared the end of the corridor, the sprinkler system spluttered on. Reflexively, I looked up and saw that two ceiling panels had been dislodged. Had he climbed up through them?

Or was it further manipulation?

I spun to my left as the killer of dozens emerged from behind the wall of smoke, his gun in his right hand, his left arm across his eyes.

With a suddenness that stunned me, Wolf snapped his weapon into firing position. Both hands gripped the .44 Magnum. Wolf scanned the corridor as if he had been impervious to the dense black smoke. Then his eyes fixed on mine.

I squeezed off a single shot that slammed into Wolf's face, sending up a mist of blood and brain. The killer went down. His gun clattered harmlessly on the floor.

Wolf lay in a sodden heap. I watched as his blood spread in a pool around his head, diluted by the spray from overhead.

I was confident that I had removed him from this life.

I walked through the mechanical rain to his side.

Most of the back of his head was gone, but still I touched my fingers to his throat and glanced at my watch. "Time of death," I muttered to myself. "Twelve-forty A.M. No resurrection this time, lad."

I turned and walked back toward the hallway.

"It's almost over," I said to Darla Michaels. "Few more seconds."

I gently nudged Wolf's bomb back onto the table and gazed down at a battery housing, three wires, the stacked sheets of cyclonite, and the timing mechanism. In ninety seconds, we and the BSU would be history.

"Cut me out of here," Michaels said.

"No time."

Landry staggered into the doorway, holding his shoulder.

"What do you know about bombs?" I asked him. "Wolf snapped the red wire in place last. That mean anything?"

"That's the one to clip first," he said. "You can't get into the battery housing?"

"It's sealed."

I grabbed Wolf's wire cutters, closed them over the red wire, and snipped. The small wheel in the timer continued to spin.

"Sixty seconds," I said. "Black and yellow are left."

Sweat slithered down the back of my neck.

"There's no way to know," Landry said. "It doesn't sound like sophisticated work. It shouldn't matter."

Forty-five seconds. What if it did matter? I clipped the yellow wire.

"It's still going," I said.

"Jesus Christ," Michaels yelped.

"There have to be two strands to the last wire, two

separate connections," Landry said. "Otherwise, it would have stopped."

With thirty seconds remaining, I examined the end of the black wire and saw the two small fragments of plastic coating where they connected to the timer. "One's white and one's green," I said.

"Clip either one," Landry said, "but don't let the metal cutters touch both wires at the same time."

Twenty seconds.

The tool slipped out of my sweaty hands and dropped to the floor. I wiped my hands on my pants, retrieved the wire cutters, and examined what I had to do. There wasn't much space to work with. I angled the clippers into the housing area from the side, slipped the pointed ends over the fragment of exposed copper, and squeezed.

The timer stopped. Eight seconds to go.

"That's it," I said.

I crouched to cut the tape from Darla Michaels's ankles with my pocketknife, and help her to her feet. Then I looked at Landry.

"Go introduce yourself to John Wolf," I told him.

"Landry, you sonofabitch," Michaels yelled. "You nearly got me killed. That fucking maniac called you. He practically told you who he was. You hung up on him."

"No," Landry said.

"Roger Curlew?" she challenged.

"A crank. We get those calls all the time."

The agent moved by us, deeper into the room.

As I walked back through the hall, I could hear Michaels still screaming at Landry. "I *write* about this shit, you asshole. I don't fucking *live* it."

I took the elevator up and left the building.

EPILOGUE

POP

I MADE MY WAY THROUGH NATIONAL AIRPORT and found the Lear. Lane was standing beside the small jet as I walked up.

"Wolf is dead, isn't he?"

I nodded.

"I made the calls. Should we wait until the fireworks are over and talk later?"

"I think that's best," I said, watching two sedans race across the tarmac toward the plane.

"You must have raised a few eyebrows in the terminal."

"Why?"

"You're soaked."

"Oh. That."

One car swung across the nose of the aircraft and stopped. The second pulled up where we were standing. Hiram Jackson got out.

"You're going to have to stay with us awhile," the agent said. "At least until we get this sorted out."

As more heavily armed men got out of both cars, I watched the black Lincoln make its way toward our group. When it stopped beside Jackson's car, he looked over at it.

Senator Harry Storrs stepped out of his car, nodded toward Lane and me, then spoke to Jackson. "I want this plane in the air, with the Franks aboard, within five minutes."

"With all due respect, sir, this is an FBI matter," Jackson said.

"I know what it is."

Jackson looked at me.

"You set a trap for a wolf and caught one," I said. "You have the imagination to work out the details. You know that Landry was leaking information to Darla Michaels. That should give you some leverage in controlling the story. Although she's so pissed at Landry right now, you'll have to do some serious flak-catching."

"That's it?"

"If you want the whole story, come to Michigan."

Jackson shook his head. "This isn't going to work."

"Bullshit," Storrs said. "Your agency is better at disinformation than the Senate is. I've already made some calls. The Bureau will come out of this thing smelling like a rose. Do you think your director would settle for less? He didn't tell me that."

I watched as Jackson waved off his troops and moved back toward his car. He hesitated before getting in, turned, and said, "You don't trust anyone do you?"

"No one."

Jackson stared, nodded once, then got into his car and drove back across the tarmac.

BY THE TIME WE WERE IN THE AIR, I HAD changed my clothes—dry jeans and a warm sweatshirt.

The plane banked in a slow arc around the Washington Monument and the Lincoln Memorial, then headed northwest. The view was impressive. Cities always look aseptic from a few thousand feet.

"I thought that this would be appropriate," Lane said, sitting across from me and handing me a bottle of ale. "It's from the Magic Hat Brewery in Burlington, Vermont."

I sniffed, then sipped. "Excellent. There are some things that they do well in the mountains."

"I looked through Wolf's box, Pop."

"At the story of my life?"

"He was always out there."

"His mistake," I said.

ABOUT THE AUTHORS

JOHN PHILPIN is a nationally renowned forensic psychologist—a profiler. His advice and opinions on violence and its aftermath have been sought by police, newspaper writers, TV producers, mental health professionals, private investigators, attorneys, and polygraph experts throughout the country. He is the author of *Beyond Murder*, the story of the Gainesville student killings, published by NAL/Dutton in 1994, and *Stalemate*, which tells the true crime story of a series of child abductions, sexual assaults, and murders in the San Francisco Bay Area. Along with Patricia Sierra, he is the author of *The Prettiest Feathers*, the prequel to *Tunnel of Night*. He lives in New England.

PATRICIA SIERRA is an award-winning writer whose short fiction and poetry have been published in several small literary magazines. She has written three young adult novels as well, all of which were published by Avon Books. Her interest in crime and law enforcement led to a brief career as a private investigator. An avid lifelong fan of true crime books and mysteries, Sierra lives in Toledo, Ohio.

A seductive serial killer…

A trail of victims…

A single taunting clue…

The Prettiest Feathers

by John Philpin and Patricia Sierra

A man like John Wolf feels nothing. He is moved only by vengeance. His mind is primal, a black hole. For years he has hunted, stalking and killing his human prey with such care that investigators have never linked his victims. His murders are repayment for the injustice he has suffered. Now, he has found the perfect victim…. ___57555-4 $5.50/$7.99 CAN